Home

'[Ronan's] brilliant novel opens in 1960s Devon with a bold flourish: Coorg starts his life in a hippy commune called the hOme . . . So delightfully sharp and funny are the commune passages that I felt a certain amount of resistance to the move to familiar fictional Ireland. But in Ronan's hands, that world is just as surreal'
Suzi Feay, *Independent on Sunday*

'A very funny tale about loss, isolation, neglect and cruelty. Yet, there is no better way to experience a story than through the non-judgmental eyes of a child. Coorg's loneliness and confusion become almost incidental to the humour and freshness of his take on life in White's Hotel in Duncannon. His own sense of wonder and zaniness always manages to supplant the awfulness of what is really happening . . . Coorg is so good and endearing you'll follow him to the end to see how he fares'
Catherine Foley, *Image*

'Ronan brings a canny lightness of touch to the material . . . and as [Coorg] struggles to grow up, the twinkly tone deepens, via impressive lyrical flourishes, finally reclining gently into irresistible melancholy'
Face

'We identify completely with Coorg as he's pulled from one religion to the next, searching for the truth and a sense of self. From his Holy Grail-seeking mother to his alcoholic auntie, the array of conflicting characters add to the mayhem and give Ronan a free hand to create a series of hilarious and touching scenarios. Definitely a trip worth taking.'
List

'Ronan has a true and firm handle on childhood confusion, teenage angst, and repressed small-town Ireland in that truly dismal decade, the 1970s. The commune section at the start of the book is so vivid and often hilarious that it deserves a book of its own.'
Bernice Harrison, *Irish Times*

'Writing from the perspective of an intelligent though lonely and bewildered child, [Ronan] uses incisive humour to expose the lunacies, vagaries and hypocrisies of traditional and alternative belief systems . . . full of grabby descriptions and witty, off-the-cuff dialogue . . . It's easy to empathise wth [Coorg], partly because of Ronan's careful and welcome lack of sentimentality. But *Home* is touching as well as funny . . . Ronan constructs his story with freshness and sensitivity.'
Joanne Hayden, *Sunday Business Post*

'What could have been cliché is saved here by Ronan's intriguing and humane approach to his characters, his low-key and quixotic style, and a satisfying desire to avoid melodrama. Indeed, one could say that he really has quite a unique style, which creates an atmosphere of strange images and acute, wistful longing. He is particularly effective at recreating a child's view of the world'
Eamon Delaney, *Sunday Independent*

'Ronan expertly satirises the suffocating repressiveness of rural Ireland . . . this is a lovely book'
Big Issue in the North

FRANK RONAN

Home

SCEPTRE

First published in Great Britain in 2002 by Hodder and Stoughton
A division of Hodder Headline

A Sceptre Paperback

1 3 5 7 9 10 8 6 4 2

A CIP catalogue record for this title
is available from the British Library.

ISBN 0 340 81904 9

Printed and bound in Great Britain by
Mackays of Chatham plc, Chatham, Kent

Hodder and Stoughton
A division of Hodder Headline
338 Euston Road
London NW1 3BH

Home

Being concealed in Mervyn was the best feeling ever and, one way or another, I've been looking for something like that feeling ever since. I've tried everything, from love to religion and all there is between those two extremes, but nothing has come close to the completeness of that warm evening in 1968.

Through the walls of his body I could hear Brenda asking where I was. I felt Mervyn's answer before I heard it. The drone rose in his belly as he told her that I was with him.

'Where?'

'He's asleep.'

I closed my eyes tight to seem more asleep if they looked.

'Isn't he hot?'

The heat was one of the best things about it; a heat so fully enveloping it made you dizzy and disinclined to move, so incapacitating that you felt you couldn't move if you wanted to. I didn't want to. I was suspended in a nest of hair. Encasing me on every side was downy arm hair and scrubby leg hair and matty chest hair and silky belly hair, and I was nestled and naked in this pocket of damp fur. Sweat trickled between my skin and his pelt, both upwards and downwards on the capillary principle, a sensation that was pleasant enough in itself as mild tickling went, but made exquisite when combined with an inertia that gave immunity to tickling. Better still were the seldom times when Mervyn spoke and plangent vibrations in his trunk spread through all the fibres and fluid and enfolded me in droning.

Sound was the only impression that penetrated from the outside world. Light was blocked by Mervyn's beard and hair, hanging in gnarled bunches and kinked curtains; yard-long hanks that draped over us on every side and gave the squatting Mervyn the appearance of a yurt with a face on top. The warm stench of his armpits built steadily, periodically laced with whiffs of his lesser sweats and excretions, repelling any other smell that came near us.

'He'll suffocate.'

'He's cool.'

'Let him out. I want him to see this.'

Mervyn shifted and unlotussed his legs and parted the beard and fired his hair over his shoulders. The perfect universe disintegrated. Flinch-making bright light and wince-inducing clear noise and lung-scorching fresh air came pillaging in. Worse was the cool of Brenda's hands either side of my ribcage as she hauled me out of Mervyn's lap. Another child might have wept and howled, but I had long since learned that crying was a waste of effort among people who would only stare in blank wonderment as if my shrieks were a sudden prophecy in ancient Greek.

'Man.'

Brenda put me on my feet and pointed to a distant stage, holding my face by the chin to stop me gazing backwards into Mervyn's lap, where the cavity of hair was re-forming and disappearing as he rearranged his limbs and tresses.

'Man that was like giving birth man.'

'Man.'

Brenda was whispering in my ear. 'Look. Keep looking. If you keep looking you'll see the great wizard appear.'

'Why?'

'On the stage. Look. He's coming.'

Across all the heads: the backs of all the long-haired heads in rows and rows of folding wooden chairs, and the headbands and hats of groups of real hippies like us squatting on the ground, disdainful of the serried masses, and the threading flittering of naked children like me, and the occasional cosmic dancer, moving to music perceptible only to themselves. Away on the stage, a plain ugly stage made suddenly luminous in horizontal light from a lowering sun, two minute figures, as small as the earlobes of the man sitting in front, walked to the centre and sat down cross-legged and waited for their audience to quieten. Brenda told me to listen hard. She said that the sounds they would make would cast a spell that could set the world to rights if everyone listened. She said that the wizard was chanting to bring in the New Age. He would stop the wars and the money and make the children happy.

'Is he the one with the tom-toms?'

'Bongos. No. He's the beautiful one.'

In the distance he looked a bit like me. He was little and he had black curly hair. The noise that he and his friend made was faster than music, but even the cosmic dancers let the sunbeams fall from their hands and sat down to listen. The beautiful one leaned forward and began to sing. His voice was weird enough to be a wizard's, and his words made little sense if you didn't know it was a spell.

Everyone, as far as I could see, was happy. Brenda was

transported. Shining crows' feathers hung over her ears and her hair dangled in shiny black plaits. Her face was as shining and white as her smock. From beneath the circumference of her purple hat she whispered to me from time to time.

'It's him. He's come to save the world, and us from ourselves.

When the cross-legged wizard in children's shoes had finished singing and left the stage, Mervyn stirred.

'Let's go now man. Right now, before the next number starts. This is what we came for. We should keep the vibe.'

Bronwen seconded him. 'And we wouldn't be caught in the crush at the end.'

The men turned on her with sneering looks. The women kept their eyes to the ground, ashamed to have had the same thought and relieved not to have been the one crass enough to express it.

Had Bronwen not spoken we might have left on the spur of Mervyn's suggestion, untainted as that was by practicality. Now there was uncertainty. Some were easing themselves cautiously to their feet as if they might be doing no more than stretching their legs, others were gazing abstractedly at the stage as if they were unaware of the predicament. A man who called himself Emperor and wore white trousers was talking about who the next group would be, but his microphone shrieked back at him and the noise from the speakers was like electronic whale song.

'Never mind what the chick said. We should be gone man.' Mervyn made his appeal general, though no one would look at him. All eyes were on Julian now, to see whether he would shift or stay.

'We are reeds blowing in a circular wind.' Julian drew himself upright, into a more mage-like posture. 'We should ask the spirits.' He reached into his mirrorwork satchel and drew out a roll of dirty chamois leather.

'Can't we use coins?' Mervyn was trying to sound reasonable but there was agitation at the edge of his voice. 'If you use the stalks we'll be here for an hour. The question is should we leave now? Not should we have left an hour ago.'

Julian, unperturbed, continued to unroll the yarrow stalks, making the chamois into a mat on the ground in front of him. 'Coins give a symmetrical result.'

'It's a symmetrical question.'

'We all decided that the use of money in the I Ching is disrespectful to the spirits. We voted on it.'

'It's more disrespectful to waste their time by asking them if you should do something you've already done. You can't ask if you should stay when you're staying to ask. We should be out of here man.'

Julian rolled the yarrow stalks between his palms, then placed the bundle on the mat. He removed one stalk, held it up and muttered, then set it down so that it pointed at the bundle. 'The witness is in place. Are you going to get into the vibe, Mervyn, or are you going to disrupt it? We have a decision to make.'

Mervyn acceded by sitting down again and turning the tor of hair that was his body so that he was facing Julian and the I Ching mat like everyone else. The irregular circle watched as Julian divided and counted the stalks again and again, oblivious to the renewed music from the stage. When they talked about it afterwards, everyone claimed that they

6

had heard no music at all during the divination. Julian said it was because we were under the protection of the spirits.

Meanwhile, I had wriggled from Brenda's side and sidled over to Mervyn, hoping for re-entrance to the lap of luxury. I perched on the edge of one of his enormous knees and sank slowly backwards, gradually disappearing into the hairfall; into the heat and stench and comfort and fur, knowing that I was safe from disturbance for a while, now this I Ching business had got going.

Julian was a slow worker, and the others sat with the stillness and silence and fixation of cats looking into a pond. The only person to speak was Bronwen, who, half-way through the process and hoping to redeem herself from her earlier indelicacy, recognised the first trigram. Her voice was heard as an earnest whisper, addressed to no one in particular. 'The open. The stimulating mist.'

A tremor of Mervyn's approval rolled through me. It was impossible to find the exact position that had been so comfortable before. The elements of the hiding place were as good as they had been the first time, the smell and the feel and the heat of it, but the sense of floating was elusive. I could have asked the spirits to help me into the right position, but I knew that they would be busy answering Julian's question.

At last, the hexagram was declared and Julian read the text from the oracle. 'The open gorge. Articulation. The mist swirls below the stream. The nodes of the bamboo. Separate what is separate and make the connections clear. Express things. By measuring the measure the city will be safe.'

'Is that a yes or a no?' It was Steve who spoke. The others

would have been looking at him with smug amusement. Steve was the most recent arrival and it was his role to ask the more naïve questions.

I was squashed violently as Mervyn's stomach expanded and contracted with sudden force. 'Tcha! It said we should separate ourselves man.'

'Not so fast man. I wasn't finished.' You could tell that this was Julian's favourite part of divination. 'There was a transforming yin above. Harshness and bitter speech. Do not do what is asked. Provide whatever is necessary.'

'You're making it up now.'

'I wouldn't meddle with the spirits man.'

'Anyway, it depends whether we asked if we should go or we should stay.'

'I asked if we should go.'

'I didn't. I asked if we could stay. Jimi Hendrix is on later. What did you ask, Colin?'

'Stay, I think. I can't remember.'

'I was the medium. It's what I asked that counts.'

Mervyn exploded, all his flesh making a lovely wobble as he ranted. 'So what's the point of the rest of us doing it, then? Or maybe the spirits think you should stay here on your own. The rest of us can go.' There was shushing from some of the people round us, and Mervyn lowered his voice, but the trembling was all the more intense for it. 'If you're the medium man you're the medium. What the questions pass through. Otherwise we're all just sitting here while you ask whatever you want. Which might explain, for instance, why when we ask what vegetables to plant it always turns out to be things you like, so we get a garden full of sodding cabbages and nothing else. Because you sneak off in your head and ask about cabbages. Is that how it works man?'

'Of course not.'

'Then let's find out what we all asked. How many asked go and how many asked stay and we'll know what the answer is.'

The ripples of Mervyn's anger must have sent me to sleep, and it was late and cold when I woke, and I was being carried through the dark, towards the bus. The music had finished and the stage was dark and most of the people had gone home. The field was lit by a scattering of bonfires made of piles of the wooden folding chairs. There was bad feeling among us, and I could tell that we weren't leaving because of a consensus of interpretation of the oracle. We made our way along a flickering plywood fence, and someone pointed out where it had been pushed over and suggested we take a short cut back to the bus, and then we stumbled in the dark, parallel to hedges and through dubious gates until we reached a road, and stood for a moment in sullen relief before someone opened their mouth to produce the embryo of a discussion about whether to turn right or left.

Bronwen made a spluttering noise. 'Ask the bloody I Ching, why don't you?' Then she set off noisily in what proved to be the right direction.

The bus, when we eventually found it, carried us nearly home, and broke down on the wrong side of the village, and we left it there to be dealt with the next day and walked the last mile across the fields on familiar territory now and sure of our way in the thinning darkness. Mervyn led, balancing me on one shoulder. We made our way in single file through the long spinney and paused on the edge of it, inhaling cold air and the smell of foxes, and looking down-hill towards a rambling, grass-roofed house in an otherwise houseless dell. There was a candle lit in every window. This was the hOme.

'hOmmmmmmmmmmmmmmmmmmmmmmmmmmmmmm mmmmmmmmme.'

The chant rose simultaneously and spontaneously from all of us, fading separately as the breath of each gave out, until there was only Mervyn's profound bass continuing to roll down the hill. A door in the house opened and a figure flitted out, black in the yellow light. Torches were lit along the path to the end of the garden and the barking of dogs intruded from the next dell. We hurried down the hill, the shock of each footfall bouncing me higher on Mervyn's shoulder, until I was spending more time in the air than on the flesh, and thought I was flying home through the darkness.

Debora's face was split in two with her grin of welcome.

She stood in the circular door with a candle held in front of her and the light pouring out of the house behind her. The sky beyond the roof was paling and the air was thick with birdsong. I couldn't help shouting.

'Guess who we saw?'

'The wizard?'

'How did you know?'

'Did he sing?'

'Debora? Why did he call you a zebra?'

By now I was folded in her arms and whispering in her ear and she was nuzzling at me. 'Zebra yourself.'

'What's for tea?'

'Has the child not had anything to eat?'

The question was directed at Brenda, who, tired though she was, still took the trouble to assume an air of casual indifference. 'I told him he could have something when he got home.'

'Did you now?'

They stared at each other for a moment, and then Brenda pushed past us, her head thrown back to show her state of superior unworldliness. 'We have been having a mystical experience. If you had taken the trouble to be there you wouldn't have been thinking of your stomach either.'

Now that we were on the threshold, with an aroma of brown rice seeping out from the kitchen, the ache of hunger that had occupied my stomach for most of the day gave way to acute pain. The others must have been undergoing a similar process because, suddenly unmysticled, they all vanished in the direction of the food, leaving Debora on the path, holding me to her hip, and muttering.

'Mystic pisstic.'

She managed, by using her elbows, to secure a plate of food for me. I ate most of it, then fell asleep with the spoon clenched in my teeth. I was woken by Debora trying to ease the spoon out of my mouth.

'Time the lamb was in bed.'

'Time we all were man.'

'Whose turn is it to keep watch tonight?'

'Brenda.'

Brenda yawned. The candles were fading as daylight began to permeate the room. 'Can't we skip a night? There's not much night left. I'll never keep awake. Missing one night won't kill us.'

Julian took a moment to assemble his face into a patriarchal expression. Then he turned it on Brenda and dropped the lower half into a viscid smile. 'We can't risk it. There hasn't been anything for a while now. For weeks man. The bus needs mending. If we don't get something soon we'll be eating into the stake money.'

'We could ask the I Ching if there's going to be anything tonight.' Brenda sounded desperate.

There was a harmonic groan from Bronwen and Mervyn, which Julian cut through. 'That is setting prophecy against prophecy. It could be dangerous. And you know the I Ching won't let itself be used for getting money.'

Brenda opened her mouth to argue, but Mervyn quashed her with a threatening rumble. 'There's no way man the rest of us are staying up all night with the I Ching just to ask if you can go to sleep.'

Debora stood up, me in her arms, my eyelids smarting from the fight to keep them open. 'I'm putting the boy to bed now.'

Brenda snorted. 'Lucky him.'

'Some mothers might want to kiss their son goodnight.'

'What's this? Pick-on-Brenda night? Why is it always me that has to do everything?'

Brenda flounced off. The men drifted towards their beds and the women began to clear the table. A ball of tortoise-shell fur sped howling through the kitchen, ricocheting off Bronwen's ankles so that she overbalanced and dropped the plates she was carrying in a clatter of wood on stone. She watched one rough-hewn disc roll in the wake of the now vanished cat.

'Time that bloody thing was put out of our misery.'

'Don't say that in front of the child. It's not the cat's fault she's the way she is.'

'Well, don't look at me. I didn't do it.'

'You didn't stop them doing it either.'

Debora and Bronwen glared at each other. It was rare that one of them was provoked to address the other and, once it had occurred, each seemed unsure what to do next. The stand-off was cut short by a whimper from me, prompting Debora to resume the way to my bed.

We passed Julian's room. His door was open and we could see him sitting up in bed in his robe of prophecy, waiting for Brenda to come and start her vigil. He was smiling beatifically at the clunks of plates from the kitchen. It was a pleasure to him to know that others were going about their tasks. Julian was the founder of the hOme and, though we were technically leaderless, our leader. We depended on him, for guidance through the I Ching, and for money through his gift of prophecy.

Julian, the hOme ruler, had begun his adult life working as a stable lad in Newmarket. It was there that he first read *Lord of the Rings* and discovered his strange abilities. Those who shared his dormitory had begun to complain that their sleep was disturbed by him sitting up in bed in the middle of the night and shouting. At first this eccentricity made him unpopular. He was tied in a haynet and lowered through the ice in the water trough as a deterrent, though it was noticed that every dunking only increased the volume of his midnight rantings. Then the lad in the next bed but one, while taking advantage of the comparative privacy of the small hours to indulge in a more relaxed bout of self-satisfaction, witnessed the entire somniloquy and noticed that only one phrase was being used and that it consisted of the name of a runner in the 3.45 at Kempton Park the following day. The horse, a rank outsider called Merry Feasting, won.

Julian began something of a celebrity on the yard, until the trainer enquired into the unusual number of his employees who were falling off their horses during morning gallops. Hangovers were blamed, and Julian was pinpointed as the source of funds that made the hangovers commonplace. He was sacked.

By this time, between one headache and the next bout of

14

consolidating his popularity in the King's Arms, he had begun to suspect that he had a calling in life. Tolkien had affected him deeply, and it seemed more than a coincidence that the book had come into his hands at about the same time as the oracle had entered him. He stopped spending his winnings in pubs and bought a dell in Devon, and recruited settlers to help build the first hOmestead in the New Shire.

Mervyn, whom Julian had found meditating under a laburnum in Nonsuch Park, Cheam, was the only survivor from those early days. They lived in a shepherd's caravan at first, and then a teepee, while making experiments in structural integrity that failed more often than they succeeded. Their incompetence as builders was accentuated by Julian's insistence that all the doors and windows should be round, as they were in Hobbit dwellings, and mitigated by the interdiction against staircases. The idea that the whole building should be in the shape of an Om came from Mervyn, who had a friend who had been to India.

Others came and went during the years the commune formed. Some left their mark on the place. An alcoholic Welsh poet called Dylan brought the I Ching and the yarrow stalks and bequeathed them when he moved on, ever mobile in his resentment at not being the alcoholic Welsh poet called Dylan who had been elected for literary immortality. An American biologist called Judy introduced her personal theory of macrobiotic eating. In her system one could, in the first instance, eat anything that was incapable of flight from the consumer. So mussels were permitted since they were tied to rocks, but snails were not because they were free to slither away. Beyond this basis there was a steep gradient of nutritional purity to be scaled, from stage ten, which allowed one to gorge on a sheep if it were found with its legs already broken, to stage one, in which all food was tabu with the exception of brown rice. Most of us remained stuck at stage three, where carrots and cabbage were permitted, though Debora would see to it that I got regular doses of illicit rations. Judy herself achieved stage one while living at the hOmestead and maintained her purity for several weeks until she collapsed and was carted off to Exeter hospital to be treated for malnutrition, from where she was deported to a mental institution in her country of origin. Her personal failure was interpreted as nothing more than that, and her dietary principles kept hold of our imagination. Other hOme-steaders came to regard their visits to hospital as temporary setbacks in a greater social experiment.

David arrived silently, on his own. I can't remember ever hearing him speak, and wondered sometimes if he had a voice at all, but now and again you would hear him laugh, and it was a deep, powerful laugh that could cross two fields and come at you through the soles of your feet as if all the things he never said had been boiled down inside him.

Debora and Bronwen arrived together and shared a room, despite the palpable dislike that fizzled between them. They rarely spoke to each other in public, but voices could be heard coming from their room late into the night, where a well-thumbed copy of Mary Wollstonecraft topped the pile on the bedside table. Bronwen was an enthusiastic member of the community, thrilled by every new rule and prohibition, while Debora disapproved of so much that the mystery of her remaining with us was often discussed, though never in her presence. Neither was it ever admitted that the reason such a disruptive and cynical influence was tolerated was probably because she did more work about the place than all the rest put together.

The sexual code by which we lived had been defined by Ash, the disaffected younger son of wealthy Bangaloris. He had brought with him the teaching of the tantras. In Ash's version the only fantasy allowed to either partner during intercourse was the leading of a white horse down a Kashmiri valley in springtime. Orgasm was to be avoided under any circumstances, and merit was earned by endurance rather than satisfaction.

Love among us was free, in theory. In fact it was a rare occurrence. A new arrival, of either sex, could go through the residents, in various combinations, like a dose of flu, bringing down the last of them just as the first was getting its breath back. But an unsalted diet of horses in Kashmiri valleys soon dulled the appetite of anyone but the most libidinous, and the most libidinous never stayed long. Ash, our sexual godfather, stayed, and mostly stayed in his room, honing exercises that were neither yoga nor sex, but some goalless amalgamation of the most disgusting aspects of both. His door was always open and, in the end, it may have been the sight of him through that circle of wattle and daub, torturing his genitals in slow motion, an absent expression on his face, that neutered the sexual charge of the hOme. My most prevalent thought whenever I saw him was always one of relief for not being an adult and for having a body that was more functional than recreational.

Though I was not excluded from the sex life of the hOme, Debora saw to it that I was never included either.

Brenda, my mother, the fairy child of the dell, as they sometimes referred to her when she wanted something and was in a mood to charm, was the mascot. She had arrived one day out of nowhere, all eyes and no flesh, with bones as thin as hair and hair as fine as cobwebs, barefoot and bedraggled. Everyone who lived there at the time was sitting in a circle in the top field, on a day of autumn brilliance. They had been experimenting with fly agaric, and Brenda's arrival seemed as natural as rain. She was asked no questions, but offered a tincture of the fungus and shown how to rub it into her armpits and groin.

I was inside her. She was fifteen and I was the reason she had run away and hitched to the south-west, sleeping in hedges and with truck drivers, until she abandoned the road, light-headed with hunger, and took to woods and fields, with nothing to keep her going but a determination that her back should remain turned on the despair she had left behind. She stumbled into a circle of smiling people dressed for a pantomime, but her life had been so odd during the previous days that nothing could alarm her. She assimilated the effects of the fly with the equanimity of a shaman, and decided that she had arrived wherever she was going.

And I, while still the size of her thumb, was given my first hallucination.

I was born an hour before midday on the fourteenth day of Taurus in the month of Beltaine and the Year of the Rabbit at the end of the Age of Capricorn. It had been a portentous winter since Brenda's arrival. Deep snow had covered and smothered the normally mild countryside of Devon, bringing hardship to those dependent on electricity and roads. The hOme fared better, although with temperatures below freezing for seventy consecutive days, and the house in darkness under snow, with one tunnel dug into the bleak world outside, it must have seemed like the end of something; if not the world exactly, at least the end of things as they were. During these seventy days the I Ching, no matter how often it was thrown, always gave the same result: the hexagram of nearing, or Lin, with a nine-at-second. Something enormous was about to happen. Then, at the thaw, my eight-months-pregnant mother was stretching her long-confined legs in the bottom meadow when a white horse came galloping towards her. She screamed and Mervyn, who was near by, hauled her to the top of a bank just in time. The horse reared in front of them, wide hooves bashing the air and black balls aquiver. No one knew how it had got there and it was never seen again.

The entire community was present at my birth, some

burning herbs and some swinging crystals. Julian sat, cross-legged, beside Brenda's head, hunched over his charts.

'Push now and he will have Cancer rising. He will be a nurturer as well as nurtured. He will be perfect in his yin and yang.'

Brenda pushed and her narrow hips dislocated long enough for my head to squeeze through. Debora's hands were waiting to receive me.

'His head is here. Push again. Push again and we will have him.'

They knew, from the I Ching, that I was to be a boy. After several days of debate they had interpreted the reading, by a majority of two, as indicative of my maleness. Had I been a girl it would have been a failure of interpretation and not a sign of inadequacy in the spirit world, which had, quite plainly, predicted that three foxes would be caught with the yellow arrow.

'There's something wrong. He's caught.'

Brenda screamed as Debora forced her fingers between my head and the labia, already taut and inflamed beyond endurance.

'Push, you silly bitch. PUSH!'

I slid out and jackknifed backwards like a fish lunging on a line, strangled by my own umbilical cord. There was screaming and confusion, but Debora kept her head and freed me and coaxed me to breathe.

Beside her, when everyone was quiet, Bronwen was thrown into a trance, and spoke.

'The child is a mage. He is born with the signs of the seer on him. He will be great and his life will be lived in pain, but he will know everything and he will always be right.'

Julian had begun to count the yarrow stalks.

'You must name him. You must name him now before the sticks are counted. He must have a name to make the oracle true.'

The story of my birth and the omens around it was told to me so often that it became like a memory. At times I think I may have been born sentient because there are details I know that I could never have heard; the smell of the room and the expressions on the faces, the flicker of eyes that betrayed thought. Maybe I was aware of what was going on, and hearing the story recounted so many times by so many people only prevented me from forgetting. How else could I remember what Brenda was feeling?

She wanted to sleep or cry. She wanted to cover herself and be alone, and to be held in the arms of her own mother. She wanted a drink of water. The last thing she wanted to do was think of a name for me. Despairing, she looked in the only direction where no one's eyes would meet hers, through the circle of the open door, to the kitchen table where a jar of honey stood from breakfast-time. Honey was the last thing she had eaten. It was honey brought back from India by Ash, who had been spending the spring in a Kashmiri valley and then had gone to Bangalore to touch his family for some of their despised money. So there was a jar of Coorg honey from Karnataka, and Brenda craved a spoon of honey.

'Coorg.'

The murmur escaped from her involuntarily, but the news was lobbed about the room as everyone took their turn to say the new name in quick succession.

'His name is Coorg.'

'What does the oracle have to say for Coorg?'

Julian was sitting in silence and astonishment. The witness was broken. The yarrow stalk had snapped in two, apparently of its own accord, and at the moment that Brenda had named me. Such a thing had never occurred before and Julian, now being a yarrow stalk short of the quota, was at a loss to interpret it. It was Bronwen who was the first to rouse herself from the wide-eyed immobility that pervaded the room.

'He has broken the oracle.'

'The spirits will not speak of him.'

'He is a mage-child.'

'His powers are beyond the spirits' knowing.'

'He will be the seer of the New Age.'

'Merlin has come back to guide us.'

'I thought we decided that Sartre was Merlin.'

'Fuck Sartre, man. This is real.'

So my entrance was made. It wasn't long before some of the wonderment wore off, erased by the realities of baby-care. Julian acquired a new set of yarrow stalks to replace the set that had, if the truth were told, been worn to the point of spontaneous breakage by years of use.

Impervious to her maternal instincts, Brenda considered her responsibilities towards me to have been discharged with my delivery. Her nipples hurt and she refused to go on breast-feeding; went back instead to being the fairy child, as useless and enchanting as the son she had produced and, secretly though not unnoticeably, jealous of my rivalry in the winsome stakes. Fortunately for me Debora's maternal instincts were so overwhelming that her hormones were affected and she found herself expressing milk from virgin breasts. I, naturally, was allowed to take advantage. The phenomenon was accepted at the hOmestead as an ordinary proof of my extraordinary nature and as a sign that, since my welfare was safely in the hands of higher powers, everyone else could go about their business without troubling themselves unduly about my survival.

Cut off as we were, there was no reason for my birth to be noticed in the wider world. No district nurse came to call and no registration was made. Debora suggested that I might, one day, find it useful to be in possession of a birth certificate, but Julian said that the Age of Aquarius was at hand and bits of paper would soon be superfluous. The matter was never raised again.

Infancy passed. Vegetables were planted, harvested and eaten and digested. The consequence of their digestion was dug back into the earth for the following crop. More people came to try living in our experiment every year and fewer stayed. No one was ever turned away, even though the nature of what we were doing was more attractive to the mad than to the sane. But somehow the truly gibbering mad couldn't stand us for long. Perhaps they were restless or perhaps they really needed a sane environment in which to practise their madness. Or perhaps the rules of our freedom were too strict.

Sometimes children were brought in, and this I resented. It was my job to be the child. And children had a tendency to treat me as an equal, whose function was to collaborate in their games of imagination. I had been told that whatever was in my imagination was the future reality of the world, and was too precious a commodity to be wasted on games of Doctors and Junkies. But in the end the children who came were ephemeral, and I was the one who remained, having wished them away.

In my earliest memories we were oddities when we went out into the world; stared at in the street by people who must have thought us as odd as I thought them, with their tamed hair and tight lips and monochrome clothes and packaged cigarettes. Some would laugh out loud and point and some would pretend they hadn't noticed us at all, sliding their eyeballs sideways with a nauseated expression on their faces. By the time I was four things were changing. The straight people remained, but we freaks were multiplying, and the more of us there were the less freakish we seemed. Soon, allies could be spotted in every gathering; long hair and tattered velvet loped on every pavement. You could tell who was a kindred spirit and who wasn't by the cut of their jib more than by their clothes, which was essential since the way we looked was beginning to be fashionable, and not everyone who wore hippie gear was necessarily hip. Ordinary people were trying to be extraordinary, and in the process making the extraordinary ordinary. Still, a fellow believer was distinguishable. There was the dirt in their fingernails and the happy glaze of their expressions. There was something proud about the men and something humble about the women. You could walk right up to a real cat and, without preamble, plunge straight into the depths of a conversation about *The Wizard of Earthsea* or *The Hobbit* or the best way to achieve oracular hallucination from bay leaves (Julian had tried eating a whole bag of them and was sick in the moonlight), as the sibyls had done when the earth was wise.

There was a buzz in our Council meetings then. It seemed

as though people everywhere were beginning to agree with us: that no one could possibly deny our truth once the light was shone on their faces. When the Grand Council made a decision, it was no longer for the hOmestead alone but for the world in general. The spirits were communicating our thoughts to the insurrecting masses. When students took to the streets of Paris for the establishment of a new society, it was we who were directing their energies, and inspiring their ideals. In the papers we would read what we had done, Julian and the I Ching and I. If we thought it, so it would be. It was an exciting time.

As she approached her twenty-first birthday, in the disquieting spring of '68, and some months yet before we went to hear the wizard sing at Woburn Abbey, Brenda found herself growing restless. She had been six years at the hOme and the novelty of eternal childhood was wearing thin. In a regime of free love, what had been her charming indifference to sex, her couldn't-care-less willingness to engage in any erotic activity suggested by the men, was turning to repugnance. This led to an unharmonious meeting of the Grand Council, during which I lay across her lap and felt her flesh turn to stone and heard the sullen withering of her voice to silence, while she was accused of no longer being in on the vibe through her frigidity. Julian was her chief accuser, the other men collaborating in monosyllables and looks. Debora might have defended her without much trouble. Everyone knew that Julian had an ulterior motive; that Brenda was the only woman to have allowed him to walk the horse with her a second time. But Debora was away in Paris for a while, and the remaining women, Bronwen, Alice and Marge, looked away and said nothing.

Not long after that, without the situation improving from anyone's point of view, on my fifth birthday Colin arrived. There was something funny between Brenda and him from the start; a look from one to the other that was almost accusing, before a word had passed between them. He was as ethereal as she. Fleshless bones were held high in his body, and black hair grew long to his waist, straight and lank as water. He arrived in the morning and a grand piano followed him in the afternoon, carried into the house by grumbling men in brown coats, one of whom gave me a packet of sweets in the shape of cigarettes.

The piano was set in the centre of the biggest room, the room where we gathered in winter and bad weather, with rugs and cushions thick across the whole floor and a fire-place that stuck a ragged blackened tongue out at the ceiling. On that first day, when Colin sat down to play, with all the windows open, the garden was filled with music and there was a sense of completeness, as if this was what we had been waiting for to round off our lives. Everyone sat still under the trees and no one talked. When Brenda stood up I slipped my hand in hers and went with her into the house, where we watched his white fingers flit over keys as black and white as his skin and hair, until he noticed us and stopped.

'You're very beautiful.'

She said it to him as though it were an explanation for our presence, and then lowered herself on to one of the big cushions, her now clammy hand still in mine. He smiled and returned to the keyboard, and at the fall of his hands the air was fat once again with music.

After a time he stopped again and rose from the stool and drew his kaftan over his head and dropped it to the floor, before reseating himself to carry on where he had left off, now unselfconsciously nude, without so much as a referring glance in our direction.

Nudity was not remarkable at the hOme. Nonetheless Brenda was agitated. She spoke over the music.

'Why did you do that?'

'Because you wanted me to.'

'What makes you think that?'

'Because you thought it.'

'In that case what am I thinking now?'

'Nothing that I can help you with. I've never had those inclinations. Not for a woman. I'm sorry.'

I had never seen her embarrassed before. Her face reddened and her hands began to shake and she almost tripped over her dirndl in her hurry to be out of the room. I stayed, puffing on my cigarette sweetie and watching the air thicken with sound.

He had been a professional, but he had had a breakdown, at the diminuition of which he found that his hair had grown, which led to chance conversations with other long-haired people, which led in turn to an awareness of a life alternative to the world of concert halls and recordings; an existence in which the pleasure of making music had nothing to do with competitions or reviews or making money. For a while he lived in a commune in Hampshire, which was entirely male and where the only rule was that every member had to go to bed with a different member each night. Though it was a fair attempt to address the demons that had driven him into his breakdown, it didn't suit him, and someone he met in a bookshop in Salisbury told him about the hOme. Without further enquiry or prior arrangement, he and his piano came to us. In those days, to follow your instincts and pitch up out of the blue was always the most acceptable course of action.

Before long Colin was referring to Brenda as his sister, and they were sharing a bed, into which I could climb in the early morning while they were both sleeping. I had never been tempted into my mother's bed while Debora was available as a resort for comfort, but Debora was away still, fomenting revolution on the streets of Paris on our behalf. Meanwhile Brenda, under Colin's influence, had become a person with whom one could almost share affection.

In the clean light of early summer morning I would settle between them and count the breathing of one and then the other, trying to guess who would wake first. It was usually Brenda, and she and I would watch Colin together, reading the dreams that flitted across his features, wondering what stories he would tell us once he was half awake. Sometimes it would be a story from his dream and sometimes from his past. I liked the stories of the commune in Hampshire, where all the men had to do the work of women.

One morning, more atmospherically perfect than the rest, when a Holly Blue butterfly came gliding through the round window from a circle of blue sky and landed on the pillow by our heads, twitching pensively on stained linen, while we waited for Colin to open his eyes and tell us something, Brenda spoke to me of her past for the first time.

'We used to do this when we were little. On a Saturday morning we'd get into my mother's big bed and Daddy would still be asleep and me and PJ would get under the covers at the other end so we were like kings and queens on a playing card, and then Daddy would wake up and make tea for us all and it was like a picnic in the bed. And we'd laugh.'

'Who's PJ?'

'Your uncle. I suppose.' She laughed.

'Will Colin make tea for us when he wakes up?'

'You could ask him.'

Colin woke and shifted his head, sending the butterfly off on a circuit of the room, and looked across at us with his treacle-black eyes, purged of all expression by sleep.

'Your mother. I saw her. She looks like someone I know.'

By this time Brenda was too accustomed to Colin's telepathy to be spooked by it. Her reply was calm.

'I was thinking of writing to her.'

'Why?'

'She doesn't even know she's got a grandson.'

'Why now?'

'I need her advice.'

'About what?'

'About why. About why anything. I think she always knew more than she let on. She might be able to tell me why I lust for a man with no lust.'

His arms reached across my head and he brushed his thumb against her lips. 'I have lust. Lust is the worst part of me.'

'Not lust for me.'

'What I have for you is the best part of me.'

'Colin?' I raised my head so that it broke the line of sight between them. 'Will you make us tea?'

In a way it was Debora's return which sent Julian off on the trip where he found the wizard for us. They locked horns within minutes of her arrival, towards the end of the month of Beltaine.

There was a lot of hugging and kissing and loud talk and some weeping. Debora stood at the centre of it all, wearing a daisy-chain chaplet that Marge had put on her head. Anecdotes were spilling out of her, of Castin in the rue this and blood flowing on the rue that, and the more she told the more thankful we were to see her alive and in one piece. In all of this, from the second she had appeared in the lane, I was clamped to her hip with my face spliced into her neck, taking a half-share in all the embraces.

Julian prowled on the periphery.

'What's the matter, Julian? Are you not glad to see me back?' Whether she meant it as a taunt or not, it was a taunt to him.

'Things have been happening while you were off enjoying yourself.'

'I can see.' She beamed at Brenda and Colin, who were hand in hand.

'Man.' The syllable strained beneath a load of derision.

'Woman. Please.'

'Woman. Exactly. That's the whole fucking point. If you were a man you might have some idea what was going on. And I'm not talking about the True Romance with Rachmaninov here. And I'm not talking about a lot of froggy eggheads disappearing up their own arses with petrol bombs.'

'Oh? Really? Do tell.' Her rigidity and trembling would have dislodged me if she had not been squeezing me like a set of bagpipes. 'Do tell what world-shattering event that I somehow missed is more important than people with the guts to stand up for what they believe dying in the street, to win freedom for ungrateful stay-at-home shits with no balls and a yarrow stalk for a prick.'

The last allusion was unkind. It was a joke among the women that Julian had a thing like a knitting needle. Alice used to call him the Abortionist behind his back. No one would explain that to me satisfactorily, and I used to think that an abortionist was no more than a lousy fuck, and wonder what all the fuss was about, particularly when people claimed to be in favour of it.

'You are pathetic. We don't need all your dried-up man-hating lesbian crap here. Just because you've been to Paris and seen something bigger than your sodding washing-up rotas doesn't make you any more important than you were before. You are a cog. A little cog. A menial. You might have got above yourself, but you don't even know where the real revolution is happening. You can't see that Paris is a sideshow; not even a sideshow. Paris is a distraction to keep all the squares and their newspapers occupied while the real revolution gets under way, and the reason you can't see it is because you're a square in disguise. You are a counter-revolutionary. I denounce you. You have no right to be here and we don't want you.'

He started to walk away. Had he kept on walking the effect of his words might have been devastating. I was sobbing at the thought of Debora being sent away for ever. Everyone else was staring straight ahead in that pole-axed kind of way. No one had ever been told to leave before. That wasn't how it worked. If anyone was really unpopular the spirits made it impossible for them to stay.

Had Julian left it at that, everything might have changed, but he couldn't resist turning round for a parting shot.

'At least I've got a prick, you fucking dyke.'

Alice sniggered and Bronwen smirked and Mervyn put his hands over the minute portion of his face that wasn't concealed by hair and his shoulders began to shake. Brenda whispered something in Colin's ear and he tittered squeakily. By the time Julian had marched out of sight, though not necessarily out of hearing, his head thrown back in the attitude of a vanquishing orator, the air was punctured with suppressed, multiple, staccato laughter. Debora, though not yet cooled enough to be amused, was coaxing me out of my distress with assurances that she wasn't going anywhere and I was to take no notice of Julian.

Ash put one hand on Debora's shoulder and rubbed the snot off my face with the other. 'Don't worry about it. You know what he's like. He's stressed. All these years he's been doing the come-the-revolution stuff and now the tower has fallen and he thinks the weight is all on his shoulders.'

'The tower?' Debora put me down and knelt to unpack the rucksack, ferreting for my present among pamphlets and paperback philosophies. 'What tower?' She took out a piece of flat metal, cut to the shape of a cat and painted tortoiseshell. The eyes were two beads of glass that flashed in the sunlight.

'The tower fell. Two days ago. Julian threw the I Ching to ask about the revolution and it said that the true beginning would be at the falling of the tower. The next day Ronan Point collapsed.'

'What's a block of flats got to do with us?'

'It's the signal. Things are moving.'

I was holding my present by its string, watching it twirl and catch the light. There was a yowl and a ball of fur hurtled through the air and knocked it out of my hand. It was the real cat, who then shot up the nearest tree, where she crouched on a branch and angrily demonstrated her entire vocal range. Some sniggered, and some glanced nervously at Debora. Debora demanded an explanation.

'They dosed the cat.' Bronwen shrugged. 'I told them not to.'

'They what?'

'It's cool.' Ash, though sounding nonchalant, was backing away from Debora as he spoke. 'That is now the coolest cat on the planet. We gave her a little trip. What other cat can say she saw God?'

'Can't you see what you've done? That animal is now insane.'

'Out of her fucking tree man.'

There was another snigger at this, albeit a lone and truncated one.

Debora, still squatting by her rucksack, put her hands in her head and sniffled. 'Maybe he's right. I don't belong here.'

I showed her a scratch that ran the length of my arm and was beginning to sting. She looked at the scratch in a helpless way as if, for once, she didn't know what to do. Colin came over and picked me up and did the kiss-it-better thing and looked at her in his mind-reading way.

'Maybe you shouldn't have gone away.'

That evening Julian called a meeting of the Grand Council. Everyone was there except Debora, who had spun herself into a silent tornado of housework and scrubbing and rice-cake-making. The oracle was thrown and told Julian that he had to go away on a mage-trip, alone. He commandeered the bus and left that night. Mervyn told him that he didn't have to go and that things would be cool with Debora by the morning. He replied haughtily that this had nothing to do with that cog: the oracle was only concerned with higher things and if everyone had the same respect for the spirits as him people like her wouldn't be tolerated anyway.

There was an air of gloom as we went to bed that night. The yowling of the tripped cat ripped sporadically through the darkness, and rain hammered on the parts of the tin roof that were not yet turfed. I lay awake and worried that the morning, if it ever happened, would be worse still.

Then everyone slept late. The day was bright and freshly washed, and there was the return to food cooked by Debora, who was the only one who could make a satisfying meal out of the ingredients we were allowed. And no Julian, of course. Calm descended and reigned supreme for a while.

It was Colin, in his gentleness, who introduced us to the practice of shouting at vegetables. Since the days of Judy the macrobiotic, a theory had lingered that vegetables were living entities that screamed with pain when they were yanked from the ground. The screams were on a subsonic level, only audible to other vegetable matter and such hypersensitive beings as Judy. Others were reluctant to leave the hOme in her company, since the mere sight of a lawn being mown could induce hysteria. She would press her hands over her ears and rush at the astonished gardener, while bellowing about the National Socialist Party and holocausts in general.

Though the belief survived her, the emphasis changed from a compassion for the plant kingdom to a suspicion that brutal harvesting practices were affecting the yield in general. How could cabbages be expected to thrive when they were daily witnesses of the end that was in store for them; when they were being raised in their own charnel house? Various strategies were tried to circumvent the problem, culminating in the ritual of carefully digging out the required vegetable as though it were to be transplanted and carrying it, root ball intact, to a copse on the far side of the house, where it was dispatched cleanly with a pair of secateurs. Though this system was time-consuming, wasteful of topsoil and not easily adapted for Brussels sprouts and other subjects that required regular amputation, it was the best we could come up with for several years. It fell into abeyance just before the arrival of Colin, when Alice had a breakthrough communication with the vegetable fairies. They told her that suspicion was rife in the potager. That the vegetables who went to the woods were being mourned, and spoken of as the Disappeared.

The first meal that Colin took with us was a reluctant affair. People picked at their food and tried to talk of other things. It was the first screaming harvest of spring cabbages and there was a general feeling of wrongdoing, not aided by Bronwen's attempts at cooking in Debora's absence. I couldn't eat at all for thinking of the suffering that had been inflicted, and sobbed onto my oatcake. Julian, who was having yet another go at stage one, was smugly tucking into his brown rice, and it was then, to cheer us up, that he proposed the cat should be dosed with acid. Until that night the cat was a docile, staring creature that made few demands of life. Julian argued that a bit of chemical enlightenment could only make her life more interesting. With the green carnage on our plates, everyone was too dispirited to argue with him, except Bronwen, who was making a lip-smacking show of eating everything in front of her and looking insulted at the same time. Colin said he thought it was a bad idea, but Colin was new and his opinion counted only in the negative sense. His objection was all the more reason for doing it.

She must have known something was wrong to be stalked through the kitchen by someone who normally ignored her, but she was never unwilling to make new friends and let herself be caught, and hardly struggled as Julian held her mouth open with one hand and put the tab at the back of her throat with the other. He rubbed her gullet for a bit, and then checked to see whether it was gone before letting her go. Still she didn't run away, but washed herself, and stared back at us in puzzlement at being the subject of such unusual attention. It was a while later, and we had almost forgotten what had been done, when she began to make strange noises, stared at nothing for half a minute and then fled in a scattering of involuntary urine. There was some laughter, but not as much as may have been intended, and it was a little forced. Before that evening her name was Eekamouse, but afterwards she was only ever referred to as the cat, as though she had lost her name along with her mind.

Maybe it was the failure of his intervention to save the cat from enlightenment that spurred Colin into thinking of a solution to the cabbage problem. The next morning he looked particularly thoughtful, and went and stood at the end of the rows, and yelled his intentions at the top of his voice.

'RIGHT, YOU CABBAGES! I'M GOING TO KILL ONE OF YOU AND EAT YOU!'

His theory was that the shock of such an announcement, delivered with such force, would cause the cabbages, to a brassica, to faint clean away. Alice later confirmed that this was true and that, furthermore, the attendant fairies fainted alongside them. So while they were all anaesthetised and none the wiser, Colin would nip in and whip out the heads of his choosing. This came to be considered a milestone in hOme technology, and earned Colin respect and acceptance which his introversive nature might have precluded.

Debora, when she had returned and Julian was gone, expressed some doubts about the necessity for such drama in the cabbage patch. She had never taken the issue of plant sensitivity very seriously. I had often seen her pull a leaf of lovage and eat it in full view of the mother plant. She watched Colin perform his ritual with something suppressed on her face that might have been a smirk. Her questions were asked in a grave tone.

'Isn't it worse for them when they wake up to find one of their friends is missing?'

'Cabbages can't count.'

'Really?'

'Besides, each cabbage is so relieved to find itself still in the ground on waking that it becomes perfectly content. So long as they haven't heard the subsonic screaming they are fine.'

'If we can't hear them screaming, how can they understand what you are shouting?'

'I speak perfect cabbage.'

'I see.' Debora surveyed the rows. 'Can you ask them to stagger their growth a little? It looks like we're in for a glut.'

'I'll do what I can. But I'm not very popular with them since I started the shouting thing.'

I was in the ash tree above their heads while this conversation was going on. I used to hide there every morning among the new leaves to watch Colin's harvest. Sometimes Brenda would be with him and sometimes they would sit in the seclusion of that part of the garden and talk for a while before Colin did the dirty deed. I don't think they ever knew that I was above their heads, though it was hard to say what Colin knew and didn't know, what with his telepathy and all.

She told him one morning that she loved him and he replied that the time was coming when everyone would love everyone. Everything love everything.

'That's not what I'm talking about.'

'Then what?'

'Call yourself a mind-reader.'

'It's not as though you're thinking very clearly.'

'I don't think I can stand this any more.'

'Do you want us to stop?'

'I want us to be unstoppable. All this coolness is driving me mad.'

'So we go up the valley with the white horse or however the thing is done around here, and then what? We become as others and lose everything?'

'We could go away.'

'Where?'

'Anywhere. There must be places.'

'I've been places. Believe me, here is better. And I've only just arrived. Don't ask me to leave.'

'And I've been here too long. Since I was a child I've been nowhere else. I want to go to San Francisco and Paris and Kathmandu. I wrote to my mother.'

'What did you say?'

'I haven't posted it.'

She drew a postcard from the pocket of her skirt and handed it to him. Although I could hardly see it at the time, I came to know it backwards in later years. The picture was of a golden spaniel puppy crawling out of a shiny coal scuttle. The message read: I'M FINE AND

HOPE YOU ARE SORRY I RAN OFF BEST WISHES B.

He spent a long time studying it, then began to question her while still turning it over and rereading it. 'Did your dad have a bad fringe?'

'Why?'

'Was he a builder? Did your mum lisp and smoke Woodbines? Did you run off from Cherry Road without leaving a note; in your school uniform on the day before their wedding anniversary when your little brother was sick with jaundice and for all they knew you were murdered in a ditch?'

Brenda was crying and nodding her head. 'Stop that. Stop it now. You shouldn't know any of that. You can't be reading my mind because I never think about those things. What are you trying to do to me?'

He put his arms about her. After a while I found myself watching them take the white horse for a walk, his white bottom clenching and unfurling in the dappled shade of the ash. It went on for a long time and I got bored and slithered down the other side of the tree, and went off looking for Debora or Mervyn, or anyone who might talk to me and stop me thinking.

Later, the same day I think, I was helping Colin to hunt caterpillars among the vegetables. We would put them in a big tin and walk down the lane a mile or so to release them at a safe distance from the crops.

When our catch had wriggled away into the woods, and after we had had a paddle in the stream, he asked me whether I felt like walking on to the village. As we went he gave me a long talk about the roles of men and women in the revolution. He explained that it was the duty of us men to change society and the job of women to make life as comfortable as possible during the change. Women, he said, didn't like change, and if it wasn't for men there'd be no progress in the world and if it wasn't for women there'd be no stability to balance the progress.

When we arrived in the village we went to the post office, where Colin bought a stamp and posted my mother's post-card to my grandmother. All the way home he was silent.

Brenda and Colin were walking the horse incessantly by the time Julian got back from his mage-trip. I had stopped clambering into their bed in the mornings, because they were always too busy to talk to me, caught up in the dull rhythm of their new pastime: he with his eyes closed and his head in the clouds, and she motionless, gazing up at him like a daisy that turns its face to the sun.

Though they were too wrapped up in each other to take any notice of what the others thought, they may yet have been encouraged by a general approval of their carry-on, blushing appropriately at remarks they were intended to overhear.

'They look more like brother and sister every day.'

'How Greek.'

'Isis and Osiris at hOme.'

'I meant how Egyptian.'

'Man.'

Whether Brenda and Colin caught the infection or started it, there was a bit of an epidemic of that sort of thing at the time. You could hardly turn a corner without coming across a bout of necking or groping, if not actual equine perambulation. Alice and Mervyn; Mervyn and Bronwen; Bronwen and David; David and Marge; Marge and Ash; Ash all by himself as only he knew how. Colin and Brenda stayed true to each other, though careless of where they did it or who saw them. They were at the hub of it, with the others kaleidoscopically combining and recombining about them. Only Debora and I remained aloof. We barricaded ourselves into the kitchen and created a mush-free zone. Mush was the word that Debora would vent and I echo as we were driven indoors by the sight of yet another set of buttocks oscillating in the sunshine.

'Why is everyone so mushy now?'

'It's the summer.'

I thought about that. 'They weren't all mushy last summer.'

'This summer is different.'

'Is it the summer of love?'

'Depends what you call love.'

'Will it be over soon?'

She bent her legs and hunkered so that her eyes were level with mine and there could be no doubt of her seriousness. 'There's nothing wrong with it. I don't want you to think that. It's a natural thing. When you're older you'll want to do it as well. Everyone does.'

'Then why don't you?'

She paused to construct her sentence. 'Because I'm no good at doing things the same time as everyone else. I either want to do it too soon or after they've all finished. And because of Paris.'

'What happened in Paris?'

'Nothing. Anyway, they'll stop soon. You'll see. As soon as Julian gets back it'll all be packed away again.'

She was right. The return of Julian brought about the end of the saturnalian part of that summer. His face shone with a fervour that cast the libidinous thrills of his absence into petty shadow. Not only had he seen the light: the light had been exactly what he had expected it to be and was now in his possession. He had also acquired Steve along the way, not so much as a new recruit for the hOme, but as an adornment for himself.

As with any vehicle that approached us, we heard the bus long before we saw it, and by the time it came to a clanking rest at the top of the lane we were all gathered in welcome. Julian stepped out, his nose held high above our smiles, and then he turned with a courtly gesture and handed his new friend down the steps as if they were a knight and lady in a storybook.

'This is Steve Brandybuck.'

A gasp, though common in fiction, is not a sound that you often hear in real life, and when it is produced simultaneously by a group of people surprised by the same amazement it is a remarkable sound. You could almost feel the vacuum as all the lungs drew sharply on the air at the sight of Steve Brandybuck and the sound of his hobbit name.

We were used to strange-looking people with names to match, but this was a creature straight from myth. There was a little pointy yellow beard and a lot of yellow hair that flew about on hardly any wind at all, obscuring the greater part of a weathered face, and occasionally revealing a magenta nose the size and shape of a marble, and eyes so recessed as to be colourless and only indicated by the occasional refractive gleam. His hands and his bare feet were flat and square and hairy, and his toenails were yellow pebbles set in leather. His face was slashed by an involuntary, lipless and narcotic grin. He was no higher than Julian's shoulder and had no fat on him to speak of.

What questions were mustered were brushed aside by Julian, who announced, in a drawling voice, without looking anyone in the eye, that there would be a meeting of the Grand Council that night. Then he and Steve stepped through us and retired to his room, where they stayed for the rest of the day. If there was any talk between them it was in voices too low to be heard by loitering outside the door, an observation made at various times by several people. By the time darkness had fallen, when Julian emerged in his mage robes and processed to the Council Circle with Steve in his train, the rest of us were irritable with mystification.

The Council Circle occupied the middle part of a redundant cider orchard, among gnarled and mistletoed and lightning-split, near-fruitless apple trees. We sat on grass that, the meetings being nocturnal, was always wet with dew. Flaming torches marked the circle boundary and a bonfire the centre. Lit candles in jam jars hung from branches throughout the orchard, glowing and flickering and sometimes burning through their own string to fall portentously to earth like meteors. There was something called a magestone; a flat piece of granite big enough for the counting of yarrow stalks, which Julian sat behind. The rule was that the Council met whenever the spirits called on us, through Julian. Somehow this never happened when it was raining, or in the cold dead of winter.

It had been usual for Mervyn to sit on Julian's right hand, but this was the evening when his position was usurped by Steve. Mervyn stood by the fire until everyone was settled, staring hard at the interloper until Julian was forced to ask him whether he had a problem.

'He's sitting in my place man.'

'This is a circle. We are all equal in the eyes of the spirits. It doesn't matter where you sit.'

'I always sit there man.'

'Do you?'

Julian's vague dismissal of past custom was given in an airy voice, and then he withdrew his attention from Mervyn and rearranged the folds of his robes. Mervyn, dumbstruck, looked around for a sympathetic eye to catch, but all were trained on Julian. Defeated, he sat in the only space available, to the right of Steve, and for the rest of the meeting made his objections by loud and frequent farting, taking care to lift his backside in Steve's direction for each exertion.

The rest of us were in our usual places. Ash, David and Colin sat on Julian's left, in that order, making the male half of the circle, or what Julian sometimes called the upper hemisphere. There were two almost imperceptible gaps between that and where Brenda, Debora, Bronwen, Alice and Marge sat, counted clockwise. The gap between Colin and Brenda would close steadily as she sneaked her hand into his, while the gap between Mervyn and Marge would increase as the odour of his dissatisfaction intensified. I was spread across Debora's lap, where the predominating smell was of an old goatskin which she had spread on the ground to save herself from piles.

'I have travelled far and have many things to tell.'

Julian began the formal proceedings in a voice that was pretentious, even for him. Mervyn responded with a timely ripper and a facetious apology.

'My journey took me north, as the spirits directed.'

'Man.' Mervyn shook his head in mock wonder. 'Those spirits really know their stuff. Any other direction and you'd have needed a boat. You're so lucky man.'

Julian snapped. 'Are you going to get with the vibe or not? I've got a tale to tell here man.'

'I'm all ears man.' Mervyn let off a boomer that made the ground vibrate.

Though she was suppressing laughter more successfully than anyone else, I could feel that Debora was close to breaking point. Her stomach muscles had gone hard and shaky. Her voice crossed the circle, stern in reproof. 'Let him get on with it or we'll be here all night.'

Julian cleared his throat. 'I left it to the spirits to decide the limit of my journey. Wherever the bus broke down would be the end of the quest. You know what that bus is like. I was lucky to get to Shepton Mallet.' He was speaking in his normal voice now, the telling of the story taking over from his own importance. 'But there was something going on. The engine held out through all of England and Scotland. Then, on a high, lonely road beyond Inverness, looking out over the Black Isle, steam began to belch from the bonnet and the engine made a noise like the song of dragons. I pulled over on to the verge and collapsed on to the wheel, exhausted by days of driving, and I stared into the empty distance, afraid of what I had come to and happy that the quest was near an end. I waited for a sign from those who had led me there.

'That was when I heard a banging on the mudguard.' Here he paused, and looked at each of us in a way that heightened the suspense, and then spoiled the effect by

letting a blank expression cross his features, before igno-
miniously reaching into his robes and drawing out a sheet
of paper, which he ran his eyes over while moving his lips
rapidly. He stowed the paper and continued. 'Then I
wrested my eyes from the horizon, and, looking down in
trepidation and wonder, saw Steve Brandybuck, who had
materialised from nowhere in my hour of need.'

'I was just hitching man.' It was the first time we had
heard Steve speak. His voice was high pitched enough to
be nearly a squeal. Somehow, unearthly though it was, it
robbed him of some of his otherworldliness.

'I know man. But the point is I didn't see you. We've been
through this. As far as I was concerned you just appeared.
On an empty road.'

'I was behind a bush. Having a slash.'

'We've already discussed this.'

'Sorry man. You're the man.'

Julian relocated the sonorous tone with which he had
begun. 'It was weird. The way it happened was definitely
weird, whether he was pissing in the bushes of not. Weird
I broke down there and weird he appeared that moment,
wanting a lift. Weird he should be the man who can mend
buses.'

'It was only the fan belt man.'

'The man who mends buses! And I knew the whole thing
was a sign I was close to the Grail, and when he said his
name was Brandybuck I knew he would lead me to my
destiny. I asked him where he was going and he said he
was following a wizard and then I got the weirdest feeling
like every hair on my body standing out like spines on a
thistle man. Like my head flew off and my bowels went

loose and I had to rethink the whole breathing thing.

'Man.' He paused, and everyone was silent and rapt. The air became still and even the flames of the fire and torches and candles were steady and expectant. A bat flicked low through the circle. 'A wizard! I said that I too was on a quest man and he said what's yours man? and I said all quests were the same man there was only one grail, one ring for the fellowship and he was the keeper of the gate man and I need to see this wizard you got man so where's he at man? and he told me the wizard was singing in Inverness and I said a singing wizard man? and he said wait'll ya hear him man and all the time he was mending the bus like in seconds and we were rolling down to Inverness and I didn't even see the road in front of me like the spirits were driving the bus to take us to the wizard.

'So I asked him how he found the wizard, like where do you go for wizards, and he told me he found him gigging in Middle Earth and I was sold man.'

'What was he like? The wizard?' Colin asked for all of us, leaning forward, mouths open as wide as nestlings, even Mervyn and even Debora.

'Like the wizard. Like Gandalf but like a kid. Tiny. In the middle of a stage sitting down and singing all his spells in a weird voice like an animal. Like you could hear the cosmos changing while he sang it. Like you couldn't take your eyes away from him and all the songs went through you and stayed in your head. Like he never stopped singing and I can hear him now. I can hear the songs now, rearranging all the electricity in my brain.

'We followed him, all over the land of Alba: Motherwell; Dundee; Glasgow; Edinburgh; like every night the vibe grew. There were chicks everywhere for the taking but like we didn't touch them because we were on to something higher.'

'Amphetamines.' Steve nodded in agreement, and licked his lips at the memory of it.

'Yeah well, like I didn't mean that man but we had to keep awake man. We weren't going to miss anything just for sleeping. Everyone was on stuff, except Marc, I mean the wizard man. The wizard never took anything. He had his own energy. Wizards have their own chemistry going on. The rest of us were doing stuff with Peregrine Took. What Took took we took.'

'Peregrine Took?'

'The dark Steve.' Julian said it as though it were explanation enough, and not even Colin was prepared to show himself up by asking more.

Fortunately Steve saw the chance to fill some gaps in the narrative and cut in. 'Took's the dark Steve and I'm the pale. We go a long way back. We were doing stuff man before stuff had names. He was the kind of cat you stuck around. You could see he had destiny. He was marked man. Then he told me he was in this combo with a guy called Marc and they had a gig at Middle Earth and I went along to Covent Garden and they blew my head away man. Tyrannosaurus Rex man. And Steve was Peregrine Took because Marc said so and Marc was the man man. And the first thing Marc says to me is I should be a Brandybuck, and he was just laughing his head off like it was some big joke, but like man when a wizard gives you a handle the handle sticks and that's how you know he's the wizard man.'

Steve finished in a squealing crescendo that seemed to leave him exhausted, which gave Julian, who had been fidgeting on the sidelines, the opportunity to reclaim our attention.

'You've got to hear him. This cat's the mage. He's got an incantation that's bringing in the new enlightenment. This is worldwide redemption by musical spells. This is Merlin back in the world preaching and the gospel is the ancient one. This is the man the oracle's been telling us to watch out for.'

'Hang on.' Brenda reached over and pulled me out of Debora's lap as she made her interruption. She held me in a possessive grip to which neither of us was accustomed, one hand fiercely round my ankles to stop me kicking myself free.

'I thought Coorg was going to be the new Merlin. The oracle said it would be him. We can't have two Merlins. That's silly. You said I was the Mother of Merlin. And who is this Tyrannosaurus person anyway? Does he have a mother?'

'Cool it!' Julian's voice came sharp across the Council Circle. 'You know nothing. Remember what you are and where you are. You're a chick. What right have you to question the cosmos? Things change man. Change. Don't you get it? The oracle is the book of changes. Things have never been changing faster than they are now. When Coorg was born there was gonna be time for him to grow up and be a mage. But the battle came sooner than we expected. The revolution is now and Coorg is still a kid. Merlin is needed now and Merlin comes when the need is greatest. You think the establishment, you think all the banks and the governments and armies are gonna be brought down by a five-year-old kid? Don't think they don't know what's happening. The establishment know what's up and if the revolution doesn't happen now they're gonna crush it for ever. Don't think we haven't talked about this. We sat up all night and talked it through with Took and the wizard. We don't have another twenty years to wait for Coorg to grow up and be Merlin. The time is now man.'

'Did this guy say he was Merlin?'

'Why should he? He doesn't need to. He's not going to declare himself now just like that so the establishment know where to get him and nobble him, is he? He's got to keep it under wraps while he sings his spells and gathers strength. He doesn't need to say who he is. The people who know can see who he is. That's the whole point of us being the people who know.'

'So Coorg isn't a mage any more?'

They were all looking at me.

Steve narrowed his eyes and took a big hit, sucking loudly to gain everyone's attention and letting the smoke out in little wisps as he spoke. 'Man. Merlin is many. You've got a mage kid here. Anyone can see that. You think Merlin is gonna put all his eggs in one basket man? If Marc fucks up, if things go bad for the singing white wizard this kid is gonna be next in line for the battle with the dark forces. You gotta treasure this kid man. Keep him safe. He's our insurance for the future. He may be needed yet.'

'And what if he isn't?'

'Hey, lady, in the New Age a mage is gonna be the thing to be. What more do you want man? After the revolution you're gonna be a fuckin' Queen Mum.'

That was how come we all, except Debora, crossed the south of England to hear the wizard sing at Woburn Abbey. Brenda had recovered from her demotion by then, and was as shiny-eyed as anyone at the prospect of imminent heaven on earth with the bonus of excursions to pop festivals, though the irony of the first one being where it was did not escape her.

'Why me? Why do these things always happen to me? The first chance I get to go anywhere and it's back to bloody Bedfordshire. What's wrong with London or Bristol? Bedfordshire's a hole. I should know. I spent my whole life trying to get out of it. What if I meet anyone I know?'

Julian said that she could stay behind if she wanted to. Someone had to.

'You're joking. You think I'm gonna stay here on my own while the rest of you are having the time of your lives? You think a future Queen Mother should miss out on a thing like this? Fat chance. But we're not going anywhere near Luton, right?'

Debora said that she would stay behind. She muttered something about having better things to do than travel hundreds of miles in a bus to pee in a trench with a lot of weekend hippies.

It felt very grown up to be going with no Debora to see the Wielder of Words as he put his hex on the old world and enchanted the new. There was no question of me being left behind. Steve told me it was part of my apprenticeship.

I had never seen so many people in one place or been so fazed by anything. If I hadn't, eventually, found sanctuary in Mervyn's lap I might have had to dig myself a hole in the ground.

'Is this everyone?'

'Everyone who?' Bronwen was snappish in her answers and crushing in her grip as she led me through the crowds in the wake of the others. Brenda and Colin were lagging farther behind, stopping to chat to strangers and to snog in the interstices between strangers.

'Is it everyone in the world?' I dodged around a lit joint being waved erratically by a hand wearing rings like eyeballs.

'Of course not. Walk properly.'

Later I asked Colin how many people there were in the world and he told me about London. 'There are so many people you can walk for a whole night and a whole day and still not be on your own. You can even drive a car all day without getting from one end to the other. And everyone is miserable because there are so many of them and no one says hello. And nothing can grow, only things called plane trees that can grow in soot.'

I looked at all the people on the grass and chairs around us in the light of this new information. The idea that it could be worse, that these hordes could multiply until there was no escaping them, was what first drove me under Mervyn's beard.

It was after Woburn Abbey that I came to see how beautiful it was at hOme. The next day it seemed all new. I set about finding places, up in the woods and down the valley, from which no trace of human existence could be detected. You strained your ears, and if you could hear so much as a tractor in the distance it was spoilt. You searched every square inch of the view in every direction and if all you saw was a strand of telephone wire then the landscape was useless. You had to be able to imagine that the world was pristine and people had never come to ruin everything. Now that the responsibility for saving the world had been taken away from me by the discovery of the wizard, I was free to find myself a bit of the world that didn't need saving.

Wild places were not difficult to find in such a corner of the back of beyond. The challenge was to find ways of linking them all; a corridor of solitude in which I could slide through the landscape, like a fox. Only my task was ten times more difficult than a fox's. His concern was not to be seen by humanity, while mine was neither to be seen by it nor see it. A glimpse of a gatepost could spoil the day; make the world a tamed, deflowered place, and send me home to the complexities of adults.

They were having a whirl of a time. There had never been so many comings and goings as there were that year. They played the wizard's record day in and day out until the noise of it became no more noticeable than the clanking of Debora's bracelets as she shredded cabbages. In the autumn the wizard made a new record and that was played too, the albums leapfrogging each other through the shortening days and lengthening nights. Evan and Evelyn arrived, with poker faces and white eyebrows and a fug of patchouli.

They set to work painting the outside of the house with dragons and constellations, fungi and fairy-folk; brushes drawling from their bony fingers across the brightening walls. Either side of the front door they painted a great dream-horse: one a red pointy-toed racehorse as a tribute to the winners that Julian dreamed of to keep the hOme going, and the other a white stallion with quarters as round as an apple and the sloe-eyes of a houri, to represent the creature who accompanied lovers through the valley.

Julian had stopped smiling. His mage-robes were velvet now and he wore them all the time. Visitors were called Ambassadors, no matter what their motive was for coming. Anyone who went out into the world was an Envoy, even if they went down to the village shop for matches. We were told that nothing happened without a reason, and every small action was significant, though it might not seem so at the time. We were somewhere near a pivot; a pinpoint on which the whole of history would turn, and for all you knew it would happen between one lungful of air and the next. Julian threw the I Ching over and over throughout the day, with Steve always beside him, reading aloud from the newspapers in his blackbird's voice, and measuring out the drugs. They were gaining control of the world, and the hOme was the Pentagon of the New Age. Council meetings were held every night, when the weather was reasonable, but now it was only the men who were interested in sitting out in the orchard to reinvent politics and life on earth. Because I was no longer Merlin-to-be, only a run-of-the-mill mage-in-waiting, my presence was not required in the Council Circle. I was free to spend evenings playing canasta with the ladies or making blackberry wine with Debora. Sometimes I played snakes-and-ladders with my mother.

Colin was the only man who skipped meetings whenever he could get away with it, since that was the only time when the record-player could be switched off and Tyrannosaurus Rex given a rest, leaving him able to sit at his piano and imbue the house with less percussive airs.

When the leaves fell from the tree a lot of my coverts were blown. The more naked the land became the more evident the hand of man. Cut-and-laid hedges, ploughed fields, fertiliser bags caught on thorns and distant chimney tops all appeared as the tide of green receded. There were places I could go still, but I had to be careful on the way always to look in the right direction, to retain the sense of wilderness. Silences became more profound as the winter deepened and birds went away or lost the will to sing and there was no background rumour of leafy frottage from the breeze. When the wind blew now it caused a motto of rasping and creaking, and in the quiet between you could hear the running of an engine a mile off. The game of being the only boy in the world was up.

I was still in the habit of going out, and a day in imperfect wilderness was better than staying around the hOme, with everyone talking in slogans and telling me how lucky I was to be growing up in a world that was on the verge of perfection, while the cat wasted away from starvation because eating freaked her out more than hunger and the morsels that Debora enticed her to have were only prolonging the agony.

Then came the day when I was sitting out in the woods under the biggest tree in my range; a tree whose trunk ran in a spiral of fissures, where the ground was always dry on the downhill side. It was beside a path that ran through the woods, but I had banked up a pile of dead leaves to conceal me from anyone who might go past. Only once before had I heard footsteps while I was hiding there, and by staying still I had avoided discovery. On this day I heard footfalls that were inhumanly irregular and breathing more violent than human lungs could produce. I thought maybe it was a cow, but on the off-chance that it might be a dragon I made no movement, but compressed myself into the bark of the tree. I knew enough about dragons for fear to win over curiosity. There were some stories of children being befriended by them, but even they involved a bit of singeing along the way.

The noise stopped. I looked up to see a pert girl in a velvet hat looking down at me. Although the visible part of her appeared to be a normal nine-year-old, she towered over me like a giant, and I didn't like to think what form she took from the waist down.

'Good morning.'

She spoke with the formality of the squarest people in the village.

I nodded.

'Why are you sitting like that?'

I had no idea what she meant. To me it was normal to be in the lotus position, palms upturned on my knees. For want of an answer I was provoked into a question. 'Who are you?'

'Who are you?'

'What are you doing here?'

'Are you one of the hippies?'

She moved in a strange way, with a kind of backward-and-forward swaying. Then a rasping snort came from somewhere beneath her. Perhaps she was sitting on a dragon. If so, it had to be a small tame dragon. I stood up to have a look.

She was astride a pony. It was the whitest animal I had ever seen: chalk and paper and snowstorm white, with black hooves and nostrils and shiny glycerine-black trappings.

She watched me staring for a bit. 'Do you want a go?'

I nodded.

She kicked her stirrups away and slid down and put her velvet hat on my head. It was hard and midnight blue and too big and slid over my eyes. Her instructions were precise and elaborate: stand there, facing that way, with one hand there and one there, now put this foot in there and spring up and swing your other leg round, and good, and sit still while I shorten your stirrups.

I hardly dared move.

'Relax and you won't fall off.'

It was a different world. Every breath the pony took and every fluctuation in every muscle of its body was a vibration between my legs. The ground was so far away it seemed irrelevant. The air was different up there. If I'd known how to make the pony gallop off I would have. If I'd known how to make it fly it would have been better.

She led us through the woods, looking back and smiling at me and reminding me where to put my hands and heels and how to hold my head and back, and telling me all the time how well I was doing, until we came in a circle back to the fissured tree, where she talked me down until my feet hit the ground with an unkind jolt.

'When I'm older I'm going to be a riding instructress, so I need all the practice I can get. Meet me here tomorrow at the same time for lesson two.'

I nodded and she cantered off, dodging low branches with her bottom in the air in yellow jodpurs, the stirrups shortened still to the length of my legs, half the length of hers.

I walked home dizzy, earthbound and clumping, and decided that when I was grown up I would go everywhere by horse and never walk again.

'Can mages ride horses?' I had decided to ask Mervyn for advice. Julian was the chief authority on mage-lore, but if you asked him you ran the risk of him asking the I Ching and you'd be stuck for hours only to be told that a withered willow gives birth to new shoots.

'Sometimes. They could if they wanted. Usually they stride across the dark hills on long lean legs with a wizened staff in their hand. But they take to horses when the need is great.'

'So there's nothing to stop a mage having a white horse?'

'White for preference, yes. A white horse is very Merlin.'

Fi being a great explainer of things, I was a rider of horses by the age of six. She explained that Fi was short for Fiona, a name that had been invented by Sir Walter Scott, emphasising the Sir to indicate that that was a crucial element of her provenance. Her pony was called Felspar, his sire being a horse called Granite Gent. That took a good deal of explaining. Trees were no longer mere trees, but ashes and oaks and beeches and birch, and because it was winter when she taught and they were leafless I had to learn them by bark and bud and outline. A crow was not a raven was not a jackdaw was not a rook. She became ten that January and explained to me what a great relief it was to be in double figures and of an age to be taken seriously. There was no question I could ask her for which she wouldn't furnish an answer, if not immediately, then by the next time I saw her. She never forgot and I never had to ask twice.

She introduced the concept of weeks and weekends. Before that I had no idea that some days were different from others. I had asked why we always met two days in a row with five in between.

'School. I go to day school because we are poor and Daddy lives in Africa with a strumpet.'

I may have been looking blank.

'Don't you go to school?'

'What's school?'

'A complete waste of time for someone of my calibre. You might find it useful. Can you read?'

'*The Hobbit?*'

'Anything.'

I shrugged. Reading was easy. When I was very little Debora would sit me on her lap and read to me. At first I had assumed that she was only describing what was going on in the illustrations. Gradually I realised that she was looking at the black marks between the pictures and after that I found that I could read. Most of the books I could lay my hands on were about the Hobbit.

'You should go to school.'

'Why?'

'Because otherwise you'll be sweeping the streets when you grow up. Keep your heels down.'

We were in a clearing in the woods that we used as a manège. She stood in the middle while I trotted round her with my stirrups crossed in front of me. Once I had mastered the art of riding without stirrups I was going to be allowed to jump.

'There are no streets here.'

'Then you'll be a poacher and you'll be sent to prison. Like Jeff Christmas.'

'Who's he?'

'You know. Barrow Cottage. The Christmasses are famous. They're inbred.'

'What's inbred?'

'It means being too fond of your family. I won't tell you again to shorten your reins. Davey Christmas is in my class. When the school inspector asked him what he would be when he grew up he said he'd join the navy and feel a new man every day. You're bouncing about like a sack of potatoes. Don't you hippies hear any gossip?'

'No. We're too busy.'

'Doing what?'

'Saving the world from fascist capitalism.'

She was silent for a bit, turning on her left heel and clicking rhythmically at Felspar. I had a sneaking suspicion I had just betrayed us to the enemy. Julian always said we should be careful what we said in front of squares. Eventually she said what was on her mind. 'I think it's time you had a proper education. Would you like to read *Black Beauty*?'

'What's that?'

'A book. About a horse. It was the first book I read and I've never looked back.'

'Are there any books about white horses?'

'I've told you before. There is no such thing as a white horse. Don't let me hear you say that again.'

She lent me *Black Beauty*, and it was the most difficult book I had ever come across. It described an unlikely world, with no wizards or spells or quests or divinations, though I cried all night when Ginger died.

On my sixth birthday she gave me a kind of tea towel, which she called a stable rubber, and on which were illustrated the Points of the Horse. She told me I had to learn it off by heart. Debora gave me a mage-coat which she had made by stitching together a lot of Gujarati headdresses and sari-ends and odd pieces of mirrorwork. Colin and Brenda gave me a set of runestones and Mervyn spent the afternoon showing me how to use them.

Then, just as I had everything the world could offer, the fragmentation started. First, Fi announced that she was going to Africa to spend the summer with her daddy and the strumpet. There would be no more riding lessons for a while. Then the wizard's third album arrived and there were murmurs that it wasn't all it should be. The misgivings flowered into near-panic when the wizard wrote a book, which arrived a few weeks later. The hOme was divided at a Council meeting which, for the first time in months, was attended by everyone.

Julian stood firm. 'Mages must not be questioned. Their ways are beyond our understanding.'

'He's laughing at us. He's turning into a friggin' pop star.'

'It's a sell-out. Everyone's being bought and sold. The establishment is winning.'

Julian glared at Bronwen and Debora. 'Perhaps if these chicks came to a few more Council meetings they might have a better idea of what's going on in the world. We're winning. Everyone's in on the vibe now, even pop stars. This shows how far we've come.'

Mervyn sputtered what might have been intended to be a facetious laugh. 'The Warlock of Love? What are you on, man? Or what does he think we're on? Fourteen bloody shillings and sixpence and you too can chant the spells. This is how far we've come. Four pimply breadheads from Liverpool discover meditation, start wearing the gear and suddenly everyone's cashing in. And you think we should be glad. Suburbia fakes psychedelia and you think that's the revolution won. Everyone's faking it, man. The government's still there. The armies are still fighting. The shops are still charging money for stuff that should be free. The children still get busted for drugs. What's changed? What makes it safe for a wizard to put his spells in a book that MI5 can buy for fourteen and six?'

'Maybe it's a ruse to put them off the scent.' Steve looked around until his eyes settled on me, conspiratorially. 'Mages are devious. You never know what they get up to. If we're thinking he's sold out, they're gonna think he's sold out. You can trust a mage to be slippery. They don't tell what they're up to. I saw that one riding a white horse the other day.' He pointed at me. 'In the woods. Galloping round on a white horse like some kind of Elf-lord or something.'

They all looked at me, Debora with some alarm.

'Were you?'

My voice came out suddenly and it sounded like Fi speaking but they weren't to know that. 'How could I? There is no such thing as a white horse.'

'What did I tell you? Devious.' Steve winked at me and made my skin crawl. I took the runestones from my pocket and threw them on the grass the way Mervyn had taught me.

Julian stood up. 'What are those?'

'He's throwing an oracle. Sit down.'

'There's only one oracle in this circle. Put them away.'

'Too late now. He can't go back. He can't unthrow. If the spirits are angry they will show it by silence.'

I spoke the oracle, while Mervyn stood his ground between Julian and me. It was an oracle of separation. It said that the mage was leaving; that the circle would be broken.

'Told you the bastard's sold out.'

'It could be any mage. It doesn't have to be Bolan. Jesus, man. Since when did we run this place on the say-so of a kid and his marbles?' With a dismissive sneer Julian turned his back on me and returned to his place, where he unrolled the yarrow stalks. He worked faster than we had ever seen him work before, and we had a result in fifteen minutes. He gazed into the book for a while, as he sometimes did when the reading was not to his liking, looking for the word or phrase that would take the sting out of the rest. He shook his head. 'The bird burns and destroys his nest. All will be lost.'

Steve nudged him. 'Come on. It can't be that bad. It's never all bad man.'

'It's the hexagram of travelling.'

'Okay, so someone's got to travel. I'll travel, man. Anywhere you like. Where do you want me to travel?'

Colin interrupted in the sleepy voice of true prophecy. 'He should go and see his friend the Took. He can find out what is really happening with the wizard.'

That was the last time I saw Steve at the hOme. He set off early next day. About a week later we had a card from him. The picture was of a red bus going round Piccadilly Circus. The message took the best part of a day to decipher. It was hard to believe that someone could write so minutely and scrawl so extravagantly at the same time: Bolan's gone electric. The Took's had it. Peace, Brandybuck.

The day they came there was nothing unusual. It was bright, still and dry, though not as hot as it had been. I know because the day before we had all been driven into the river for a cooling swim; everyone splashing and shrieking, or holding on to a rock with one hand while the body undulated in the current like river-weed. The day before I thought I would swim every day for the rest of the summer, but the day they came I only got up to my knees before making a shivering retreat. You had to be really boiling for the cold of that river to be bearable.

Evan and Evelyn, having painted every square inch of the walls of the house, were executing a big and stiff willy on the door. They said it was a lingam, but it looked like a willy. Debora, Bronwen and Alice were standing about the steaming cauldron by the rosemary bush. Ash had told them that orange was the most karmically beneficial colour and they were dying every pale garment in the house with onion skins, and limited success. Only their arms had turned a rich shade of true orange, up to the elbows. Bronwen was singing in Welsh and out of tune. Not far from them, on the dingy patch of camomile he called his meditation lawn, Ash was immersed in his weekly stomach-cleaning ritual, which involved swallowing a twenty-yard ribbon of wet fabric and then drawing it out again like a magician. He had first completed the companion ritual of rinsing out the other end by squatting in a pan of water which he somehow sucked in and blew out to the accompaniment of the inevitable noises. It was all, he would say with some complacency, a question of sphincter control. Behind him, Marge and David were enjoying a post-coital kip in the hammock, three legs dangling from one side and one from the other. To the left of them, from where I was, Mervyn sat, patient and naked, if someone so clothed by nature as Mervyn could ever be considered naked, while Brenda styled his hair. She was trying to make plaits that went all the way down, from the top of his head, through his beard and into his body hair. He winced a lot as the hair grew finer and the plaits grew tighter as they descended, but he said nothing aloud and Brenda seemed happy in her work. I was having a mage-duel with Julian, he with his stalks and me with my stones. From the house there came the mixed sound of Colin's piano and the wizard's album. Since the postcard from Steve no one objected if Colin played variations along with the spells. It broke the monotony of them without anyone having to admit that they had become monotonous. There were no Ambassadors staying with us that day. It was just ourselves being ourselves.

They may have been standing for some time, watching us in silence. A man and a woman, at the turn of the lane, by the thorn tree that had been hung with magic stones and prayer-bells to welcome good spirits and scare away the bad. The woman wore a pale outfit of a kind of puce colour and a rubbery-looking material that Debora told me afterwards was Crimplene, spitting the word out as if it was sour in her mouth, and all topped off with a hat of net and artificial roses. In front of her she carried an enormous white handbag. Her lips were moving in some kind of silent mantra. She was an ordinary-looking, ageless, shapeless woman, without make-up or novelty. The kind of woman who would be nice to me and call me a poor child and be snippy with the adults when we went into the village. By her side the man stood dumbfounded in a suit and cap. The suit was navy blue with huge lapels and turn-ups, and the cap was speckled tweed. His shirt was brilliant white and his tie greasy. Beneath the dust, his brown shoes betrayed the glow of daily polishing.

I was the first to notice them, and I watched them watching us. His eyes darted erratically over the scene while hers moved in smooth uneasy curves until, by uncanny timing, each came to canvass the other with a simultaneous, momentary, questioning glance. Their eyes flickered back in the direction from which they had arrived, but she touched him on the elbow and they stood their ground.

By that time, in the moments they were distracted, they had become visible to all of us, and mine was just one of a dozen pairs of eyes that were fixed on them when they looked our way again. They froze, his mouth open for a word of greeting that could find no exit. Then one faint noun, spoken in Brenda's voice, came rolling out from us to them, and made them sway as though their ankles had turned to rubber.

'Mam.'

All eyes shuttled from Brenda to the strangers by the thorn tree and back again.

'Breda?'

'Mam. Dad.'

'Breda.'

Now that they mentioned it you could see the relationship. The angle of his chin and the turn of her mouth and
the spacing of his teeth and the scission of her eyes and the
small tics of shock-induced posture displayed in both of
them: all were seamlessly combined in their daughter, who
now abandoned the mound of plaited hair that moments
before had so enthralled her.

'I'm Brenda now.'

'Breda.' He said it patiently, but firmly and correctingly
and cynically, loaded with the ballast of past conflicts.

'No.' Brenda met the tone with her own, inherited,
version. 'Brenda. I changed my name.'

'Did you change your manners too while you were at it
or are you going to ask us in and give your poor mother a
cup of tea after we came all this way and introduce us to
your friends while you're about it?'

'How did you find me?'

'That's a fine question to be kicking off with not that it
was easy with the postmark smudged and we've been
hunting every weekend the past year through Devon but
we're here now and there's an end of it thank God.'

While he spoke his wife and daughter, walking and
crying, drew into one another's arms, where they said
things that were lost in the muffling of snot on shoulders.

After calm had reasserted itself, and introductions had
been made, and tea had been produced, though not a brew
that was recognisable to Bridey or Willy, and when the
mother and daughter were deep in the awkwardness of

finding questions to ask that would not lead to outright conflict at this early stage, Willy looked about him and, finding nothing else in the garden of hippies on which his attention might happily linger, fixed me with a glare and a smile.

'Well hello you youngster and what might your name be when you're at home?'

'Coorg.'

'Coorg, is it? Well, and if you don't mind me asking since with that class of an up-to-date hairstyle it could go either way, is that a little boy's name or a little girl's name?'

His question made no sense in itself, even after it had been picked out from the speed of its delivery. I decided that the best thing would be to stand behind Debora and be shielded by the fullness of her skirts.

'There's shy now did you ever see the like of it hiding behind the mammy like that and what age is the child if you don't mind me asking?'

'He's six.' Debora put her hand to my head so I could feel all her rings around my skull. 'Brenda? Don't you think it's time you told your parents about Coorg?'

Brenda flushed a shade of underripe raspberry pink. 'What's to tell?'

'Let me look at him.' Hands turned me round and eased me out of Debora's skirts and then I was face to furrowed face with Bridey. 'Jesus Mary and Holy Saint Joseph he's the spit of your father Willy. Breda?'

'Brenda. It's Brenda. I am Brenda. My name is Brenda. And yes he's mine. He's your grandson. Okay? Happy now?'

'But your wan said he was six.'

'Why do you think I ran off?'

'You didn't have to run off. You could have told us.'

'Who's the father?'

'See? See? That's why I had to run off. Not how terrible for you, what can we do to help? But who's the father? What'll the priest say? It was an immaculate conception, okay? Coorg is the new baby Jesus. He's going to save the world.'

'There's no call for blasphemy.'

'Now, Willy. Don't mind your father, love. He didn't have a proper breakfast this morning. Six? I'm not old enough to be a grandmother.'

In the house the record had finished and the piano-playing had stopped. I was facing that way, pinned by Bridey's hands as she scanned me through watery eyes. Colin emerged and made his way towards us. He wore nothing but a small cheesecloth lungi tied low on his hips and a dropped pearl in his left ear. He had a swaying way of walking when he dressed like that, one hand shading his eyes from the sudden light of outdoors.

Willy spotted him. 'Does no one wear a stitch in this place? Don't look behind you, Bridey, there's another one coming over in his pelt.'

Bridey looked. 'Colin?'

Colin peered. 'Mrs Scully?'

Willy glared. 'Colin? Is it yourself?'

'Mr Scully.'

'Will you pull your skirt up, boy. Mrs Scully doesn't want to be looking at your curlies and have you no shame and what would your mother think? She'd die not that she'd recognise you with that hair all over your face and your yoke bobbin' about in a net curtain.'

I made the most of the distraction and wriggled from Bridey's hold, and slipped into the woods, where I stayed until dark and hunger made it worthwhile to come back and peer through the windows to check whether everything was back to normal yet.

I was looking for Debora, so it was the kitchen window I tried first. She wasn't there, but Julian and Mervyn were, having an argument that, by the sound of it, had been going on for some time. They were repeating themselves more in exasperation than anger.

'He should have told us his old man was a pig man.'

'Why? Why should Colin be judged by his father more than anyone else? Do you go round telling everyone what your father is?'

'My father's not a pig man.'

'So what is he?'

'That's not relevant. I'm not the potential spy here.'

I slid on round the outside of the house to look for her in her room, but she wasn't there either. I heard more raised voices from Brenda and Colin's room and found her there. All three of them were sitting on the bed: Brenda and Colin at diagonally opposite corners and Debora in the middle. I went round and crept inside by shadows and walls, and got into the bed in the empty top corner and pulled the sheets up to my nose to make myself unnoticeable. Debora didn't turn to look at me but quietly put her hand behind to stroke my hair in greeting, as if she had eyes in the back of her head.

'He knew. He just knew all the fucking time and he was laughing at me.'

'I wasn't laughing at you. I know a lot of things. I'm telepathic, remember? Tell her I wasn't laughing at her.'

'And he posted that card. He had no right to post that card. I hadn't made my mind up.'

'Yes you had.'

'Tell him to stop talking to me. Tell him to get out. I don't want to see him. Ever again.'

'Yes you do.'

'And what's all this stuff about PJ? He knew stuff about PJ the whole time, and I used to say to him I wonder how my brother is, and he'd say nothing, just be laughing at me.'

'I'm sorry, Okay? I'm sorry. I didn't want to freak you out. You think it didn't freak me out when I worked out I was knobbing PJ's sister? How was I to know your parents were going to turn into bloodhounds and track us down?'

'Funny how he's only telepathic when it suits him. And tell him to leave my family out of this. He's done enough damage.'

'All right, Breda.'

'I'll kill him.'

Brenda lunged across the bed at Colin, nails first, but was caught by Debora before she landed on her target.

'Now, children.' Debora pushed Brenda back into her place. 'Remember where you are. This is the hOme. We may be fucked up, but we don't use violence.'

Brenda took a few deep breaths and looked as near to contrite as she got.

'Where did you get that N anyway?'

'I'm not saying.'

'Oh, come on. You can tell me.'

'I don't want him to know.'

'Oh, go on. He doesn't matter.'

'You're right. He doesn't. It was nothing. Just a creepy guy I got a lift off when I ran away. I told him I was up the pole because I had to tell someone and he was a stranger and I didn't think it mattered and he said something horrible. Breda by name, breeder by nature. So I made it Brenda. Breda was a stupid name.'

'Don't say I don't matter. I love you.'

'You have a funny way of showing it.'

'Well, now we're all talking to each other again, I take it I can go to bed?'

Debora picked me up and carried me to my bed, where she lay down with me for a while, stroking my hair. I fell asleep, and then she must have too, because I woke in the night to feel her rings still hard against my skull.

Willy and Bridey came back the next day, and the day after that, always in their Sunday clothes dusty from the lane. When you got used to them they weren't too bad. Bridey kept pushing the hair back off my face and telling me how handsome I'd be with a bit of a trim. Willy showed me how to make a catapult.

'What's it for?'

'Anything you like. You could pelt cats or birds with it.'

'Why?'

'Jesus, Bridey, the child isn't natural.'

The day after that they asked if they could take me for an outing. Brenda shrugged. Debora was suspicious.

'An outing where, exactly?'

'Oh, anywhere. A little spin in the car. We might go into

Exeter maybe and buy him a toy for himself. He has nothing to play with but the stones in his pocket.'

'I'll come with you, I need to go to Exeter.'

'For what?' Brenda sounded put out.

'For stuff.'

'You never wanted to go to Exeter before.'

'I do now.' She turned to Willy. 'I'm coming.'

Willy and Bridey exchanged a look. Then Bridey spoke in a voice too cheerful not to be covering for some kind of disappointment. 'Why not? Of course. The more the merrier. You're more than welcome. Isn't she, Willy?'

We set off in their navy Cortina, which had been left every day at the top of the lane because the summer-hardened ruts were too deep for anything but the bus or a tractor. Inside, the car smelled of tobacco and mints. I sat in the back with Debora, who leaned forward to make conversation.

'So how long have you lived in England?'

'Oh, twenty years or more. We came over after the war when the building trade was booming, wasn't it, Bridey?'

'Do you like living in Luton?'

'It's grand, isn't it, Bridey? You couldn't ask for better though it's not the same as home not that any place could be. That's always the way.'

'Would you ever go back, to live?'

Bridey made a rapid interruption. 'I thought we might take little Coorg for a feed of fish and chips when we get to the town. He'd like that, wouldn't you?'

Debora made a face. 'Fish are living creatures and potatoes are members of the family *Solanaceae*, which includes deadly nightshade. Bad karma and poison in one meal.'

Bridey snorted. 'No wonder the child hasn't a pick on him.'

Assuming an unlikely serenity, Debora smiled. 'It's funny about Colin, isn't it?'

Willy crashed a gear. 'His father'll give him funny when he gets to hear of it.'

'You wouldn't credit what that young fella threw away. Children would scald you though it's no good saying that to someone until they know it themselves.' Bridey paused under the weight of her own wisdom, before giving herself a little shake and setting off in another tone of voice. 'They were as proud as peacocks of him when he was getting on so well with the piano. He could play anything you'd care to mention. Not that it was the same as a proper job, though he'd look lovely in his tail-coat. Do you remember, Willy, when we went all the way down to London to see him playing? That was the first time we met Robert and Mavis. They're a lovely couple and he just got promoted. What was it? Detective something or something detective? Something big anyway. But as I say, they were devastated when he had his break-down and they hardly mentioned him since. We'd have thought he was put away in a home if it wasn't for PJ telling us he wasn't. The two of them were always great, weren't they, Willy? That's how we got to know Colin to start with. He was always coming to the house. Thick as thieves those two. Great friends altogether. Though Colin must have been older by a year or two. God knows what they used to get up to above in that bedroom. They'd be up there for hours with the door locked and the music blaring. But that's young people for you, and he was always very polite, young Colin. Wasn't he, Willy? Very clean and presentable he used to be. Very artistic.'

I didn't like Exeter. We wandered in and out of shops and Bridey kept trying to get me to like things, but I held fast to Debora's hand and just kept thinking what a better place the world would be without all the people. We were standing at a big window full of plastic boys and men in grey clothes with sharp creases, and I was shaking my head savagely as Bridey was yet again enticing me to let her buy me a new set of clothes to replace my mage-coat. She said it was fine for cowboys and Indians but not to be seen dead in the street with. I felt Debora's grip change and heard a hiss come out of her, and then she said that she didn't believe it, and we all looked across the street and saw what she saw.

In the café across the street, on his own, Julian sat in profile, raising a Mars bar to his lips and taking off half of it in one bite.

Just recently Julian had been lording it over everyone with his dietary rigour. About the time that the postcard came from Steve, he had gone to stage one and, as far as anyone could tell, had eaten nothing but brown rice since, without losing any weight. He had begun to talk about giving up food altogether, saying that he could absorb all the nutrients he needed through reverse circle breathing. He said that he had achieved cosmic balance and he sneered at the rest of us for being so dependent on vulgar carbohydrates. That he had, at about the same time, taken to leaving the hOme on a daily basis to place his own bets did not arouse suspicion. Going to the bookie's had never been a popular task and anyone who volunteered to do it would not be questioned.

Now there he was, cheeks bulging with chocolate and a plate smeared with red and yellow stains before him. Shaking in anger, Debora loosened my hand from hers and ran across the street, where she began banging on the window.

The next thing I knew was that my feet flew from the ground as I was swept up in Willy's arms, and then he was running. I could hear the clatter of Bridey's shoes and her panting breath behind us. Debora was still banging on the window and I shouted to her, but she can't have heard, and then we had turned a corner and she was gone. Another minute and we were in the car and driving out of Exeter.

'Where are we going?'

'We're going home. Be a good boy.'

'Why isn't Debora with us?'

'Debora's busy. She'll find her own way back with that other fella. Be a good boy and stop asking questions.'

'Why?'

'We'll get you fish and chips later if you're good.'

I slept. I woke. In the evening we stopped outside a house like all the other houses around it and I was told to hide down on the floor of the car or the bad man would get me, and Bridey ran in and ran back out again with a big suitcase, crying, and Willy told her it was only for a few days until they saw how things were, and she said that anyone with eyes in their head could see how things were and that poverty and riches could never be hid.

Realising that there was something illogical about my position, I popped my head above the seats, hoping, maybe, the bad man would see me and take me back to Debora.

'No. Get down. He'll put you in a sooty sack and take you to jail.'

'He's as cute as cut-the-bags, that child.'

'It wasn't off the grass he licked it.'

I slept. I woke. They bought me fish and chips and I was sick out of the car window, down the side of the car, and I felt a sting on my leg as if something had hit me, but I couldn't think what, and Bridey said I was bold out and I could tell from her voice that being bold out was something I should avoid if I wanted her to be nice to me. In the dark we drove into a great hole in the back of a ship that stank of petrol and whiskey and sick.

In the morning we drove off the boat into the rain.

'Where are we?'

'Home.'

'What are those?'

'What are what?'

'Those things floating on the river.'

'Don't point. It's rude.'

'What are they?'

'They're buoys.'

'Why are they there?'

'To show the ships which way to go.'

'Why do they have to do it?'

'Who?'

'The boys. Why do they have to live in the middle of the river?'

'They asked too many questions and the bad man put them in his sack.'

The shelterless middle of the brown river in spate looked like no place to be condemned to, for the sake of a few questions. I could still remember a time when I asked what I liked. There wasn't always an answer; sometimes only a lot of stoned nodding, sometimes a lofty non sequitur, but nobody would try to stop you asking.

I could still remember, but I was less sure of my memory. I wasn't sure whether days or weeks had passed. My hair was gone now, and my mage-coat. Every night I dreamt of Debora and every day I waited for her to find me. I worried that she might see me and not recognise me, since I no longer resembled myself, so I scanned the street and the horizon, knowing that I would always recognise her. I listened perpetually. The clank and jangle of her bracelets might be the first sign that she was coming for me.

On top of that was the small matter of survival in the creamed cage to which I had been brought, and the impossible problem of working out how long my sentence would be. Sometimes they told me we were just here for a visit. Sometimes they said that this was my home now and I had to get used to it. Mostly they told me the terrible things that happened to boys who asked questions.

'What's hell?'

'It's where boys who asked questions go.'

'Is it where the answers are?'

'Don't be smart now and sit up straight or I'll redden your legs for your answer.'

We were at somewhere called the Parish, a building that was bigger on the inside than you would have thought possible, and this, apparently, was Mass. There had been a lot of talk about Mass, and whether I should or shouldn't be brought. There was a choice, seemingly, between somewhere called the Convent, which they also called the Augustinians, and this Parish place. Because the Convent was the place where everyone liked to go, it was thought safest if Bridey took me to the Parish first to see whether I made a show of myself, which was strange because all the talk had made me nervous and the last thing I wanted was to be noticed, and I wouldn't have wanted to go at all had someone not pressed a penny into my hand and told me it was for buying a black baby.

We were high up, at the front of the gallery at the back of the church, looking down on the pews as the rows filled with hats and scarves and heads in their hundreds, and hands bound with beads and hands gripping black books with coloured ribbons caught in the pages, all supervised and directed by painted statues with bleeding wounds and expressions of incurable sadness. I stood to lean my chin on the wooden balustrade and gain a clearer view, and Bridey gripped the back of my jacket.

'You have to be good now. Baby Jesus is going to appear on the altar.'

'Where?'

'Look. You have to keep looking. If you keep looking you'll see Our Lord appear, but only if you're good enough.'

She explained that Baby Jesus could save the world if only everyone would behave themselves and be good Catholics and do whatever the Pope said and say a prayer to Our Lady every day.

'Is that him?'

'No. That's the altar boy lighting the candles. You could be doing that if you behaved yourself.'

'Is Baby Jesus black?'

There were sniggers from the row behind us. Bridey reddened and flustered and let a shish out of her that was so loud people in the nave below turned to look up at us.

'Don't ever talk about Our Lord like that.'

She raised her hand at me and I looked at it and realised what had caused the sting on the back of my legs when I vomited down the side of the car door. I found myself flinching and quickly tried to think what I might do to avoid being hit. I whispered that I was sorry, and she put her hand down and whispered back, hard.

'Baby Jesus couldn't be black. He's God.'

'I can't buy him, then?'

'No. Our Lord is not for sale.'

'Where is he now?'

'He's on the altar. Behind that little curtain at the back there's a gold door and he's in there.'

'How do you know?'

'Because the lamp is lit.'

'Will he come out?'

'You have to wait for the priest to do everything, and the bell will ring and he'll elevate the host, and if you're good you can see God except if you're good you'd be saying your prayers and not looking, and you have to make your Holy Communion first.'

'Is he a kind of wizard?'

'No. He's God. He's very, very holy.'

'Is that why you can't see him?'

'Yes. Now be quiet or you'll make Baby Jesus cross and he'll turn you into a shellikapooky.'

I peeled my eyes for this baby full of holes that even Bridey was afraid of, and thoughtfully chewed my penny.

'Don't put that in your mouth. A dirty black man might have touched it.'

'Is he the one selling his babies?'

She was going to shish me again but there was a great rumble as everyone got to their feet at the same moment. A man in a kaftan came out on to the stage, with a lot of boys in smocks like the one who had lit the candles, and everyone started singing the worst kind of song you ever heard to the

accompanying drone of the loud and rhythmless instrument behind us.

When it was over, and we had come outside again in a
slow coughing flood, the sun was shining, and it was such
a contrast to the crippling gloom behind us that for the
first time in that town I was nearly glad to be where I was.
Bridey instructed me all the way back to Mary Street.

'You've heard the word of God now and you've no
excuse. Your heathen days are over. If you died while you
were still a heathen you'd just go to limbo, but if you die
now and you have a mortal sin on your soul you'll go to
hell, and there's nothing you can do about it.' She described
hell to the best of her knowledge, and said that if I didn't
want to go there I had to pray to God and his mother all
the time until the day I died, which could be any minute. I
somehow found that I had run out of questions or, at least,
lost the desire to know any more. We were on the shady
side of the street and the town was shouldering in around
us.

The town was called New Ross and it was famous for
having a curse on it. It loomed over the River Barrow with
all the luck draining down the hill and into the sluggish
water. People, even the proudest townsmen, would joke
that the best thing about the place was the road out of it. I
couldn't understand why anyone stayed in the town when
there were fields and woods a short walk out of it where
you could live a decent life, and I thought all the people
must somehow be trapped in it, as I was trapped in it for
the whole of that summer.

The Barrow had been spanned by a bridge of wooden
planks that rattled like the teeth of an old piano, as I was

told by several wistful people. Now all that was left were the amputated stumps at the end of Bridge Street and the beginning of Rosbercon, while a new bridge of concrete vaunted itself at Kilkenny and the Waterford road. The Kilkenny people were, apparently, as sly and treacherous as cats and we were supposed to hate them, and it was no good saying that I liked cats because I'd only be laughed at. We, on our side, were the Yellabellies. If you called anyone else that it meant they were a coward, but when we used the word to describe ourselves it had an altogether opposite meaning, as if anyone brave enough to say he was a Yellabelly was excused from the slur.

From the stump of the old bridge the Quays ran along the river, away from Bridge Street, and you were supposed to imagine that it was all crowded with ships once, before the curse on the town took a hold; and there were big empty warehouses with the town pressing behind them. Like Bridge Street, most of the roads in the town had been given names that you might have guessed if you hadn't been told. North Street went north and South Street went south. Mary Street went up to St Mary's, past Barrack Lane where the barracks used to be and Brogue Lane where the shoe-menders used to live. Above that the Carmelites lived, and they were so holy that no one could look at them, a piece of information which reinforced my confusion of holiness and holes and made perfect sense at the time.

Back in the eye of the town, at the bottom of Mary Street, the second shop up on your right, if you had your back to the river, was a sweet shop, also selling toys and novelties and fancy goods and cowboy suits and rolls of caps for pistols and lucky bags and toilet paper. Above the door there was a sign which read:

2   J. SCULLY   2

There were three floors of living space above this sign, and that was where I had come to be, among three strange women, two of whom I was invited to call Anti-Netty and Anti-Sally. They were said to be Willy's sisters. The third and weirdest was called Granny Scully, and she was Willy's mother and so my great-grandmother.

Granny Scully lurked on the second floor in a rocking chair that barely moved and constantly creaked, fingering her silks and embroidery in the dim light that struggled through layers of lace and net shrouding her north-facing windows. A single lamp, clamped to the back of her rocker, illuminated the circle of cloth on which her spidery fingers sewed dull-coloured flowers and withered leaves. Sensitive to any intrusion on her domain, she could distinguish between the noise of the front door and that of the shop door and would shout down as soon as she heard it to know who was there. Powerless, the visitor was drawn up two flights of stairs to stand in the gloom and be drained of all the information they had. There was no escape until she was sated and you saw her eyelids droop and her stitching fingers fall idle.

The top floor was divided into two smaller bedrooms, one for Netty and one for Sally, but while we stayed they moved in together, and Willy and Bridey and I shared Netty's room, with Netty's things strung about still and her lavender-water permeating everything and her Infant of

Prague smiling from the windowsill. I was jammed into a baby's cot that had been got down from the attic, the bars of which were rusted into position and had to be climbed over morning and night.

Netty's real domain was on the first floor. There was a big pale sitting room where she dusted her ornaments and polished the furniture, and a tiny kitchen off it where she cooked, to the accompaniment of instructions shouted down from the floor above and the softly playing radio that she lied to her mother about, claiming that the noise must be from the butcher's next door and there was nothing could be done about it.

Netty was tiny and sprigged with floral patterns and diminutive movements, and she would grab me for a muted dancing lesson whenever Andy Williams came on the radio to sing that she was just too good to be true.

Sally was her opposite, as much over the mean in size as Netty was below it. She had a voice like a man compared with Netty's gentle trill, and bottle-end spectacles that gave her monster eyes. She spent all her day in the shop, terrifying the children who came in holding their pennies in front of them; making them tremble by the tone in which she asked them what they wanted, before giving them twice as many sweets as their money warranted.

Apart from the occasional waltz with Netty, and the conscientious eating of the chips she liked to fry incessantly, there was not much to do in the day. I would have thrown my runes but they had been taken away from me as soon as Bridey began to suspect a pagan connection. There were windows to look out of, but nothing to see out of them but the street and the people in it, and the rival sweet shop opposite and the people getting their hair cut off in Lar the barber's, and the mud-spattered cars that pulled up in front of Fogarty's for the weekly shop. There wasn't a tree to be seen in any direction and, for the first few days, while I was kept hidden inside, I thought that I might be in a place as urban and terrible as London.

At six the television was switched on for the angelus. That was my first experience of television. A black-and-white painting came on the screen, showing two hippies kneeling either side of a depressed-looking woman with a baby, while a bell tolled slowly and profoundly. Everyone in the room fell to their knees with their hands tied in beads and began muttering at each other with their eyes shut. The first time I thought maybe they'd all taken something, and it was best if I got out of the way until they'd come down from it, so I retreated upstairs.

Granny Scully heard me trying to slink past her door and called me into her room. Her hands too were tied in beads, and she had a piece of black lace draped carelessly over her head.

'Why aren't you below saying your angelus?'

I shrugged.

'Is it a heathen you are?'

I let her take that shrug as read.

'What class of a name is Coorg anyway? Is it a nickname? Do you not have a proper name as well?'

I said the first thing I could think of. 'Mage?' I knew it wasn't right, but I could feel her feeding on my silence.

'That sounds like a girl's name. Or a disease a dog would have. You can't go to school with a name like that. They'll be laughing at you enough with your accent as it is. Little

91

Lord Fauntleroy. Would you like to be called Joseph, after your great granddaddy?'

'Can't I just be called Coorg?'

'We'll call you Joseph so. That's settled.'

STRANGE ORCHESTRAS

When I think about it, there must have been a certain amount of consternation at 2 Mary Street upon the unexpected arrival of a child who was both a bastard and a pagan. Granny Scully must have been giving Willy and Bridey a hell of a time. If only I had known, I might have been able to take some pleasure in their discomfort, to relieve my own misery. The Scullys, however, were not a family to show weakness to an outsider and, although I was now a Scully in name, until I had been trained in the reticence and conduct of a decent society I could not be considered an insider.

That much I would gather from the fierce whispering that would pass between Willy and Bridey in the thick dark of our room when I would wake to cram my legs into a new position against the bars of the cot and hear them hiss their resentments along the bolster between them. The talk was mostly of shame and of money. I gathered that the shame of me was nearly unbearable, but nothing compared with the shame of having no money, and the speculation as to what might happen if Granny Scully ever found out was always followed by a silence and then the hollow assertion that there was no reason why she should.

Sometimes Willy would say that he was sorry and Bridey would answer that it was much good sorry could do her when she didn't have a home to call her own and what good was sorry to a woman whose new three-piece had been left to them vultures? And Willy would tell her that God was good, and didn't God send them the child when it was wanted. To which Bridey would reply that that was just the sort of thing you could expect from God, to be sending down a loaf of bread to a drowning man. And Willy would point out that if it wasn't for the child it would look as if they were home with the tail between their legs and their hands hanging and the whole town laughing at them. And Bridey would say that she knew, but why couldn't something nice happen for once in her life, hadn't she done enough to deserve a bit of peace? And Willy would say he was sorry.

I understood that I was the child, but the rest of it made no sense at all.

Meanwhile I was being repackaged to local standards. First I was taken across to Lar's for a proper haircut to mitigate the pruning that Bridey had given me in the back of the car as we waited to get on the ferry that night. Willy escorted me over the street and Sally watched from the shop, while Netty on the floor above waved a little handkerchief out of the kitchen window throughout the entire operation, turning back now and again in a running commentary to Bridey, who was sitting for a home perm on the kitchen chair. Lar put a red leather plank across the red leather arms of his chair and I was lifted on to it and strangled with a sheet and told to keep my head still. I counted packs of combs stacked against the glass of the mirror rather than watch the denuding of my ears reflected in it. Willy sat with his back to the window and the women, telling Lar that you couldn't beat a short back and sides for value no matter what the quare fellas were getting up to in England where you couldn't tell a man from a woman any more without shaking it to see if it rattled. Lar laughed, gravely and politely, and if he had an opinion he kept it firmly beneath his own well-greased quiff.

Then we had to go to Joe Lawler's to supplement the outfit I'd been jammed into in Wexford town on the first morning. Dickey bows were chosen and knee socks were picked over and white shirts had their seams scrutinised and itchy jumpers were haggled for and scratchy shorts lauded, and the pile on the counter was crowned with indispensable matching pant-and-vest sets. Bridey supervised all this, and while she peered for loose threads that might bring the price down she fended off questions about my origins.

'He's just over for his holiday. Aren't you, Joseph?'

And prevaricated over her own intentions.

'We might be staying for a while, the weather's so nice this year for a change and please God it'll stay that way. You may as well throw those in for nothing as I'm buying half the shop off you.'

And on to McKeowan's for brick-hard shoes to replace the binder-twine-bound sandals that Bridey said a tinker wouldn't be seen dead in.

'Aren't you the little gent now?'

'Do I have to be called Joseph?'

'You can always tell a gent by the shine on his shoes. What's wrong with Joseph? It's a lovely name. You should be proud of it. Don't fidget or the woman'll cut the legs off you.'

I had never been accused of fidgeting before, so I don't

know whether I did and nobody minded, or whether I was beginning to react to all the gobstoppers and jawbreakers and chocolate bars that Netty fetched up from the shop to keep my mouth busy in the short intervals between plates of chips. Sugar had been an unknown substance in the hOme and I had no resistance to it. In Mary Street I succumbed to the addiction within hours, crunching through slices of bread and butter heaped with white sugar while Netty stood ready with a bag of Emerald toffees.

'We'll soon fill him out.'

'I spent a fortune on clothes and he's bursting out of them already.'

'There's boys for you.'

'Can I have another one?'

'Little word?'

'Can I have another one please?'

If you burped you had to excuse yourself, but if you farted the only way to get away with it was to deliver in silence and deny all knowledge. If you used the lavatory, which you had to call the bathroom even if there wasn't a bath in it, you had to shut the door and lock it in case anyone saw you and started shouting. Bottoms were rude but the front bits were ruder, although what came out of bottoms was ruder than what came out of front bits. None of it should ever be seen by anyone, and the front bits were not seen to be mentioned. If the Devil heard that kind of talk it was as good as a ring on hell's doorbell.

The Devil lurked in all sorts of places. He hid in mirrors and could jump out at you if you stayed looking at yourself too long. You had to give a quick glance to make sure your face wasn't dirty, because dirt was the Devil's friend.

There was a great deal of the Devil's work also on the television. When two people started kissing each other on the mouth you were told to look away while everyone else clucked and said that there was no call for that sort of behaviour. If a woman on the telly had a dress that was low at the front, or a woman in the street had a short skirt like they all wore in England, she was doing the Devil's work for him. The Devil loved nudity, and when you went to bed at night you had to be careful to change into your pyjamas without exposing yourself. First you took off your top half, then you tied your pyjama top around your waist like an apron, then you slipped off your bottom half and put on your pyjama bottoms, keeping your back to the wall in case anything should show through the slit in your pyjama apron. Then you put your top on and you were ready to say your prayers.

Prayers didn't count if you said them in the comfort of the bed. You had to be kneeling to say them properly, all the way from three Hail Marys through God bless everyone you could think of. Except that I never mentioned Debora or anyone at the hOme in those prayers because I thought they would be better off if I didn't draw God's attention to them. Then, because you might die in your sleep and go to hell, you had to pray for your guardian angel to keep watch over you, and then the prayer to God himself to take your soul if you died before you woke.

'What's a soul?'

'It's invisible. Only God can see it.'

'Can God see everything?'

'Everything.'

'Can he see your bottom?'

'You have a very dirty mind. God has better things to be doing than be looking at the bottoms of rude little boys. Get into bed now before I redden yours for you.'

You had to fall asleep with your arms crossed over your chest as a final precaution against being dragged down to hell if you died in the night.

Even with my arms crossed I dreamed of the hOme, but no one there would talk to me or recognise me or acknowledge me. The ones who were naked were now devoid of body hair, even Mervyn, who had come to resemble a giant nude cherub. The ones that were clothed were clothed in grey. Then I'd give up trying to get one of them to talk to me and I'd go into the woods and find Fi, and ask her where the white pony was, and she'd tell me there was no such thing.

Then I'd wake to the fierce whispering from the bed across the room and Bridey asking why they couldn't have gone where no one knew them, just the two of them and PJ maybe, and Willy saying he was doing the best he could, and at least he had a family that could take them in. She would ask him what was meant by that and he would say he meant nothing, Bridey, nothing. But she would be quiet for a while at least.

In the morning you had to polish your shoes on a sheet of newspaper while eggs and black pudding were being fried in the kitchen, because a gentleman wouldn't sit down to breakfast without polishing his shoes first and breakfast was the most important meal of the day.

Willy went away. There was something abrupt about his leaving. Bridey said that he'd gone to fetch her a few stitches of clothes from the house in Luton, but she said it too often for it to be true. Sally said that he'd probably had his fill of a household of women.

In his absence Bridey took long walks. Sometimes I went with her, down the Maudlins or up Rosbercon or out on the Rocky Road. In a good mood she would tell me stories, about when Brenda was a little girl and they thought she was going to die because she had the poliomyelitis and all the nuns in England and New Ross prayed for her until she got better, and how she wouldn't take anything to drink until they tried her with a drop of lager in desperation and she kept that down so the doctor said she should have as much lager as she wanted and thcy had a terrible time weaning her off it afterwards. Or stories about dancing to the big show bands in Tramore, with sand in their hair from a day on the beach, or when she and Willy were courting and they had to pretend to Granny Scully that she was a friend of Netty's come over to play cards, and Granny Scully had treated her ever since as if she were in the house under false pretences.

In a bad mood she would walk fast with her lips set and say nothing except that she wouldn't stay where she wasn't wanted.

99

More often she went off for the day on her own, usually having emerged from Granny Scully's room in the morning with tears in her eyes and the big white handbag clamped across her chest. Those were days of relative freedom. After what had once been lunch and was now called my dinner, Netty would go for her nap and I would go down to sit on the stairs behind the shop, where Sally would give me money to play with. There were animals on all the coins, and I would make a farm, herding them from step to step.

Between her customers Sally would talk to me, and eventually cajole me into coming out of the dark stairway to stand behind the counter with her, where she taught me the prices (Dairy Milk sixpence and thruppence the small bar) and new ways to say my prayers (Hail Mary full of grace, the cat fell down and broke her face) and the delights of muttered mispronunciation (lick your arse for liquorice).

When adults came in she was reticent and monosyllabic, but with youngsters she was booming and informative, shouting out intimate details of their lives as they cringed on the other side of the counter.

'What do you want, Sean Breen?'

'Sher—bit, Miss Scully.'

'Did I hear you fecked a cigarette off your daddy and got sick on the Convent Steps?'

'I don't know.'

'A big bag or a tuppeny bag?'

'Big, Miss Scully.'

'Show me the money.'

'Here.'

'Where did you get that?'

'Off me mammy.'

'I'll be asking her after and she'll redden your legs if you fecked it out of her purse.'

Unflinching, Sean Breen held the tanner out and met Sally's glare until she gave him the sherbet. Then, instead of fleeing with his booty as another child might have, he paused to consider me for a minute, twizzling the lollipop in his bag of powder. 'Can he come out to play?'

Sally pushed her bottom lip against her upper dentures and blew down her nostrils, making her glasses slip to the tip of her nose so that her eyeballs were magnified beyond their containment. 'What are you playing?'

'Cowboys.'

'He hasn't a gun.'

'You could give him the loan of one out of the shop.'

I was fitted with a holster and given a black Luger and shown how to load the caps. In all of this I was silent and acquiescent. I had a vague memory of being told that when I was grown up there would be no more guns in the world, so maybe I wanted to make the most of this, my first chance to play with one. Or maybe I was in awe of Sean Breen and his cavalier treatment of Sally, and I wanted to see how he survived in this place where I knew nothing.

Sean Breen lived higher up on the other side of Mary Street, and his house had a garden at the back that ran up the steep slope parallel with the Convent Steps. There was broken glass along the top of the wall and there were bees that could be caught between two jam jars. He taught me the rules of Cowboys, the most important of which was that he always had to be Trampus. The main object of being a cowboy was to tie up girls in Barrack Lane and whip their legs with nettles. But girls were not that easy to capture, and we used up all our caps in trying, and Sean said we couldn't go back to the shop to get more because Sally might not let me out again.

'That wan your Anti Sally is a right oul hoor.'

So we retreated to his garden to torment the bees and then his mother called us in for our tea. I realised that, for the first time since I had arrived in Mary Street, I was hungry.

Mrs Breen had a hairdresser's shop, full of magazines and the noise of driers and the smell of chemicals. We were sent upstairs where a plate of bread and jam and a jug of milk were set out on the table. Sean Breen ate the white of his bread only and piled his crusts disdainfully beside his plate. Timidly, I informed him that I had been led to believe that if you didn't eat your crusts all your teeth would fall out. He answered by opening his mouth and pushing out a tongue loaded with the mashed pulp of bread and jam.

'My mammy says you have no mammy.'

I couldn't deny it. There had been no one in my life so far who fitted into the mammy parameters which, at that moment, stretched from Sean Breen's hairdressing mother to the obese slave women in Shirley Temple films every Sunday afternoon.

Mrs Breen delayed us on our way out. She was acting casual, but all her customers were twitchy and staring over the tops of their magazines. She asked me where I had lived in England.

I said that I had lived at the hOme.

The magazines were abandoned and there was a lot of face-twisting and nodding. 'God love ya. Aren't ya well out of it?'

'Did you never have a mother, love?'

'There was Brenda?'

'Who was Brenda?'

'Bridey calls her Breda.'

There was the noise of magazines hitting linoleum, and all the women were making a kind of chewing noise, except they seemed to be talking to each other. Over these masticated exclamations came the sweetened tone of Mrs Breen's next question.

'And do you know who your daddy was, love?'

Unwilling to disappoint such an expectant audience, I decided to hazard a guess. Steve had sometimes referred to Julian as Daddyo, and he had been a kind of head of household.

'Do you mean Julian?'

They moaned encouragement.

'What did Julian do?'

'He drove the bus. And he threw the oracle in the Council.'

'The council? Urban or county?'

'And he dreamt the horses we put the money on.'

'Did he bet on the horses much?'

'Every day.'

'Was he married to your mother?'

My expression may have shown that I wasn't sure what was entailed in the concept of marriage. They seemed to be holding their breath and I thought I should say something that might throw light on the relationship between Julian and Brenda.

'She wouldn't walk the horse with him after Colin came and starting sleeping with her and Julian said she was a prick-teaser.'

'Jesus and His Holy Mother, child, don't ever use language like that. What else did he say?'

I was cornered, terrified that anything I might say would provoke another reaction as violent as the last.

'I want to go back to Aunty Sally now.'

'Who's Colin?'

I ran.

The day Willy returned was the day hell broke loose and we moved to Duncannon, which was also a Sunday. He was back early enough in the morning to be able to scratch the tops of my ears off with a hairbrush and check the toecaps of my shoes for a good reflection before we set off for Mass.

Of all our interpretations of Sunday Best, Sally's were the least successful. The more she dressed herself up the more wrong she looked in it. Feet that wallowed happily in slippers all the week were now cracking out of shoes that spread at the sides into puddles of navy leather. Her frock, having lost the battle with her bosom, was engaged in guerrilla warfare with the rest of her, and refugee threads fled in every direction while the hems had quarrels of their own. Her hair was a barbed-wire tangle on which her hat, identifiable as a hat only by its position, was bludgeoned and impaled with a rusting pin.

Netty, by contrast, would make a garden of herself. Silk bluebells nodded at the insteps of her dainty shoes and her frock was of a print as solid and intense as a seed packet. Her gloves were daisies crocheted together and her hat was more posy than straw. Beneath it, her face would shine with the recent effort of having peeled a stone of vegetables for the Sunday dinner.

Bridey wore a thing round her neck made of the fur and

paws and faces of dead animals. She smelled strongly of all the extra talcum powder she had dusted on her neck to stop it breaking out in a sweat in the summer heat. Apart from that she and Willy were dressed in more or less the same kind of clothes they had worn since the day they first appeared at the hOme, not yet having had a reason to change out of their best.

There was a spindly table at the top of the stairs, the drawer of which was opened only on a Sunday to extract white gloves and white handkerchiefs that were ironed to sharpness, and the black missals with gilt-edged paper and coloured ribbons. When all this was distributed, we only had to wait for Cissy Casey, who was always on time. Cissy went to seven o'clock Mass, and sometimes the eight o'clock one as well, and then came to sit with Granny Scully while the rest of us went at ten. As soon as she knocked on the door Sally would clump down to let her in, while Willy stood on the stairs jingling his car keys.

On this occasion she was twittering more than usual. She stopped by Bridey, who was straightening the paws of her tippet in the mirror, and asked how Breda was and whether there was any news of her. Bridey froze and, without waiting to see what demeanour an unfreezing might bring, Cissy prattled on. 'A lovely little girl she was. I remember her well. It must be a blessed relief for you to be in touch with her again.' Then she bent over me so I could see the fine moustache on her lip as she pinched me on the cheek. 'Isn't he the image of his grandfather?'

Willy hadn't heard, twirling his hat and rattling his keys on the stairs, and making a clucking noise to encourage the women past the mirror. Netty hadn't heard either, running in and out of the kitchen to recheck the oven. Cissy Casey, having wished us a lovely Mass, blithered her way up to Granny scully's room, while Bridey caught my hand with a distracted ferocity and dragged me down the stairs with her.

By this time I was an old hand at Mass, knowing when to stand and sit and kneel and genuflect and cross myself, when to look at the priest and when to bury my face in my hands. I could get through the whole performance without a single clip on the ear or pinch in the small of the back from Bridey. I was beginning to understand some of the gravity of the proceedings, as well as my own good fortune in having been plucked off the road to hell. I began to wish that there was some way of letting Debora know about Jesus so that I could meet her again in heaven some day, if all else failed.

After Mass the women went straight into the house to get the dinner under way. I went with Willy to Jimmy Hanrahan's for his Sunday pint and a hand of cards. Past Cullen's on the corner and Kiely's cigar divan and French's pharmacy, we disappeared into the gloom of the closed grocery at the front of Hanrahan's, over the sawdust floor and past the stand of glass-topped biscuit tins, through to the bar which, having no windows, was in a permanent state of comfortable shade.

There was a poker game in progress on the bar. Nobody spoke more than one word at a time, and that without expression or much in the way of lip movement.

'No.'

'No.'

'Openers.'

I was allowed to go where I liked, as long as I stayed quiet: behind the bar or into the shop or up the stairs at the back to see the greyhounds.

'Check.'

'Checkwitcha.'

'Raise.'

Dickie the greyhound man came in to do the feeds, and I went with him and watched the bowls of cornflake and raw mincemeat and raw egg and brown bread mixed and distributed among the various kennels. The dogs I liked best were kept in cages set into the wall on an L-shaped staircase. Staircases were still new to me, there having been none in the hOme, and these broad, shallow and glimmering steps, smelling of straw and liniment and housing brindled sneering fabulous beasts with high collars, added glamour to the novelty. More than that, there was a kind of holy spookiness on those stairs, something tabernacular. I wanted to win the greyhounds over to my side in the same way that I needed to woo God and Our Lady and the other new gods into whose presence I had been dragged.

Back in the bar I tugged on Willy's sleeve. 'Can I get a greyhound?'

'Shish. I'm playing cards. Do you want another Fanta?'

I was cloyed already from three Fantas and three packets of crisps, so I said nothing but went back to watch the greyhounds.

Our Sunday dinner, Willy's and mine, was always a bit drier than weekday dinners, from being kept warm in the oven between two plates, the women having eaten theirs long before Willy could prise himself away from

Hanrahan's and the Devil's prayer book, which was his name for a pack of cards. But that Sunday we didn't get any dinner at all, for Bridey was waiting for us inside the front door, her suitcases round her ankles.

'What?'

'We're not staying where we're not wanted.'

'What?'

She handed two cases to him and pushed him out of the door and a minute later we were all sitting in the car. Willy started the engine and put it in gear, then switched the engine off again.

'Would you ever mind telling me what's going on?'

'You can ask him.' She flicked her head in the direction of the back seat, and me.

'The child?'

'He's been going round telling the whole town that his mother was a whore and a communist and Cissy Casey brought the whole thing back to your mother and no woman should have to endure what I've had to stand and listen to off that old witch this day while you were out polishing a bar stool with the arse of your trousers. I'm not staying in this feck of a town another minute.'

'Bridey. Language in front of the child.'

'Child? Do you want to ask that child what kind of language he was using above in Breen's? Start the car.'

'Where do you want to go?'

'I don't care. So long as I never have to set foot in this hole of an excuse for a town again. I want to go back to Luton.'

'You know we can't do that.'

'They all know now. Every single one of them knows he's a bastard, or worse.'

'What did you expect them to think he was?'

'Just drive the car to Rosslare. We'll find somewhere in England we can live. We should never have left it.'

'How can we? Haven't I just come back on the skin of my teeth with what was left of the money? Do you want me to go to jail? And what if those hippies told on us to the police? Would you like to go to jail, Bridey?'

'Breda wouldn't do that on us. Not our own daughter.'

'Come back inside, Bridey. You don't have to go anywhere near Ma. I'll talk to her.'

'Drive the car, Willy. I'm not getting out of it until we're somewhere else.'

She turned to me and I turned to look out of the window to escape her withering. We turned left down South Street, past all the shops closed for Sunday, and out past the town limits on to the windy road to Duncannon. Nothing was said, but it may have been that Willy thought an afternoon at the seaside would cheer Bridey enough for her to be enticed back into his mother's house by the evening.

They had to buy me a bucket and spade and togs and a towel. We had fish and chips for a late dinner down on the strand, with Willy talking all the time softly, and Bridey saying no at intervals and in the same flat tone.

That night we stayed in the White Hotel, in the biggest room I had ever seen. The curtains flashed on and off in time with the beam of Hook lighthouse, and seabirds made lonely noises. Next day Willy booked us into a holiday house a few doors along the seafront from the hotel. Then I began to find places, up on the cliffs and out in the dunes, where nothing could be seen of human damage, and nothing could get at me but the gentle heat of the sun.

I woke, feet cold on lino and mouth full of candlewick bedspread, and had to start again from the beginning. This could happen as much as three or four times a night so that I couldn't get into bed for a proper sleep until three or four in the morning. Once, I had remained kneeling on the lino all night until I was called for school. Years of school stretched behind me now, and it was hard to imagine I'd ever been free of it. Willy had taken a notion to buy the hotel that we'd taken refuge in the summer Bridey put her foot down, and the lumbering pile was our home now, though sometimes, in sourness, Bridey said it was his mother who bought the hotel for Willy and we were only there on sufferance. Whatever way things were arranged, the sufferance seemed to have become permanent. Maybe that was how, for want of hopes, I had become dependent on prayers.

As far as I could gather, the chances of getting straight into heaven were slim. Only saints were guaranteed a place, so you had to take all the precautions you could. It was possible that God had a particular favourite prayer, but there was no way of knowing which one it was, and to leave it out might be tactless. On the other hand, I worried sometimes that by first drawing God's attention to myself with prayer and then falling asleep on the job I was doing my cause more harm than good. It would have been unexpectedly fair to earn marks for effort.

So, as usual, I did my best to make amends by going back to the beginning of the sequence of prayers every time I woke. You had to say them all in the right order to be sure that you'd said them all, starting with the rosary, which could take up to an hour in itself. You could say it faster, by rattling through the Hail Marys, but, as the priest said, what was the point of doing it at all if you didn't think about the meaning of every word? And there are a hundred and fifty Hail Marys in a basic rosary, and it's not easy to think about the fruit of thy womb Jesus a hundred and fifty times when you're not sure what a womb is or how it came to make a fruit of Jesus.

After the rosary was out of the way the worst was over, the repetition of it being more soporific than anything that followed. Also, as you got closer to the completion, you had more to lose by falling asleep and so more incentive to stay awake. The next great hurdle was the Apostolic Creed, the words of which I always had difficulty remembering, and getting stuck in that could set you off thinking about all kinds of things. That was as bad as falling asleep in a way, except that I didn't think distraction incurred going back to the beginning, just a quick apology.

Jesus was a great mystery. You kind of felt that he was a bit constrained by an unusually stern father and a goody-goody mother, and that if he was left to his own devices he'd probably be very nice. Probably look a bit like David Cassidy. David Cassidy's posters outnumbered all the others on the walls on my side of the bedroom. I had a lot in common with David. We could both sit comfortably in the full lotus position and would almost certainly strike up an instant friendship should we ever meet. A chance meeting was most likely to occur when he was passing through Duncannon and was suddenly set upon by a horde of hysterical female fans, which I understood to be the invariable result of his trying to walk down the street like the normal person he actually was. I, as luck would have it, would be just coming out of our side door at that moment, perhaps crossing to the shop to collect my weekly copy of *Music Star*, and, seeing David running in fear of his life before a flood of full-throated, scissor-armed, souvenir-hunting teenagers, would be in the perfect position to save the day.

'Psssssssst! David, in here, quick!'

'Phew! Gee, thanks! Would you mind if I hung out with you a while until things cool down out there?'

'Not at all! Stay as long as you like! There's plenty of room and so much to talk about!'

'Hey! I like you already! You're my kind of guy, pal!'

To my certain knowledge, somewhere in Los Angeles, David Cassidy was entertaining similar fantasies about me. Not about me specifically, of course, but about the one exceptional person among his millions of fans who could be his friend, which was me. You could tell what he was thinking from his photographs. He was always smiling, but if you stared hard at the eyes for a long time you would see that there was something missing in his life. He needed me.

It was hardly my fault, then, if his name kept cropping up in the blank spaces of the Apostolic Creed. The almighty creator of heaven and earth and his only son David.

Though the bedroom was dark, I knew that his face was smiling down at me twenty-two times from the wall.

Once I had got past David, and through the God blesses, I had to cross myself, get into bed, cross myself again and say the As I Lay Me Down to Go to Sleep. You had to be lying down to say that one, or else it didn't make any sense. Then I crossed myself again, to make the crossings even. It had recently occurred to me that God couldn't possibly be making fine moral judgments about everyone in the world every minute of the day, and that he had probably evolved a simpler system. He could get angels to keep a tally of the number of times people crossed themselves, and the even crossers would go to heaven and the odd to hell. Although I had no reason to believe this, it was a possibility, and it was better to err on the side of caution in these matters. God himself, after all, was an unproven possibility upon whom one erred on the side of caution.

A thought like that would bother me. They were always saying how important it was to love God independently of any desire for personal salvation, otherwise your faith would be judged insincere and you wouldn't be saved, but what other motive could you have for loving him purely? It wasn't exactly as if he was taking you out and buying you ice-pops on his day off. And even if he did there'd still be a secret bit of you that hoped being palsy with the boss man was going to get you into heaven. The only way to overcome the whole mess was by sainthood. But could you qualify to be a saint if your primary motive had been to save yourself?

It was on loops like that that I would, finally, fall asleep, arms clamped firmly in an X across my chest. As I slept on my stomach this was a position that usually led to cramp, but I'd be so tired from all the praying that I could have slept on a crucifix, and what was a bit of cramp compared to having nails driven through your hands? And to sleep without the added precaution of crossed arms wasn't worth the risk. I didn't know the statistic for the number of ten-year-old boys who died unexpectedly in the middle of the night, but it was a prospect that was always being laid before me, and didn't seem any less likely than the imminent visit of David Cassidy to Duncannon.

Tonight, however, sleep was elusive. I'd had no problem nodding off with my knees on the cold floor and my head tipping forward on the candlewick. When I fought sleep, sleep fought back, and won. Now that sleep was welcome it was shunning me, and there was something else amiss.

On the wall, two-thirds of the way down the side of my bed and four feet above it, there was a new poster. Surrounded by the Sweet and Alvin Stardust and Marc Bolan, an eyebrowless David Bowie, with a big gold spot on his forehead, cut the darkness with lizardy eyes, biding his time until I was asleep.

I had no idea what any of these people sounded like, apart from David Cassidy, who sang in the Partridge Family on the telly. The rest of them had earned their places on the wall by dressing up alone. We hadn't a record-player in the house, and if we had there wasn't a record shop nearer than New Ross, and you'd have to be a Jim Reeves fan to want to set foot in there. Just as you had to be keen on Frank Sinatra and diddley-I music to listen to Radio Eireann. Bridey had a radio that you could get the English stations on, but if anyone else touched it and *Waggoner's Walk* failed to come through when she pushed the button we'd all be for the high jump. As for telly, that was RTE, and RTE could be depended on to keep our screen free of the cross-dressing incubi that passed for musicians across the water. If it hadn't been for Kieran and his footballers I might never have got the glam rock bug in the first place.

Two years before, maybe about a year after Willy had bought the hotel and Bridey had settled in it, Kieran had arrived from Dublin. I was told that he was my brother, though he plainly wasn't, and that his mother and father were dead, which was unlikely because that was exactly what I heard them tell him about me. But that was as much information as I could get out of anyone and more than I got out of him. Long afterwards I worked out that he was a sort of cousin, but at the time I assumed that he was someone who had been stolen from his home as I had been. That, at least, explained the anger in him. He was a year older than me and a lot bigger, and he didn't say much. He liked more physical forms of expression and, as often as not, I was the canvas upon which his emotions were manifested in browns and purples.

Somehow we never got round to comparing notes and finding out what, if anything, we really had in common. I had resented his coming, but not nearly so ferociously as he had, and by the time we had learned to put up with each other we had already decided that we couldn't. In the winter that was fine, and we could keep ourselves to ourselves with every bedroom in the hotel to choose from, but during the season we were forced to share a room above the bar, a room with wood-panelled walls that took drawing pins easily.

It was hard to say how much Kieran liked football. He never played it or watched it, but all the same his half of our room was covered from floor to ceiling with pictures of footballers, with row upon row of men with folded arms. That was how you knew where his territory was and you didn't enter it, except to cross to the door, without risking a tap of his knuckles. I felt I had to do something to counteract his lowering army, and then I discovered a magazine called *Music Star*, with posters of louche men in eyeshadow, and began to build my defences.

David Bowie had already been mobilised in other guises. He was always a bit scary looking, but I knew all about him and Angie and Little Zowie, who, though still a baby, would chortle his way through the gigs from the top of a speaker. So, in the light of day, there had been nothing odd about pinning this picture with him and a gold spot on his forehead into the space between Marc and Alvin. Alvin was a bit of a snarler himself, and there was something unsettling about Marc. Unlikely though it might seem, the Marc Bolan I knew of when I lived in England was a shy-looking thing, and I hadn't made the connection between this glitter-teared icon and the wizard of Woburn Abbey. It was only after dark and after the prayers and after the last of the after-hours drunks had stopped singing under the window in the not entirely groundless hope that if they made enough noise they might get readmittance, and after sleep had failed to arrive, that I began to ascribe my unease to this picture. The gold spot glinted faintly in the room and I knew that David Bowie was going to come and get me with his reptile eyes.

Disquiet turned to fear turned to terror turned to desperation, and I lunged at the poster and dragged it off the wall and crumpled it and took it out to the wastepaper basket on the landing, into which it fell with the eyes glinting uppermost. After that I couldn't sleep at all. He would certainly come and get me now, and the only way I could keep safe was by starting the rosary all over again.

That's how it is if you're picked on. They make you think that it is your duty to save the world, and just as you are coming to terms with the burdens of sainthood or messiahship or whatever it is they have in mind, the likes of David Bowie are sent along to rattle you out of it. It was nearly as bad as when I was supposed to be Merlin and everyone kept saying that the establishment would try to track me down, except of course that that was pagan times and fairytales and the fear then was nothing like the fear in me now. Could you measure the amount of truth in something by the degree of fear it inspired in you? Whether you could or not, I did. It occurred to me that the reason the world never got saved was because all the potential messiahs got nobbled before they could start. I said the prayers as fast as I could so there was no time to think of anything else between the words.

I must have slept because I woke, in response to a rabbit punch in the back, which was the usual consequence of not waking before Kieran. At least it was hard evidence I was still alive, and I had to thank God quickly for not letting me die in my sleep, while taking evasive action from the second punch.

'Get up, Nigger.'

The best policy was to say nothing, but to look at him in

a low-intensity kind of way. If you looked away he would slap you on the head and if you looked at him hard he'd go mental altogether. He didn't like to be looked at, but if you got it right and weren't too provocative he would turn away and walk off with rolling steps, indicative of a state of mind somewhere between disdain and Neanderthal confusion. He turned, picked his clothes off the floor and swaggered to the bathroom. I knew I had ten minutes to say all the morning prayers. I did them sitting up in bed for safety, biting into my thumbs as a substitute for the discomfort of kneeling. He came back before I had finished and threw his pyjamas on the floor.

'Get up, Faggot.'

He concentrated on a point in the mid-distance, lifted his right leg and farted.

'Good arse.'

Then he was gone.

It took me a while to finish the prayers. My head was fuzzy and the words wouldn't come in the right order, and it was another ten minutes before I could dress and deal with a bursting bladder. Then there was the problem of what to do with David Bowie, who was still crumpled in the bin. I could neither reinstate him nor leave him where he was. I thought I'd take him to the end of the gardens and burn him.

The gardens were a chain of walled enclosures beyond the yard, the last and largest of which was a declining orchard in which there was a peeling greenhouse bursting with nasturtiums. The air was volatile and pungent with crushed tropaeolum as I stood in it and struck a match, but one lizard eye was looking straight at me from the ball of paper and I couldn't set it alight, broad and encouraging though the daylight was. I smoothed him out, pushing the wrinkles out of his gold-spotted brow, and I fixed him to the wall of the greenhouse, among sacred tongues of red and orange flowers and strangled fruit. He looked at home there. I felt I had done right by him and I was less afraid.

I slipped back along the stable wall to avoid being seen by Bridey if she was at the scullery window. David Bowie was not the sort of thing you could explain to her.

She was in the kitchen, pouring anthracite into the Aga. I poured my cornflakes quickly and ate fast, so that when she noticed me she might think that I had been there all along.

'Where have you been till this hour? You're late for school. I don't know what you get up to above in that bed.'

She wasn't looking at me as she said it, and she said it every morning, whether I was late or not. She had changed since we had moved to the hotel. She never seemed careful of anything any more. There were ladders in her tights and knots in her hair. She never went outside, or even looked out of the windows. Her white handbag was scuffed and scratched and stood open on the dresser with the gilt flaking off the clasp.

She took two plates out of the oven and uncovered them. Rashers, sausage, fried egg, fried tomato, black pudding, all a little shrivelled and sweaty from being kept warm.

'Bring those in for me. They should be finished the corn-flakes by now.'

'Which table?'

'There's only the one.'

The first summer we had been overrun with guests; with entire families who'd been coming annually for generations. Half the girls in the village were employed as chambermaids and waitresses and washer-uppers. People swarmed in off the beach for afternoon tea and you could be cutting sandwiches for the bar until closing time. By the end of the season Bridey had lost a stone and the ability to hold a conversation.

I took the hot plates through to the dining room, where a cross-looking couple sat at the farthest window table. Two bowls, still full of cornflakes, had been consigned to the table next to them.

'The milk is sour.'

'We rang the bell.'

'Twice.'

I put their breakfasts down in front of them.

'Sorry.'

'This used to be a good hotel.'

I didn't know what to say to that, so I left them prodding at eggs and went straight into the hall to pick up my schoolbag. Bridey was there already.

'Where are you off to?'

'School. I'm late.'

'And who's fault is that?'

'They said the milk is sour.'

'That milk is not sour. The cheek of them. I smelt it myself. Who do they think they are anyway?'

'Dunno.'

She was shouting loud enough for the guests to hear, and I was sliding out of the door. I ran up the hill to the school and arrived sweating with a stitch in my side.

'Oh, and his lordship has decided to saunter in at this hour. We are honoured. And what kept his lordship late this morning? Was the maid late bringing his lordship his morning cup of tea?'

Hated though she was, Sister Vesuvia had no problem provoking a room full of her enemies to snigger in support of her jibes. She fingered her moustache and flexed her ruler. Her aim was bad, but if she missed you got a double dose, so you had to fight the reflexes that pulled your hand away, and try instead to intercept her wild flailings with your palm.

The school had three classrooms. The first contained infants and baby infants, and was taught by Sister Marina, a fat and untroubled woman, who might have had trouble maintaining discipline among older children, but found it easy to instill the necessary terror and silence into the tots in her domain. The middle classroom was taught by Miss Lacey, a nun in all but uniform as far as discipline and corporal punishment were concerned. She differed from the virgins either side of her in that she took the trouble to teach reading and writing and arithmetic, whereas the sisters stuck to the less controversial subjects of religion, Irish and music. Since I had graduated into the top classroom, the three brittle years spent under Miss Lacy's tutelage had begun to seem like a golden age of education and interest.

Fourth, fifth and sixth classes filled the rows confronted by Sister Vesuvia. It was rumoured that she had been demoted to us from the big convent in Ramsgrange for throwing stones at pupils in the playground. Whatever made her superiors imagine that the parents and guardians of Duncannon would be more likely to countenance that kind of behaviour, they were right. Maybe it was because the school was at the top of the hill and whatever went on in our playground was invisible to everyone but the parish priest, with whom Sister Vesuvia had an affinity.

We learned Irish until twelve, and had religious instruction until dinner-time. This consisted of reading and rereading a magazine called *The Messenger* from cover to cover, in silence, to the clicking and sucking sound of a bored nun who treated her false teeth as if they were a mouthful of boiled sweets.

Dinner-time lasted for half an hour. You ran down the hill feeling sorry for the children who lived too far out to go home for it, who had to stay and eat sandwiches, before donning felt slippers to skate up and down the parquet floor in the corridor until the afternoon lesson, forbidden to make noise or slide or laugh or do anything that might make the chore a pleasure.

Usually there was a stew on the Aga and we helped ourselves but that day the Aga was out because no one had fuelled it the night before and the anthracite that Bridey had poured in that morning was wet. Now she was jiggling a gas poker and calling on Jesus and Mary and Holy Saint Joseph to work a miracle of ignition. I switched the deep-fat frier on and pulled some frozen chips out of the freezer. There were cold pig's feet in the fridge to go with it. Kieran was standing by the bread bin, consuming white slices three at a time to keep him going until the chips were done.

'Could not one of you have thought of fuelling the Aga last night? Do I have to do everything? Go and fill those scuttles up for me while the oil is heating.'

Since she hadn't mentioned anyone by name there was a

split second of uncertainty before Kieran sputtered through a mouthful of breadcrumbs, 'I did it last time. I'm always doing it. Let that midget do it for a change.'

I already had the scuttles in my hands. He would win in the long run, would put more effort into not filling them than it would take to fill them. And even if he didn't, he would take it out on me later.

'Don't call Joseph a midget.'

'Why? Just because he's the pet.'

'No one's the pet in this house.'

The voices were rising behind me as I went up the yard, and they would have been screaming by the time I got back, had it not been for the distraction provided by Willy.

I was halfway with the full scuttles and had just got to the point were my arms always gave out and I had to leave them down and take them in one at a time, when I heard the big gate creak and the sound of hooves in the arch. Willy appeared, leading a grey pony by a piece of old rope around its neck.

We rarely saw anything of Willy. While the hotel had been busy he had spent most of his time in the neighbouring bars, keeping an eye, he said, on the competition. Since things had gone into a bit of a decline he had taken to the building trade again and was away from early in the morning, not usually returning until after closing time. I had gone with him once or twice, but his working day was not something to hold the interest of a companion, mostly consisting as it did of sitting in one pub or another, waiting for one man or another to turn up with something or other, and interspersed with occasional visits to the site where a couple of unshavable men would stop smoking long enough to explain why nothing had been done since the last visit. On Sundays Willy would stay home and help in our own bar for an hour in the morning, before heading across the road for a quick one. The first rule of being a publican, he said, was never to drink in your own bar, and he never broke his rule unless persuaded to.

So now, an appearance by Willy in the middle of the day in the middle of the week was strange enough. The horse that accompanied him was beyond wonderment. He tied the animal to a beer keg.

'There you are now.'

'What's his name?'

'How would I know?'

'Where did you get him?'

'Off a man in Clonroche that owed me money.'

'Can we keep him?'

'We'll have to if we can't sell him.'

The sound of Bridey's voice alerted us to her presence in the doorway behind us. Kieran was beside her, bread frozen in mid air on the way to his mouth.

'Sacred Heart of Jesus, Willy, what's that?'

'Howiya.'

'And where have you been the last three days? I nearly phoned the Garda.'

'It's a horse I got off a fella in Clonroche.'

'What are we supposed to do with it?'

Willy shrugged and looked offended. Consequences not being one of his deeper interests, he often adopted a wounded demeanour when confronted by them. There was an impasse while Bridey waited for her answer.

Meantime I was stroking the pony's shoulder to see how

tame he was. I looked at the teeth and thought he was maybe a five-year-old, though I was guessing from the colour of his coat as well. His feet were in bad condition and he didn't know how to pick them up for me. I doubted whether he had ever seen a brush in his lifetime.

'Would you look at young Joseph now. Going over the horse like a tinker at a fair.'

'Is he broken in?' For some reason my voice sounded more Englishy than it had for years.

'Is he what?'

'Can I ride him?'

Kieran pushed past Bridey. 'I want to ride him.' He caught me by the shoulder and yanked me out of the way, while jumping up on the beer keg which the pony was tied to, towering over the retreating creature before launching himself in a belly-flop across its withers. The pony reared and the beer keg came up with it and a stack of crates of Macardles empties went crashing to the ground, making a carpet of brown glass shards across the yard. Any eagerness I felt to see the end of Kieran was cancelled out by a blunt fear that the pony was going to break a leg.

Willy's flaccid knot slipped and the keg fell harmlessly. Kieran slithered off and incurred no more damage than a kick in the shoulder and a cut on the backside from a broken Macardles bottle. The pony galloped to the end of the yard, tail tucked in and body shortened and eye-whites showing, and stood pressed against the coach house where the anthracite was kept, trembling and breathing hard.

'I'll feckin' killim.' Kieran, now on his feet and purple with anger, hurled a bottle in the direction of the pony. It splintered across the yard. The pony saw the door to the garden and shot through.

'You'll feckin' clear up this mess.' Willy held Kieran by the shirt-tail to stop him running after the pony with another bottle.

'I have to do everything around here. He can do it. It was his fault.' He threatened me with the bottle. 'I haven't even had me dinner yet.'

'Jesus, the chips.' Bridey ran back to the kitchen.

Willy and I went to catch the pony while Kieran was sent to get a brush to sweep the glass. We stalked the animal through the apple trees.

'I'm going to call him Asfaloth.'

'What class of a name is that when it's at home?'

'Dunno.'

There was no point in telling Willy about Frodo and Glorfindel. Years before I had learned the wisdom of not mentioning anything connected with the hOme. I would only be contradicted and told that I was making it up and that I had a perverse imagination. Sometimes I thought they might be right, because memories were sliding and fading and taking on the qualities of remembered dreams, but I still had no other way to account for the years before the visit began. I fantasised that I could be snatched back to the hOme as easily as I had been snatched away. Now and again, in the middle of misremembrance, a word would crop up, like Asfaloth, and seem appropriate.

'Couldn't you not call him a proper name? Grey Boy or Prince or something?'

'Asfaloth. Asfaloth. Good boy. Stay there.'

He stopped beneath the fig tree and let me walk up

to his shoulder and take hold of the trailing rope.

There was no sign of Kieran in the yard, or that any of the glass had been swept. We cleared junk out of one of the stables and put Asfaloth in there with a bucket of water.

'He needs hay. And straw to stand on.'

'It'll be far from straw he was reared.'

'It's not good for his legs to be standing on a hard floor.'

'Since when did you know so much about horses?'

'Dunno.'

'I'll sort the beast out. You should be at school.'

I ran, and got there just as the bell was being clattered in the playground. The afternoon, as usual, was given over to music. All three classes stood before Sister Vesuvia and she conducted us with her ruler. Those who could play did, and those who couldn't, like me, mimed; fingering the holes of our tin whistles without blowing. Kieran, being the tallest in the school, had the job of standing at the front and turning over big sheets of paper on which the music was written. Being without a grasp of the connection between the noise of the tin whistles and the marks on the paper, he had to be reminded when to turn the page by Sister Vesuvia, who would jump up and down in an attempt to hit him on the head with her ruler. She never got much past his shoulder, and he took little notice of her until, in the course of one of her descents, she landed a blow on his wrist and smashed the face of his watch.

He looked at it and he looked at her.

'Me mammy gave me that.'

His voice sounded uncharacteristically small. He had never been heard to mention his mammy before, or acknowledge that he had one.

The expression on Sister Vesuvia's face was similar to when her false teeth went flying across the room in mid-tirade. She dropped her ruler and scrabbled for some Sellotape which she plastered across the broken watch.

'There. It's mended now. You don't have to tell your mammy about it.'

Maybe she thought he was referring to Bridey when he mentioned his mammy. She didn't live in the village and was vague about who belonged to whom, one indignant mother interrupting the class to have a go at her looking pretty much like another. After one of those interviews she would return from gesticulating in the hallway and screech to know whose mother that had been.

'Mine, Sister.'

'Go and stand in that corner for the rest of the day and that'll teach you to be running home with lies about me.'

Now, overcome by the need for diplomacy, she gave Kieran a mint to secure his discretion. He looked at it, then looked at his watch, then flung the mint in her face.

'You can fuck off for yourself and shove that up your cunt.'

We crowded to the windows to watch him leave, striding against the sparkling sea and vanishing beneath the brow of the hill. Sister Vesuvia ran up and down behind us, swiping at the backs of our heads with the ruler and screeching at us to go back to our places. But there was no one who wouldn't defy her to watch him out of sight.

I had never seen him vulnerable before, as he had been when he stood and let her Sellotape his watch. And he had got his expletives right for once in calling a cunt a cunt. I thought that when I got home that afternoon I might say something to him. Just 'Hiya' or something like that.

By the time the bell went and I was running downhill in the daily cataract of liberated children I could only think of Asfaloth and whether Willy had given him anything to eat. Instead of going through the hotel I went straight into the yard by the big gate. The floor was bare and the manger empty and the bucket of water had been kicked over and he was chewing the wood off the top of the half-door. I got him some windfalls out of the orchard to keep him going while I thought of something else.

There were some old cracked bits of tack in the loft above the stable and I managed to cannibalise enough broken bridles to make a whole one, reciting the names of the parts as I buckled them together, as if Fi were standing over me.

There was a tennis court that belonged to the hotel, across the road from it, above the wall of the strand. Since we had taken over the net had rotted and the concrete was breaking up and what had been lawn all round was now a thick thatch of grass and sweet wrappers. I brought him there first and sat on the wall, holding the reins while he guzzled.

'Wheredja get the horse, Joe?'

There was a gang from school who had come down for a swim. Now they were standing on the opposite wall in their togs, holding towels across their shoulders and shivering.

'Caniva go on her?'

'No. And he's a gelding.'

'Ah, go on.'

There was a crunch of lemonade bottle giving way under hoof and Asfaloth was in the process of trying to swallow a crisp packet. As I pulled the soggy plastic out of his mouth I realised that the tennis court was not ideal grazing. We set off down the beach to look for better fodder.

It was late by the time we got back from grazing the long acre. Everyone was out playing mob-mob in the setting sun. That was a kind of search-and-destroy version of hide-and-seek.

'Here's snobby Scully and his gee-gee.'

'What's the point of walking a horse around like a dog? I heard you're afraid to get up on him.'

'No.'

'Kieran says he rode him and he was like a bucking bronco.'

'Well, he's not.'

'Are you staying in or coming back out to play?'

That was Christo Maloney. He was inclined to be easier to get on with than some of the others.

'I'll be out in a minute.'

The yard was still glinting with brown glass and there was no sign that Willy had done anything about hay or straw. From the way Bridey was talking it sounded as if he had disappeared again.

'Where have you been to this hour? There was no one to mind the bar for me the whole afternoon.'

'Out playing.'

'Isn't it well for you?'

'I haven't done me homework yet.'

'And who's fault is that?'

'I'll go in and mind the bar so.'

'And don't give Martin Foley any more drink. He's had enough.'

Martin Foley was the only customer in the bar, muttering affectionately into the remains of a large stout. He was a bachelor farmer who came in every night to sit in the corner and drink stout in silence. When he was drunk he would start to tell his joke, endlessly repeated, the nouns mixing as the evening wore on. 'What have more holes than hairs? A dog. What have more holes than hairs than a dog? What have more hairs than holes? A dog. A dog have more holes than hairs than holes a dog.'

I propped my copybook behind the counter to get the homework done. Bridey would be going to bed by now, and there was no sign of Kieran. It was a few hours yet to closing time and I had my fingers crossed that no more customers would come in. Martin was easy to deal with, but there were still soldiers up at the fort, and if any of them decided to have a night on the tiles I might not be able to manage.

Kieran didn't come to bed that night. I got through all the prayers without falling asleep or thinking about them too much. I might have said them a bit fast, but I thought that would be all right for once. Beneath the window Martin Foley was still telling his hair-and-hole joke to the puddle at his feet. The cold would sober him for the walk home, eventually. I hadn't worked out where or how I was going to get my hands on hay and straw, but I hoped I was going to wake early enough to take the pony out for a graze before school.

So near the sea as that, winter was the best of the seasons and the storms were the best of winter. When the wind blew hard enough to keep the people off the street you could imagine that the village was a deserted place, given back to the gulls and the foxes; that the stain of humanity might one day be worn away by storms.

Duncannon swept down from the school to the strand, and the strand spread left for a mile, facing south and the lighthouse. The lower part of the village was a knob of a peninsula, the road that circumscribed it dividing at the hotel, forking right across the neck of the isthmus towards the harbour, or carrying on circumlittorally to sweep up again towards the fort, which covered the head of this member in an unretractable skin of stone. During the summer the fort was full of resting soldiers. They were a hard-drinking, towel-flicking, streaking-down-the-sands mass of crop-haired men who could be pleasant individually and amusing in pairs, but in gangs of three or more they were another animal altogether, and it was best to steer clear of their neatly ironed civvies and fresh sunburn. By winter the fort was back the way it should be, and you broke in by climbing the cliff beneath and sliding between the bars of what was rumoured to be the Croppy Boy's dungeon, from where you could sneak out on to the walls, which in the old days had been three times as high, and James II had leaped from the top of them on to the deck of a waiting ship hundreds of feet below, landing without a scratch and so proving the justice of the Catholic cause and the perfidy of the English, as if everyone didn't know that already from the way they had treated poor old Oliver Plunkett, for whom our school was named and on whose behalf we hated Titus Oates more than Cromwell himself. I worried sometimes that part of me was English and that that was the reason for all my failings.

The winter hid us from the public. The strand became a private place; a square mile when the tide was out and a long one when it was in, and the wind never stopped blowing, seasoning every breath you took and raking all the grass on the dunes and, if you ran with it, skimming you over corrugated sand on a layer of salt and air and water. The least of the winds would blow money out of your hand as you crossed to the shop and all you could do was stand and watch the pound note swoop and climb like a swallow before you returned, empty-handed and flinching, to Bridey. The great winds would snatch yourself as easily, on the way down to the harbour for a bag of anthracite, anchored to the road by the sack truck. Let go at the wrong moment and you'd be flying through the air, feet first, towards the harbour wall and the sea. The time it happened to me I only just caught hold of a lamppost at the last moment, from which I fluttered out over the water like a pennant until the gust had died away. And when the real storms began the boats came back with herring, and we roasted them on the fire in the bar and ate them with bread and our fingers, spitting bones from the oily char.

Kieran had run away on a herring boat the day he told Vesuvia where to stuff her mint. He hid until they were out at sea and then there was nothing they could do about it but put him to work. It was Pakki Purcell and that lot and he had fished with them before, for salmon in the summertime. He was away more than a week, and Bridey was worried sick once his absence was noticed, which was not on the first day or the second. He returned an adult, in his own estimation, and with a mild dose of tuberculosis, which delayed any decision about whether he should go back to school.

And PJ came to live with us.

He was like someone from a poster in a magazine. The toes and platforms of his shoes were draped in the bottoms of his trousers and his trousers ascended in parallel lines until they caught him tight about the thighs and hips and finished in a broad, five-button waistband, flat and snug as the shirt above it. He had a trimmed beard like Cat Stevens and wavy hair that fell in symmetry across his level shoulders from a central parting. His hands were bone and sinew.

I thought at first he had come for a holiday, as he had once before, brushing us with his glamour and vanishing again before it was tarnished or the week was up, but it soon became obvious that he wasn't here to enjoy himself and that he was in no hurry to get away again. He moved into the biggest room on the top floor and rarely came out of it. I would bring his breakfast to him in the morning, and you never knew what to expect. Sometimes he would be asleep and sweet, more often awake and sitting up in bed, grinding his teeth, and with dark circles under his eyes and a hunted look.

'What do you want?'

'It's your breakfast.'

'Fuck off.'

'I'll leave it over here for you so.'

His temper gradually improved and he began to come down in the evening to watch telly with us.

'What the fuck is that?'

'Language, PJ.'

'Sorry, Mum.'

'It's the news in Irish.'

'Do they have to?'

'It's your heritage. You should be proud of it.'

'One sodding channel and they fill it with this guff.'

Kieran roused himself in the big armchair. The TB entitled him to sit nearest the fire, apparently. His question came out with more eagerness than you'd think was in him.

'What's it like in England?'

I couldn't help myself. 'They don't have television in England.'

Kieran laughed the loudest, though PJ wasn't far behind. Bridey looked up from doing the fashions in the *Sunday Express* and smirked along with them, managing to glare at me at the same time. 'What makes you think that?'

'Nothing. I just didn't think they did.'

Kieran was keen to cement his alliance with PJ in the wake of my retreat. 'Everyone in Dublin has the BBC. It's only in holes like this you can't get it.'

'Of course we have telly in England. We invented it.'

'Who's this we?' It was amazing the way Bridey's lisp would disappear when her voice sharpened. 'Since when were you English?'

'Since I was born there, Mother. And don't come the Paddy nationalist with me with your *Sunday Express*. You'd go back there tomorrow if you could and you know it.'

'That's no way to be talking to your mother.'

He winked at me. Whenever I could I'd sit beside him on the sofa, and if everyone else had gone to bed I'd rest my head against his arm and pretend I was asleep. Sometimes I wouldn't get there until after the bar was shut, and there'd be just the two of us and I'd make milky coffee. He liked that.

'Proper little mumsy, aren't you?'

'Dunno.'

'Did you really think there was no telly in England?'

'Dunno.'

'We even have colour now.'

'Colour?'

'And *Top of the Pops* every Thursday. You're a deprived child. How old are you?'

'Ten.'

He counted backwards on his fingers. 'It wasn't that long ago they brought you over. You must remember something, even if they've made a complete Paddy of you by now.'

'No.'

'Nothing?'

'I remember everyone was nicer to me and we were going to save the world.'

'I remember all that. It's too late now. The planet's fucked. You might as well get on and enjoy what's left of it. Mum won't say too much about it, but I got the impression that Breda had you in some kind of commune.'

'Her and Willy kidnapped me.'

'I heard Breda asked them to take you.'

'She's Brenda, not Breda, and it wasn't for her to say. She didn't own me.'

'I thought you couldn't remember anything.'

'I can't.'

'Suit yourself.'

'Will you go back, to England?'

'I'm not hanging round this dump for the rest of my life.'

I wanted to ask whether he would take me with him, but it seemed a bit premature. 'Why did you come here so?'

'Cold turkey. Do you know what that is?'

'No.'

'It doesn't matter. I just have to stay out of the way for a bit.'

'Of what?'

'Temptation.' Exasperated, he stood up and went off without a word.

The other thing the winter brought was shrinking afternoons, and dealing with the pony became more of a challenge. Asfaloth being a bit of a mouthful, I'd started calling him Ash for short, like his ash-grey coat. I had persuaded Martin Foley to let me keep him on one of the fields on his farm, knowing that if he stayed around the yard too long Willy would find it easier to sell him than to buy in straw and fodder. We got out of school at three, and I'd already have the bridle in the bottom of my schoolbag, and I'd set off at a fast walk. I could have gone by the strand, but the road was quicker, and after two miles

I could take a short cut across the fields. I tried to avoid being seen from Martin's house in case he thought I was a nuisance, but sometimes he would be leaning on the gate with a dog, presumably the dog with more holes than hairs, lying across his feet. He'd nod, and I'd say 'Howiya', and he'd nod again, and that would be it. I'd catch Ash and brush him with two clothes-brushes and a scrubbing brush I'd stolen from the hotel and kept hidden in a bucket under the hedge, and then I'd ride him, bareback since there was no saddle. Sometimes I'd ride in a big circle, pretending Fi was standing in the middle shouting instructions, and sometimes I'd just ride off somewhere. On Saturdays and Sundays, when there was more time, we'd go down to the strand and gallop in the sea. I had to be careful not to ride on the road much, since I was still saving up for a set of horseshoes, which was why I hadn't bought *Music Star* for a few weeks now.

It would be dark when I left him, and I always came home along the strand, as there was no hurry to be back at the hotel.

'Can you mind the bar for me for a few minutes?'

I'd be in the scullery, with my head in the freezer, trying to find something I could cook and eat under a row of frozen rabbits, like babies with their heads cut off, before Bridey found me. But she always found me first. Not that it made much difference whether I ate on the bar counter or the kitchen table. It was no strain to mind the bar in the winter. There was nothing to do apart from pulling the odd bottle of stout and keeping the fire going, and you had to look in on the lounge every once in a while to make sure there was no one in there waiting to be served. Sometimes you might have to contribute to any desultory conversation that arose.

'Martin Foley is looking for you, boy.'

'For what?' I was caught off guard, and there may have been a squeak in my voice. Pakki Purcell had just come in, and made the announcement with the latch still in his hand. It sounded as though something terrible had happened. 'What did I do?'

'He says you're bringing home a half-acre of his land on your boots every night of the week.'

Pakki Purcell nearly fell off the step laughing at himself while I pulled the cap off a lrge Macardles for him. Eddy Darcy sputtered the Guinness froth out of his glass and across the counter. Martin himself was not in yet, to complete the inevitable trio of customers on a week night. I glanced down at my feet, not booted but shod. Most of the mud had come off walking down the strand. All the same I wondered whether Martin had been complaining about me, and whether he was getting fed up with our arrangement.

When he came in he nodded, as usual, and I said 'Howiya', and he nodded again, and that was it until he'd had a few bottles under his belt and started on the joke. Neither Pakki nor Eddy spoke to him the entire time, or gave any indication that they ever had, so I was hoping that Pakki had made the whole thing up after all.

Willy arrived home about half past nine, and started up a game of Twenty-one with Pakki and Eddy in front of the fire. Twenty-one was a complicated business; the higher the red the lower the black and all that, not to mention reneging. If you had a particularly good card you had to hold it high in the air first and slam it down on the table with a shout. The rest of the rules were beyond me. The telephone rang in the passage behind the bar, and I wondered whether I should go and answer it. I didn't like using the thing. It was always someone ringing up to talk to Willy and he was never there and if he was you had to pretend he wasn't. Bridey refused to answer it under any circumstances and Kieran seemed not to hear it ring, so it was usually me who gave in in the end. This time I heard PJ pick the receiver up and say hello. A minute later he opened the door.

'Dad. It's for you.'

'I'm not here.'

'I already said you were. It's Aunty Sally.'

'What does she want this time of the night?' Already he was making his way behind the bar, cards tight to his chest. As soon as he had gone through and the door was shut, PJ caught me by the shoulder and dragged me into the lounge. He was laughing.

'What?'

'Granny Scully had a heart attack.'

It wasn't the worst news I'd ever heard, but it wasn't the funniest either. 'Is she dead?'

'It'll take more than that to polish the old boot off. No, but listen, Breda's turned up at her house.'

'Breda my mother?' I could fee something slipping out of control somewhere. I put my hands behind my back to give myself a Chinese burn.

'Breda your mother. Pitched up with a spade. She walked into Mary Street with a black boyfriend in tow. Granny Scully took one look at him and keeled over.'

'Why?'

'Jesus Christ. How long have you lived in this country?'

'Is she looking for me?'

'Breda?'

'Is she?'

'I don't know. Maybe. You'll soon find out, if she isn't run out of the country for polluting her race.'

I said twice the number of prayers that were necessary that night and didn't fall asleep once. I wasn't specific about what I was asking for. I had found God to be one of those contrary characters who never gives way to a direct demand. It was better to drop hints about wanting good things to happen in general and keep your true purpose to yourself, which was difficult given that the whole thing was done by thought-transference. I did, as casually as I could, suggest a deal in which Ash and I went to live at the hOme, and in return I converted the lot of them to Catholicism. I tried to make it sound like a spontaneous suggestion, and emphasised the conversion bit as though that was what I had thought of first. I thought it was a good idea, but you never knew with God.

Bridey, Willy and PJ went into town the next day. I asked if I could go, but Bridey took one look at my shoes and said that she wouldn't be seen dead with me in that state in New Ross. She said she'd take me to Wexford the following week to buy a new pair. I was to stay home from school and mind the bar.

There were no customers that day, only a delivery of crisps. Some time in the afternoon Kieran put his head round the passage door and said I was to come into the kitchen. He was in his pyjamas still.

'What?'

'Just come.'

'I have to mind the bar.'

'Leave the door open. You'll hear anyone coming in.'

I thought maybe he wanted to talk about mothers; that because mine had come back from an implied death he would want to tell me about the one who had given him the watch. Since the TB he was more relaxed, though not necessarily more approachable. He would stay in bed all morning and only get up to steal a packet of Major from the bar to go and smoke in the stables. He had been moved to a room of his own at the other end of the hotel, and half the walls of my room were bare now where the footballers had been. I would have liked to put up more pop stars but I couldn't afford any more until the horseshoes were bought, and after that I'd probably be saving for a saddle. Sometimes I wished I had Julian's talent for dreaming racehorses, but that was probably the work of the Devil and not the best way to earn a living if your definition of the long term encompassed eternity.

Kieran had magazines spread over the kitchen table. There were pictures of girls pulling their fannies apart with painted fingernails, and of girls shoving things up themselves, and of men with huge yokes sticking them in girls' mouths and fannies and bums, and of men sticking their tongues out at girls' fannies.

'Where did you get those?'

'Above in PJ's room. He keeps them under his mattress.'

'What were you looking in there for?'

'What else is there to do? Dja like 'em?'

'No.'

'What's your oul fella stickin' out like that for, then?'

I looked down to where he was pointing and there was an irrefutable perpendicularity. I stood closer to the table. 'It's not my fault.'

His answered by stepping back to display his own wincyette excrescence. 'I already had two wanks this morning.'

I looked blank.

'You're too young. I betcha don't even have a hair on your mickey yet. Which is your favourite?'

'Dunno.'

'I like her.' He jabbed at a woman in her nip standing by a swimming pool. I couldn't see anything that set her very far apart from the others, but Kieran had his yoke out of his pyjama flies and was rubbing it. 'Go on. Pick one and have a go.'

The latch clicked in the bar and I ran off to see whether there was a customer. Kieran shouted after me that I knew where they were now, under PJ's mattress.

Bridey was watching, with arms folded and lips compressed, as Ash did complicated things in her kitchen, with flasks and sieves and thermometers. Not Ash the pony but Ash from Bangalore, though it seemed that I had invoked him, accidentally, by calling his name every day above in Martin Foley's field.

'There's yoghurt for sale in the shop across the road if you have to be eating that class of a thing. Strawberry flavour. Chocolate even, though it'd take more than chocolate to hide the taste of it.' Bridey grimaced as her throat closed involuntarily over the memory of the one time she had been persuaded to try a spoonful of yoghurt. 'Why anyone in their right mind would want to put germs in the milk. Aren't there enough germs in the world already? Did you know that's what you're doing? Putting germs in the milk?'

'Bacteria, Mum. Leave him alone.' Brenda sounded as bored as she looked.

'Well, pardon me for having an opinion.'

'You don't have to watch over him.'

'I'll watch what I like in my own kitchen, thank you.'

She had hardly taken her eyes off him since he had crossed the threshold with Brenda the evening before. She followed him around the house as though he might go into a corner and make a mess. Her frustration, when he went into the bathroom and locked the door behind him, was unconcealable.

'I hope he knows what he's doing in there.'

PJ gave her an open-eyed look and exhaled.

'Don't you be sighing at me. I'm the one that has to clean up. They don't have toilets in Africa, you know.'

'Mum, he's Indian. And how would you know what they have in Africa? And he's lived in England for most of his life. He went to a public school, for God's sake.'

'They're all the same as far as I'm concerned. They're worse than tinkers.'

'You know nothing about them. And they aren't them. We're all us, whether you like it or not.'

'Don't you be telling me what I know and what I don't. Wasn't I living twenty years in Luton and the streets crawling with them? They should never have left them in. We shouldn't be leaving them in here. The country's poor enough as it is without the likes of that fella taking the dole and the council houses.'

'He's not going on the dole. He wants to buy a house and start a meditation centre.'

'Meditation. There you go. There's not one of them prepared to do an honest day's work.'

There was a flushing noise and Ash reappeared. Bridey darted off and returned moments later carrying a whiff of bleach and disappointment with her.

'Is everything all right, Mrs Scully?' The few times that Ash took the trouble to address Bridey directly he availed himself of the chance to goad her with courtesy.

He was not the Ash that I remembered. He had short hair

now and a suit from Savile Row. The old Ash would never have locked a bathroom door behind him. I knew it was him because he called me Coorg, which made me feel a bit shaky. Whenever he caught my eye he would wink, as though his visit was a ruse to snatch me back to Devon and Debora. He did so now.

'Everything's fine and why wouldn't it be?' Bridey put on a breezy smile that did little to foil the tone of her voice. She turned to me. 'Is that fire all right in the bar, Joe? Have you nothing better to be doing than hanging around in doorways?'

Thinking that no one would notice me, I had propped myself in the kitchen doorway, from where I could keep one eye on the bar. There were no customers. Bridey glared at me until I retreated to my proper post. I put a token shovelful of coal on the fire, which was blazing anyway for nobody's benefit. I rearranged the bottles on the shelves and put all the glasses in the right order and folded the J-cloths neatly. There were things I wanted to ask.

I had tried to ask Brenda, but the question had come out more like an accusation. I don't think she recognised me to begin with. Then, when I was pointed out to her, she gave a distracted smile in my direction, though not at me. 'Well, he seems to be doing all right.' She said it to no one in particular and went on flicking through the magazine across her knee. I hung around until I was alone with her, since Bridey would have murdered me for what I was about to ask. In my mind I thought that Brenda was being as cautious as I was, and that she would open up when no one else was listening or watching. Maybe she would have, if it wasn't that the first thing I blurted out came in a voice that was irritating even to myself.

'Why didn't Debora come with you?'

'Debora who?' The astonishment on her face hardened and set as it came to the surface. 'Because I didn't ask her to.' She heaved herself on to her feet and walked away, supporting her great belly with hands clasped beneath it.

So I needed to ask Ash, but there was no chance of that while Bridey was monitoring his every move. I stayed as near to the passage door as I could, so I could hear the mumble of whatever conversation was going on.

A taut silence filtered through from the kitchen. The wave of awkwardness was followed by PJ with his face screwed up. Again he dragged me into the lounge, where he burst into snorts among the empty tables, a wiped, though not clean, ashtray set on the centre of each.

'What?'

The muscles round his mouth were going in all directions as he tried to form words through the laughter. 'That woman.'

'Who?'

'She told Breda to have an orange, for the vitamins, and gave her one out of the bowl on the dresser. Breda was about to peel it when she saw the Outspan sticker and said she couldn't eat it because it was South African, and Bridey said, "So?" and Breda said everyone knew you weren't supposed to eat South African oranges. Bridey thought about it for a minute, and she looked at Ash and told Breda she was right. "I never thought of that. For all we know a dirty black man might have picked it." And she took the orange off Breda and ran it under the tap.'

'What did Ash say?'

'I don't know. I ran. Go in and see.'

There was only Bridey and Brenda in the kitchen, glaring at each other. Ash came in in his overcoat and told Brenda he was going for a walk.

'Should I come with you?' She said it feebly and sagged in the chair so that her belly looked even bigger.

'No. But maybe you'd like to think about where we're going to stay tonight.' He turned to go.

A wave of alarm passed over Bridey before she shouted after him. 'You'll have to go out through the bar. I lost the key of the front door.'

Ash changed course like a deflected automaton and went out through the bar.

I spoke out of turn. 'There's no key to the front door. It's a bolt.'

'Be quiet, you, and mind your own business. As if things weren't bad enough without the likes of him being seen coming out of the house. I thought you were minding the bar.'

'PJ's in there. I'll see ya.'

I ran before they could catch the breath to ask me where I was going. I was still pulling my anorak on when I caught up with him on the slip road down to the strand. I tried to fall in with his manic pace. The Devlin sisters were sitting on the wall on the other side of the tennis court. One or other of them called out.

'Is that yer oul fella, Joey? Did yer daddy come to see ya?'

The two of them were clutching at one another not to fall off the wall with cackling.

The tide was out. Neither Ash nor I had said anything

until we caught up with it and the pace was broken by having to skirt shallow expanses of abandoned seawater. Our shoulders were turned into the drizzle and wind.

'That's Hook and that's Crook.' I pointed out the headlands to the left and right of the estuary. 'It was Strongbow was the first to say it.'

'Strongbow?'

'He was the one started all the trouble. He brought the English over. By Hook or by Crook. And that thing there on Crook. Do you see that speck? That's the Metal Man Monument. If you're a girl and no one will marry you, you have to hop around it three times on one leg.'

'Magic.' Ash was transfixed by the talisman across the water.

'Do you still do the yoga? I still do the yoga. And David Cassidy does it.'

'Who's David Cassidy?'

'He's in the Partridge Family.'

'Oh.'

'Would you like to see Ash? I mean Asfaloth. But I call him Ash.'

'It's a good name.' He was laughing at me.

'He's only called Ash because it's short for Asfaloth. I couldn't be calling out Asfaloth at the top of the field.'

He followed me without asking what his namesake was. Questions were piled in a bottleneck at the back of my throat, and all that could slip past them was a gabble of useless information. I told him about the witches on Broom Hill and the ghosts in the fort and the Templars of Templetown, while leading him the length of the strand to the caravan park at Ballystraw, and up the hill and through the woods to Martin Foley's land.

'You'll have your good shoes ruined with the mud.'

He looked down at the mud and crusted salt on his brogues, which had been as shiny as a gent's when he left the hotel. 'It takes more than a bit of mud to ruin good shoes.'

'Be careful. Don't walk there. Come round it.' There was a she-brier over that bit of the path; a bramble that had grown in a hoop and rooted itself into the ground on the other side, making an arch that you could pass beneath.

'Why?'

'That's a she-brier and if you want to sell your soul to the Devil you may run under it three times and call his name out and he'll appear before you and you'll be rich all your life and ride around in a carriage but you have to go straight to hell when you die. That's the bargain. And what if you went under it three times by accident and said the Devil's name by accident and then where would you be? Come round this side of it.'

He thanked me, and deferentially stepped round the peril.

'Be careful now. This field we're going to cross is a fairy field. We have to put our coats on inside out or we'll be trapped in it and we won't be able to find the gap in the hedge no matter how many times we look.'

He scanned the small field of tussock and dead ragwort. There were tall thick hedges all the way round so it was hard to see where we had come in, let alone how we could get out. Then he followed my example and took his coat off and pulled the sleeves through, replacing it damp side in. We took a pace forward and the gap appeared in the hedge opposite; a hole with a sceach across it, which he crossed as easily as I with all my practice could. Now we were at the top of Martin Foley's field. I called out and Ash came bucking up the hill with three heifers behind him, one of whom had taken to chewing his tail so it was half the length it should have been. Otherwise he was in fine fettle and armoured with a layer of dried mud.

Still none of the questions would take on a form that was fit to be spoken aloud. And what if the answers were going to be worse than knowing nothing at all? If Ash had found me, then Debora could have. So what had prevented her?

Ash the man watched me open a stolen packet of crisps and feed them to Ash the pony. 'How much do you remember about the hOme?'

I don't remember it starting. I remember his question and then the next thing there was the sound of howling and the realisation that I was the source of it. I couldn't see anything and there was a pain in every part of me and the grass was wet under my hands and face and the ground was vibrating with the percussion of hooves galloping away in terror.

The next thing I was rocking and rocking, in a shallow cup of tweed-clad legs. The air was filled with a reverberating, profound, drawn-out, becalming Om.

I remembered everything. The beat came into my head. Duggareedugandugareedugreeduh in the wizard's voice and the bongos materialised in the silent air like in a musical on the telly when the orchestra strikes up invisibly in a cornfield. Debora was made manifest; every word of her invocation in place, her sunken face still like a galleon. Just before the end I opened my eyes. We were on a rainy green hillside and I was cradled in the lap of a small rocking yogi in the gentleman's clothes. A pony and three heifers were sniffing their way back up the hill towards us, heads low with curiosity and white breath ricocheting off the grass. I looked at Ash the man's face. Streams of tears eroded the lighter film of rain on his cheeks. He sang the last word. 'Shhhhhhhhh.'

'Coorg.' Ash took the snot from under my nose with the ball of his thumb. 'His name is Coorg. The child is a mage. He is born with the signs of the seer on him. He will be great and his life will be lived in pain, but he will know everything and he will be right.'

I felt as if I were floating. It was so long since I had heard those words that I had stopped believing them. And somewhere along the way it had struck me that I knew very little.

Suddenly I realised that I was too big to be lying in this man's lap, and what if Martin Foley came along and saw us? I might have been a mage once, but now I was a dirty-minded little boy with an irritating voice whom nobody liked. I got to my feet and held my hand out to pull him to his. 'You'll get piles off the wet grass.'

He hesitated. 'I don't know where Debora is either.' He gave me his hand.

'See? It isn't true. I don't know everything.' I caught his hand tight and leaned backwards on the slope to give myself the leverage to pull him. Ash the pony licked the back of my neck.

'It doesn't work like that. You can know things and be unaware of it. Are you still in touch with the spirits?'

I crossed myself and said nothing.

'I'll tell you what I do know, though it isn't much.

Debora went to pieces after they took you away. Brenda was angry, but Debora was the one who went a bit mad. She blamed herself. She left the hOme and we thought she was gone looking for you. Everything was finished by then anyway. No one believed what Julian was saying any more. He was seen eating a Mars bar.'

'I was there.'

'You were there. Anyway, I left soon after. Debora may have gone back by now for all I know. I lost touch with all of them until I met Brenda, about three weeks ago on the steps of the British Museum. A few days later I met her on the steps of the National Gallery. She said it was fate, and I agreed. Then she told me she had nowhere to live and I let her move in. I was about to go to Wales to look for somewhere to start the meditation centre but she persuaded me that here would be even better. So we came. She never mentioned you. She's a funny girl, your mother.'

'She's not my mother.'

'It'll be dark soon.'

We retraced our steps in gloom. I made him shake Martin Foley's mud off his shoes at the boundary, just in case. He lit a hand-rolled cigarette that gave off a heavy smell I'd forgotten. I remembered Mervyn teaching me how to stick the papers together and burn small pieces of hash on the end of a pin. I remembered all the smiling there was at the hOme. Steady, deep, private smiling that lasted for days, and the gut-bursting laughter of the mushroom season, and the mush that went on in the hammock for everyone to see and nobody bothered to look. Here, the mush was all compressed in magazines stuffed under PJ's mattress.

God forgive me, I thought, I have a dirty mind. It was

because I was corrupted as a child that it excites me to think of red fingernails on hairy bollocks. And if I'm like this now, what will it be like when I'm older? Kieran said that when I'm older I'll be wanting my hole.

'My hole?'

'Yer hole. You'll be wanting a ride. Do you see them fingers? You should have had a smell of 'em yesterday. I had the four of 'em up Tracy Devlin.' He sawed the air with four fingers held rigid. 'In and out the hairy snatch and she was drippin'.'

The red end of Ash's joint preceded us in the darkness. I was glad of the dark, since it was a cover for the impure thoughts. It was just as well that Debora had not come to get me. As I was now she would have taken one look at me and gone away again in disgust. She might have had to put her hands over her ears as Bridey did. 'Will you please stop speaking to me. I don't know what it is but your voice cuts right through me and gives me a headache. Just don't say anything at all.'

I decided that if I could get away that night I'd go up to the church and do the stations of the Cross. There was rarely anyone around in the evenings, and I owed God an apology for being myself.

'How old are you now?' We were on the road at Ballystraw, leather soles echoing on tarmacadam.

'Ten.'

'You seem older.'

'I'm small, though.'

'So am I. There's nothing wrong with being small. Great men are always small. The big ones don't feel the need to try.'

'That's Tommy Whelan's house. The one with no light

in it. He'll be making baskets. He's blind. Would you like to visit him? I always visit him. He has a lovely dog and she's always having pups. He said I could have one for fifty pee but I'd never get it past Bridey and anyway I'm saving up for a set of horseshoes.'

'We should get back.'

'All right so.'

Outside the hotel he asked me if I'd go in and ask Brenda to come out to him, and bring his stuff. He said he'd wait in the car.

'Why?'

'Because I made a mistake.'

'Don't mind Bridey. Nobody does.'

It isn't that. I should have known that all Brenda wanted was a free ride home. I've just been used as a long-distance-taxi. Now that I've delivered her I can see she'll have no use for me. This is not a good place to have a meditation centre. No one in their right mind would choose to meditate here. She knew that. If only she had asked me directly what she wanted I would have done it anyway, but she had to make a game of it.'

'Why would she want to come here?'

He was supposed to say that it was to see me, to find me and rescue me. That wasn't what he said.

'She isn't a monster. She wouldn't dump her baby in any old lap.'

I may have turned red. I may have been embarrassed to acknowledge the fact that had been staring me in the face, that the space-hopper hanging off the front of her was an unusual form for weight-gain to take. Sometimes the unthinkable is invisible.

'I'll get her so.'

Less than a minute later I was back outside rapping on his car window. 'It's all right. You can come in. Bridey's gone. She took Brenda to the hospital in Wexford.'

'Is everything all right?'

I looked at him for a few seconds. For some reason I could neither understand the question nor why someone like him should ask it of someone like me.

'You may as well come in.' I did my best not to make it sound like an appeal.

I made him milky coffee and we sat up until late in the kitchen. PJ was minding the bar and Kieran was nowhere to be seen. Ash kept saying that he had to collect his thermometers and go, but I made him wait until midnight to see the scullery ghost.

At twelve exactly, the shadow passed along from the sink to the freezer, as it did every night, and then Ash thanked me and gathered his bits and pieces and left. I asked if he had a message for Brenda and he shook his head. 'Nothing I could ask a child to repeat.'

He gave me a card. 'Don't show this to anyone else, but if you want to get in touch call this number and they'll tell you where I am. Don't tell Brenda about it. She's had one free ride too many out of me. But don't lose it. Everyone needs at least one friend, even a mage like yourself.'

The card was blank on one side. The other, in curly handwriting, read: Babu 01 4383410.

'Would you not be able to think of a nice Catholic name for her?'

'No.'

'But Sarah? Where did Sarah come from? There's no Sarahs either side of the family that I ever heard of. And if there was ever a Saint Sarah they kept her quiet, so she can't have been any great shakes.'

'Sara. Not Sarah. Her name is Sara. Not Say. Sa.'

'I don't see what difference that makes. A pagan name is a pagan name no matter how you pronounce it.'

'I am a pagan.'

'We'll have none of that talk in my house.'

Bridey glared at me, as if it was my fault that blasphemy had come into her life, which, in a way, it was. It was keeping my new sister occupied with a gentle jiggle in front of the Aga while Bridey and Brenda stood their ground either side of the kitchen table.

'I hope your hands are clean.'

'They're clean.' I gently shifted the baby's weight and splayed my fingers one hand at a time to prove it.

'They better be. I don't want that christening dress blackened by the time we get up to the church. Oh, Breda.' Bridey sniffed. 'I remember the day you were wearing the selfsame dress. You were a lovely baby. I don't know what you did to yourself.'

'Brenda. Brenda. Brenda. Brenda. BRENDA!'

'Breda I named you and you'll always be Breda as far as I'm concerned.'

'Fine. Then I'll start calling you Brodie.'

'You'll do no such thing.'

'What's that, Brodie?'

'I'm your mother. Show some respect.'

'But you'll always be Brodie to me.'

Bridey turned on me. 'Wipe that smirk off your face. You shouldn't be listening to other people's conversations. I'd show you the back of my hand if you weren't holding that baby. And where's your good-for-nothing grandfather? That's what I'd like to know. We're going to be late and I'm not walking up that hill to the church. It's bad enough christening a child with no father without parading the fact through the whole village.'

Brenda leaned back and spoke in the idle voice of a happy torturer. 'I've said already we don't have to do this. It's just an initiation rite. We could build a big bonfire on the beach instead and dance around it naked. When Coorg was named we danced around naked for three days. Of course that was in the summer.'

A bunch of cherries fell out of Bridey's hat and landed with a woody clatter on the table. Brenda took a deep drag on her rolly and blew the smoke into a cloud of *schadenfreude* that hung between them. Bridey hadn't forgotten Ash nor forgiven her daughter for introducing him and all the speculation that had come with him.

Brenda, more economically, seemed to have forgotten Ash entirely without having forgiven her mother for anything.

Bridey turned on me. 'Go and see if there's any sign of Willy Scully and tuck your shirt in while you're at it. You look like a tinker.'

I carried Sara through to the lounge bar and stood in the window, one eye out for Willy's car turning into the ball alley opposite, and the other on her and the ever-fluctuating contortions of her face, humming *Find a little wood and have a little sleep sleep there*.

The day felt like a clean day. I was holding a new baby and dressed from head to toe in new clothes for the first time since my communion, bought in Wexford the day we went to bring her back from the hospital. Soft pale cord trousers fit for a christening.

When I got to the part of the song about *Love is like a beautiful girl who smiles for you* she seemed to be smiling, her eyes screwed up with the effort of it. Then there was a thunderclap of a fart, ten times as loud as you would think a creature that size was capable of. I carried her back to the kitchen.

'Well?'

'I think she needs changing. Number two.'

Brenda rolled her eyes and made a great show of drooping with weariness. 'Can't it wait?'

Bridey snapped. 'You're not natural. Dropping babies all over the place and expecting other people to take on the responsibility. Your father and I could be in retirement by now if it wasn't for you.'

Somehow, this was directed as much at me as at Brenda, but it was Brenda who answered. 'Nobody asked you to stick your big nose in and steal my child. We were perfectly happy. I could have had you arrested, if you weren't on the run from half the banks in Bedfordshire already.'

'Who told you a thing like that?'

'Who didn't? Everyone knows you didn't give a flying fart for Coorg's welfare. He was only your excuse to skip the country.'

'Don't talk to me about that child's welfare. Somebody had to take him out of that filthy place. Pigs the lot of you. Fornicating pigs. No one could leave a child in the hands of those animals and face their maker when the time came.'

'So that's it? It was yourself you were worried about.'

I tried to sneak away.

'Where are you off to, Mr Big Ears?'

'I was just going to change her.'

'If you get any shit on that christening dress I'll kill you. It's a real antique and can't be washed.'

'I'll be careful.'

I was just finishing when I heard the car draw up; had just impaled the nappy safely and successfully with the single safety pin, one hand under it so that if any skin was pricked by accident it would be my own. The nappy was nearly as big as herself. Plastic pants on and everything rearranged, I carried her to the window for her first sight of her great-aunts.

They got out either side of Willy's car. A sprightly seed packet out the left and a great navy battleship in battered condition out the right. 'That's your Aunty Netty and that's your Aunty Sally.' Jiggle jiggle jiggle. She liked to be jiggled a little bit when you talked to her. Then down to the kitchen for the presentation.

'Isn't she lovely lovely lovely?' Netty was twitching and twittering with excitement. Sally stared down silently from a broken face, breathing in snorts like a maternal pachyderm, while Netty made enough noise for both of them. 'Gorgeous. Only gorgeous. Pink as a rosebud.'

'Thank God.' Bridey crossed herself. 'Whoever the father was at least it wasn't the nignog.'

Netty seemed not to hear. 'Aren't you doing a great job, Joseph? Isn't she lucky to have a big brother like you to mind her?'

I nearly had to draw attention to myself with an answer, but Bridey cut across in a pointed voice. 'How's Granny Scully?'

'Oh, grand, grand. She's great above in the hospital, otherwise the two of us wouldn't have been able to get down for the christening. We'd have been slugging it out to see who got to view the baby first, wouldn't we, Sally? Only that's what kept us so late. We'd never have heard the end of it if we hadn't called up to see her on the way out. She has the nurses running round like greyhounds. Poor mother.'

'Poor racist old bat.' Brenda was adjusting her turtleneck over her coat collar.

'Now, Breda.'

'Brenda.'

'Now, Brenda, you can't expect a woman of your grandmother's age to be up with the fashion. It was a great shock to her, a black man appearing at the end of her bed and you with a belly on you the size of Christmas. We're lucky she didn't die on us.'

'No one can say I didn't try. Are we going to this mumbo-jumbo farce or what?'

Since we couldn't all fit in the car, Kieran, PJ, Netty and I walked up the hill. The car passengers were so long arranging themselves that we were nearly at the church by the time they overtook us. Netty turned to look at the view, over the big field with the donkeys in it and down to the sea. It was a half-fine, half-cloudy day and the breeze was what you'd call rigorous.

She clasped the upper part of my arm. We were the same height now, though most of my contemporaries would be towering over her. 'I love the sea! Don't you love the sea? Just look at it. Aren't you lucky to be living here and able to look at the sea every day?'

'I suppose.'

'Will you take me for a walk on the strand after? I'd love a walk on the strand with a handsome young man like yourself.'

Taking my cue from her, I pretended not to hear Kieran and PJ snickering behind us.

The christening went off reasonably well, considering we were late and the priest was in a temper, not that he ever wasn't, and that Brenda had decided that the child's full name should be Sara Wicca Scully, which Netty, as the godmother, enunciated with a hint of suspicion, and the priest repeated in his hurry to get the thing over with, not realising what he had said until it was too late. That PJ, the godfather, had kept a straight face was a sure indication that he had been in on the plot.

On the steps of the church, over the beautiful sea, with the gloomy stone of God's house at our backs, Bridey demanded to know where on earth and in God's holy name did a name like Wicca come from?

'She is the goddess of black magic. That is where we get the word wicked from.' The neutral superiority of PJ's tone wasn't going to improve things.

'Mother of God, don't tell me you're serious.'

Brenda stepped back, a safe distance from her mother's twitching handbag. 'I wasn't going to let you have everything your own way. At least Wicca had a bit of spirit to her, not like old mumsy Mary on the altar in there. She couldn't even admit to having a fuck.'

'You're on consecrated ground!'

'Bugger the lot of you, then.' Brenda stormed off, ankles oscillating on her platforms. I jiggled Sara in my arms. Willy and Bridey were white with sorrow. Someone who didn't know them better might have mistaken it for rage.

Netty demobilised the silence. 'Don't mind her, Bridey, Girls are often like that after a baby. I read about it in *Woman's Own*. She has the postnatal depression and you just have to put up with it until she's herself again. Mary Flynn's daughter went down the street in her dressing gown and slippers two mornings in a row. And if we don't get this baby in out of the cold the craythur will perish. I made a christening cake. It's in the boot of the car.'

As soon as we were in the door Netty started cutting ham sandwiches into piles as high as herself. Sara was changed out of the antique dress and then I fed and burped her while everyone around me softened mouthfuls of fruitcake with gulps of whiskey, until Bridey and Brenda reached a condition in which they could embark on a bout of tearful hugging, both of them magnanimously forgiving and neither seeing the necessity for any kind of apology.

Netty, having worked on this reconciliation, and thrilled

to have accomplished her mission, decided that she could take a break from thrusting plates of food under people's noses. She winkled Sara out of my arms for her turn at holding the baby. 'Lovely lovely lovely. Pink as a salmon she is.'

Sally made a ferocious face at me and beckoned that I should follow her. Out in the hall she looked around carefully before producing a bulging carrier bag from behind her back.

'SHHH!'

'I didn't say anything.'

'No. I mean SHHH! don't tell anyone. Put it up in your room quick before anyone else sees. And you're not to share it. Not one bit. It's all for you.'

I ran up the stairs, terrified by what might be in the bag. It was as heavy as a bag of spuds and shaped like a severed head, only lumpier and more sinister. There was a lock on my door but I couldn't decide whether to turn it for privacy or leave it open in case I needed to run screaming. I locked it.

The bag was full of sweets and chocolate and lick-your-arse and toffees. Hundreds of bars of everything. I tipped it all out on the bed. She must have emptied half the shop for me, I thought at the time, and wondered whether any of it would keep long enough for Sara to have some when she was older. I hid it all in the back of the wardrobe.

'What are you grinning at?' Kieran met me on the stairs.

'Nothing.'

'Did you have whiskey?'

'No.'

'I did. They're all so bladdered they wouldn't notice.'

I ducked a rabbit punch, more clumsily dealt than usual.

Netty was waiting with her hat and coat on. 'There you are. The lovely boy. Are you ready for our walk now?'

I didn't know what to say.

'You promised.' She wagged a finger at me.

'What about Sara?'

'Sara's asleep. She's worn out with the day and her Aunty Sally is minding her. Come on and you can show me all your hideouts.'

The Devlin sisters were on the wall. 'Is that yer girlfriend, Joey? Are you going off for a snog on the dunes?'

I turned and gave them the four-finger sawing sign that, according to Kieran, Tracy Devlin would understand.

'What's that supposed to mean?' Netty recoiled at the sight of my fingers.

'I dunno. It's a secret sign. It means shut up or I'll saw your head off.'

'That's not a very nice way to treat young ladies.'

'They're not very nice young ladies.'

'All ladies should be treated the same, if you are a gent.'

'What if I'm not?'

'If you're not a gent you're not a Scully. Your great-grandfather, God rest him, would raise his hat to every lady he met, whether she was a sailor's chew or a duchess.'

'What's a sailor's chew?'

'The opposite of a duchess.'

'What was Granny Scully?'

'Don't be cheeky now, young Joseph, or you won't get your present.'

'What is it?'

'We'll see if you're a good boy. Isn't the sea lovely?'

She laughed at the loveliness of the sea, and didn't stop talking all the length of the strand, as near to the edge of the high tide as she could go without wetting her feet. We came up against the stream that crossed the strand from the end of the golf course.

'And what do we do now?'

'I'll carry you across.'

'You will not.'

'I'm stronger than I look.'

'And I'm fatter than you think.'

'I can lift a sack of anthracite. That's eight stone.'

'I want to paddle anyway. I never come to the sea without taking a paddle. Sack of anthracite how are you.'

She took her shoes and socks off. I followed her example and we paddled through the sea where the stream flowed into it, and back again. The water was freezing and she laughed until the tears came and then laughed louder. There wasn't a soul to witness us on any of the blurred horizons.

She sat on a barrel half buried in the sand and looked at her wet feet as our laughter abated. 'What are we going to do about that? We'll catch our deaths.' She fished in her handbag and took out a packet of Handy Andies. 'Paper hankies. Paper hankies. Oh, how real those hankies seemed to me.' She broke into the Marie Osmond tune, substituting hankies for roses all the way through as she dried her feet with them. The wind whipped a hanky out of her hand and set her off in shrieks of giggles and more choruses of the song, tearing up tissue paper and tossing the pieces into the air so they were blown high out to sea.

I wasn't used to laughing so much and my stomach began

to hurt. When we were shod and socked again, she fished about some more in her handbag and gave me three stones.

'That's your present.'

'Thanks.' I didn't recognise them to begin with, but as soon as they were in my hand I recognised the feel of them.

'I found them above in the drawer when I was having a bit of a spring clean. I don't know what they are but they should never have been taken off you when they were the only thing you owned.'

'They're runestones.'

'You were only a little boy. Eyes on you the size of fried eggs.'

She asked me what they were for and I said I could tell her fortune with them, and she got very excited about that and wanted to see it done. I closed my eyes and threw the stones on the sand between us.

'What do they say?'

I was sure I was mistaken. Nothing so horrible could happen. 'I don't know. I've forgotten how to use them.'

The Saturday before Christmas I was allowed into Ross on the bus to buy presents. Kieran came with me, but as soon as we were out of the village he went down the back of the bus to smoke cigarettes with Tommy Maher and Smut Maloney. Knowing, from experience, that I was more likely to be a butt of their entertainment than a beneficiary, I stayed where I was at the front and watched the road.

Ross was in a lather of Christmas prosperity. Men tied fir trees into car boots and women were flustered from arguments with the butcher about the size of their turkey or the quality of their ham. Children counted money from one hand to the other in front of shop windows that outshone the day-long twilight. Everywhere everyone was saying how ridiculous it was, and at the same time flinging banknotes across counters as if there were an interdiction against taking money home with them when they went to seal themselves into their Christmas bunkers.

The high-do of the town was bewildering as I stepped off the bus and stood on the Quay. Off my guard, I invited a thump across the shoulders that sent me reeling into the path of an oncoming car. That Kieran was the source of the blow was confirmed by the sound of his derisive laughter. I tried to smile an apology at the driver, who was crossing herself wildly between failed attempts to restart her engine.

She rolled down her window to call me a hooligan and a blackguard. Kieran, Tommy and Smut had vanished. I said I was sorry but my voice was drowned out by the hooting of the car behind. 'One of the days you'll be kilt and you'll have earnt it.' She narrowed her eyes for this prediction, and her engine roared to life.

Shaken, I went the wrong way twice in the few hundred simple yards between the Quay and the shop in Mary Street. I had a sense of direction that only worked in open country. In the town there was always a building blocking the way you wanted to go, and a building couldn't be got over like a ditch, and you had to choose right or left, and whichever you chose would take you back to where you started or, worse, to some clone of a building that looked like where you started. By the time I found Sally in the shop I had had enough of the big smoke of New Ross and was in a bit of a panic about how I was going to survive until the afternoon bus home.

The shop was full of customers and Sally was red in the face and tight in the mouth, calling out prices in a defiant voice to ditherers who held up one object after another in abstract speculation. I slipped behind the counter.

'Hiya.'

'They have me plagued with buying things. How's young Joseph? That's ten shillin's, missus. Fifty new pee to you.' Everything she said came out in the same bruising shout, whether it was directed at the woman on the other side of the shop or at me beside her. 'Go up and see your Aunty Netty. Here. Wait.' She took a pound note from the till and folded it small and pressed it into the palm of my hand. 'There's your Christmas box and you're to spend it on yourself, mind.'

Netty was icing a cake the size of a car tyre, wearing an apron printed with holly and berries and robin redbreasts. All the cake ornaments were lined up on the table beside her: Santas and snowmen and sleds and reindeer and bells and ribbon and a forest of two-inch Christmas trees.

'God, you put the heart across me. Where did you spring from?'

Not to be heard by Granny Scully I had crept up the stairs, and now Netty was fluttering and breathless at the sight of me, the colour momentarily gone from her cheeks. Not knowing whether or how to answer, I waited until she was herself again. It was an awkward few moments, but she pulled a bottle of pills from her apron pocket and placed one on her tiny pink tongue and screwed her eyes up to swallow it. When she reopened them she was back to normal.

'Isn't this a lovely surprise? And I was just about to put the pan on to fry a few chips, and there's a bit of chester cake you can have while you're waiting. Did Willy and Bridey come in with you?'

'No. I came on the bus.'

'The bus? I love buses! When I was over in London to see the doctor they couldn't keep me off the buses for a minute. Top deck, up the front; there's nowhere like it. Aren't you great now to be able to go where you want by yourself? You'll be off round the world before we know it.'

'I wouldn't want to go to London.'

'London's lovely. You'd love it. You'd be worn out with all the lovely things to look at. I was there twice. My Aunty Janey Mac took me there when I was sixteen for the Christmas shopping. It was lovely. And the manners the men had. Gents, every one of them.'

Then Granny Scully called down to know who was there making Netty talk, and I had to go up to the darkened room where her spotlit embroidering fingers floated in the gloom and her chair creaked the cadence of her stitching.

'It's yourself. Come here till I get a good look at you.'

I edged closer, but not much.

'Well, you won't be breaking any hearts this side of Christmas. Whoever your father was it wasn't his looks she was after. I hear you have a sister?'

I nodded.

'That mother of yours is no Scully. It must be off Bridey's side she gets it. Knackers the lot of them. I don't suppose there's any sign of PJ getting married either?'

'No.' I bowed my head for all our inadequacies.

'That fella wants to shake himself up a bit. A good woman would soon knock the fairy out of him. How's the hotel?'

'Fine.'

'Any guests?'

'No.'

'I warned Willy when he married that chit he'd never prosper. Carpet in the bathroom, I suppose?'

She had me. I'd let slip the fact that we had carpet in the bathroom on a visit a couple of years previously. It was a failed attempt at defending Bridey's housekeeping, and now Granny Scully used it as the prime metaphor for her daughter-in-law's stupidity. I fixed my eyes on her embroidery. It was a crow in a circle of thorns.

'You're still small so. I don't suppose you get fed in

that house. Poor Willy hasn't a pick on him.'

'He's never home for his meals.' You could make as many vows as you liked to say nothing to her, but the odd thing still slipped out.

'And how could he be?' Her voice rose. 'Having to be off all over the country to keep a roof over your heads, and not one of you born with the good manners to be the right side of the blanket. If Bridey Cullen had brought up her children like Christians!' She glared at me. My very existence was proof that Willy's burden was more than a man should have to bear.

'I have to go now.'

'Where?'

'The Christmas shopping.'

'Isn't it well for some to be out spending other people's money? Here.' She scratched in her purse, wheezing, and produced a ten-pence piece which she held out to me. 'Let no one say I wouldn't give a child his Christmas box whether he earnt it or not. And would you not think to polish your shoes before coming into the town to shame us? Joseph Scully, God rest him, wouldn't have been caught dead in that state.'

'Yes, Granny. Thanks, Granny. Bye, Granny.'

Netty was waiting downstairs with a plate of fat brown chips and a big bottle of tomato sauce. 'You have to keep your strength up for the shopping. They'd mow you down if you weren't looking over your shoulder. I was down Waterford yesterday and I nearly got axfixiated.' The decorations were all crammed on to the cake and she was darting over it with an icing bag, squashing stars of white sugar between the Santas and the trees. 'Lovely lovely

lovely. Isn't Christmas the loveliest time of the year?' Then I helped her arrange the crib, which had four asses, thirteen shepherds and three baby Jesuses, not to mention an entire faculty of wise men. I asked her what she wanted for Christmas. 'You don't have to be buying me anything. Don't you love Holy Saint Joseph the way he'd put up with anything? Here, get something for yourself.'

With the two pound notes Netty gave me I was three pounds ten richer for having called in at Mary Street. The task of getting presents for everyone seemed easier than it had a while before, when all I had was just under a pound culled from the horseshoe fund. I got soap for Bridey and cigarettes for Willy and soap for Brenda and cigarettes for PJ and soap for Netty and cigarettes for Sally, all of them in special Christmas packaging. For Sara I got a thing you shook to make it snow on the Holy Virgin, which said 'Not for Children under Six', but I thought I could do the shaking for her until she was old enough. Kieran got socks and Granny Scully got soap that didn't smell as nice as the other stuff, because she was always complaining about people who smelled like a chemist's shop. After all that I still had a profit to put back into the horseshoe fund. Then I was in Sheehan's, looking through a book called *Horses and Ponies of the World in Colour*, and thinking about a day in the future when I was going to be rich enough to buy such things for myself, when I heard a familiar snorting and turned to see Kieran, Tommy and Smut pawing at a magazine for parents with a picture of a breast-feeding woman in it. The shop was busy enough for them to be unseen by the man behind the counter, and they were making a great show of being careless of the disapproval of the other customers.

Kieran spotted me before I had time to slip away, and came over to prod at the bags and packages draped off my arms.

'What's them, midget?'

'Presents.'

'Whereja get all the money?'

'I got some off Sally and Netty.'

'They never gave me any.'

'You never went to see them.'

'Creepy-crawlie pet. How much didja get?'

'I can't remember.'

'Gimme some of it. I betja they told you to give half of it.'

'They didn't. And it's all gone now. Every penny.' You could lie to Kieran without being troubled by your conscience.

'I'm telling.' He pinched my upper arm.

'Telling what?'

'That you stole my half of the money, nigger.'

'If you go and see them they might give you some.'

'Some hope. I'm not the pet like you are.'

'They were asking after you. They said they'd love to see you.' I could have just told him that they were my aunties and not his and he had no right to expect anything off them, but that would have led to violence, even with so many witnesses present. Kieran was touchy on the subject of his relations. I held my tongue about his non-Scullyness and he satisfied himself with knocking the packages out of my arms, before strolling off with Tommy and Smut, the magazine with the breast-feeding picture stuffed up Smut's jumper and unpaid for.

There was still an hour before the bus and I made my way

back along North Street, frosty now and spangled with coloured lighting that kept the darkness overhead at bay. When I got to the shop Sally was so distracted with customers that she didn't notice me, even when I was standing beside her at the till.

'I got you and Netty presents, but if I leave them now you're to promise not to open them until Christmas morning.'

'What?'

'Hiya.'

'It's yourself. You'll never guess who's here. Go up and see.'

In the kitchen, Netty said the same thing. 'Go up to Granny Scully's room and see who's here. It'll be a lovely surprise for you.'

Willy was sitting in the chair opposite his mother. She was saying something to him about women who put carpet in their lavatories and thought they were better than anyone else, and he was punctuating her discourse in the tones of a dutiful son, albeit one forty years younger. 'Yes, Mother.' He seized on the distraction of my entrance with the enthusiasm he normally reserved for a glass of whiskey. 'Here's Joey the man. I heard you were up painting the town red. Would you ever look at him, isn't he the spit of yourself, Mother?'

To my relief, she declined to agree.

'Whoever he's the spit of it's no one I was ever introduced to but that's the way nowadays I suppose if people want to rear their children across the water with carpet in every room in the house and no sign of a holy water font inside the door to keep the people out of harm's way when they go out of it. In my day a good family kept their name and the daughters didn't go whelping until they changed their name for another. I suppose the people down the street are all saying it's my fault I didn't rear you to know better than to marry outside your class or warn you what might happen once the wrong class of woman got her hooks into you.'

'Yes, Mother.'

'Yes Mother me arse. There's no blame to be laid on my doorstep. You were better reared than the quality and all the good it did you.'

'Yes, Mother.'

'I have to get the bus now.' My voice sounded very quiet.

Willy seized on the change of subject. 'Why would you be wasting money on the bus when you can come home with me?'

'I got a return.'

'Go down to your Aunty Netty and wait for me. I'll be down in a minute. I have to go now, Mother.'

'I hear that hotel of yours is failing.'

'Who told you that?'

'Never mind who told me. You can't shit on your own doorstep and expect your own mother not to smell it. Is it true?'

'I'm owed a lot of money, Mother. You know yourself what it's like getting money out of people. Things are looking up now. Please God by this time next week we'll be in the clear.'

I went downstairs and Netty offered to put chips on for me, but I said we were going in a minute. Eventually Willy appeared, looking thirsty from his interview. He said he had a few little messages to do down the town and he'd be back to collect me in five minutes.

Four hours later, when he returned, I was playing snakes and ladders with Sally. She said her feet were swollen the size of plum puddings and she didn't care if the communists took over tomorrow and banned the whole of Christmas. Meanwhile Netty marshalled squadrons of mince pies in and out of the oven and made sure that I tasted at least one from each batch to see if it was up to the standard. Then Willy had to have a Christmas drink with his sisters, but that didn't take long and we were soon on the road.

'That's a long face for the season that's in it.'

'I'd be home long ago if you'd let me get the bus.'

'And what's your hurry to be home all of a sudden?'

My hurry was that I was worried about Sara. Sometimes they forgot to change her when I wasn't there. Bridey would think Brenda had done it and Brenda would think Bridey had done it and neither of them would bother to check. I couldn't say that to Willy. He thought I was cissy enough as it was.

'Nothing.'

Willy was in singing form. We took what he called the scenic route, along skiddy roads, via Ballinaboola, where he had to see a man in the Horse and Hound, and by way of Cassagh because he had a message for Tom Morrissey, and through Campile where we had to stop at the Rendezvous for a minute, and Arthurstown where we were lured inside the King's Bay Inn. By the time we got home the hotel was dark and cold, our own bar long drained of its own after-hour drinkers. We let ourselves in through the yard and the back door, which Bridey always left on the latch.

The wardrobe door in my bedroom was swinging open. I was so tired I didn't notice it until after I was in bed. I should have ignored it, but you can't go to sleep with something like that unexplained. Not that I couldn't guess before I looked that the carrier bag full of chocolate would be gone. I hadn't eaten any of it yet because I was saving it to have a proper birthday party in May, like the parties in comics where everyone stuffed their faces with chocolate and jelly.

I knew it was Kieran who stole it, and I knew what I would get for accusing him. I was too angry to say any prayers that night. I decided that I'd had enough of trying to be good and being made a fool of, by God as much as anyone else. It was time to try another survival tactic.

CHANGE

To be properly bad, the first and most obvious accomplishment to be mastered is the smoking of cigarettes, preferably stolen or, failing that, bought with stolen money. So, the next morning being a Sunday, and the most appropriate day of the week for such an undertaking, I decided, first thing, to initiate myself in the rites of boldness.

First thing, that was, after I had got Sara up and changed and dressed her and given her a bottle and winded her. She had, as I suspected she might have, a bit of a rash from the day before, but she seemed cheerful enough. Her knees were fat now and her blonde hair silky. She liked to be carried around a lot, though Bridey said that I was spoiling her and that babies should be left to cry. But she knew me, and whenever she was in my arms she was happy, and that seemed reason enough for her to be there as often as I could manage.

The next delay to badness was that Bridey gave me a cup of tea to bring up to PJ. She said he'd been out at a dance the night before and he might never be up in time for Mass if a hint wasn't dropped. That PJ had never yet been up in time for Mass on a Sunday wasn't worth pointing out. In Bridey's eyes PJ was a saint led astray, and if she held the gate open for him long enough he'd return to the fold and be counted among the blessed.

'What was Ross like yesterday?'

'Black. You couldn't move for people.'

'And it not Christmas Eve till tomorrow. I don't know what the world's coming to. Hurry up with that tea or it'll go cold.'

The mug was full so I walked carefully and, I suppose, silently up the three flights of stairs and down the long landing to PJ's room. The door was ajar and I was about to push it open, but I remembered what a loud creak it would make and that he would likely have a hangover. I started to slide through the gap, mug first and then my head, and then I stopped.

The room was dazzling with all the light of a frosty winter morning bounced off the sea and thrown through the big windows. There was a smell of stale beer and cigarettes. PJ was awake, which was unusual enough in itself. He was propped up on his pillows and, notwithstanding the cold of an unheated room the size of a small carpark and a linoleum floor, he had kicked back the bedclothes to the foot of the bed. In his left hand smoke wandered from a freshly lit cigarette. His right hand supported, at the base, a horn.

The dimensions of the thing I could not tell you objectively. It seemed massive to me at the time, but I was a boy of ten who had studied none but his own since early childhood. At the hOme a sight such as this would have been an unremarkable occurrence, but in the intervening years I had jumbled dream and memory and become uncertain about what I had witnessed and what I had imagined. I had, for instance, come to doubt the existence of pubic hair, which had been cultivated in abundance in Devonshire but was nowhere to be seen in County Wexford. Kieran had sorted out that dilemma, with his insistence that I should witness his first sprouting. And the pictures in the PJ's magazines had filled a lot of gaps, though in the grammar of a sexual rhetoric that was plainly the exclusive province of foreigners.

Now, the object of PJ's attention dominated mine. He beheld it with an expression on his face not unlike the look of stupefaction worn by women who are inspecting the contents of another woman's pram. Taut and rigid, it nodded at him with a pulsing movement and he smiled in response, as if under the impression that his knob was a separate entity from him and that communication was possible between the two of them. Beneath the spread of his fingers his balls shifted and curled like sleeping infants under a blanket.

If I had waited to see what would happen next I might have gained a more accurate, though prosaic, impression of the relationship between a grown man and his pizzle, but because I was starting to tremble a bit I knew it would only be a matter of time before I was detected. I withdrew and crept back down the landing.

Now I knew what all the secrecy was about. It was a thing to be adored in private; an icon, the contemplation of which brought serenity to the face of the beholder, the way staring at the stations of the Cross was supposed to and didn't. And it was a rite of badness that could be conducted simultaneously with smoking, if PJ was anything to go by. As I had lifted Sara out of her cot that morning I had had doubts about my resolution to be bad. What if I was a bad influence on her? That didn't seem to matter now that I had seen the proof that badness and happiness went hand in hand, or knob in hand even. I took a big gulp of the rapidly cooling tea and stamped my way back to PJ's room, knocked loudly on his door and called his name. He was pretending to be asleep, blankets to the chin, and told me to fuck off in a convincing rendition of his usual greeting.

'What are you grinning for?'

'Nothing. Bridey says it's time for Mass.'

'Tell her to fuck off too.'

There was still time, before Mass, to slip into the darkened bar and steal ten Major and a box of matches. I sneaked through the yard to the far garden and stowed the booty in the greenhouse where David Bowie still presided with a gold spot on his forehead, an altarpiece of badness if there ever was one, and where nasturtiums still flowered and stank under the protection of glass.

Because neither PJ nor Brenda ever went to Mass and Kieran was being let off going because of the TB, it was only Willy and Bridey and I who made the short journey up the hill in Willy's car, the moulting head of Bridey's stole snarling at me over her shoulder like eyes in the back of her head.

For the first time I didn't sit with Bridey, but syphoned myself off to join Christo Maloney, the younger brother of Smut, up in the gallery. Willy always stood in the porch with the other men. Christo taught me the coughing game. You waited until the congregation was quiet and then you coughed, loudly. Six or seven other coughs would immediately break out around the church, from the polite ahems of spinsters to the raucous hawking of heavy smokers. It worked every time, and the only difficulty was in keeping a straight face so you wouldn't be suspected. Had I known that badness could be so entertaining I would have started younger.

Christo hissed the summary of his philosophy in my ear. 'Dontcha hate people?' Everyone else was singing a high-pitched carol at the time.

'Yeah. I do.'

Back at the hotel, having ascertained that PJ was occupied elsewhere, I made my way up to his room and looked under the mattress. The magazines had been plaguing me since I had first been told of their existence. I couldn't understand the hunger in me to have another look, but I knew that it would be a sin to give in to it. Now, as a bad person, there was nothing to stop me.

There were six or seven and I chose the one that seemed to have the most variety. The fall into hedonism might as well be educational while I was about it. I took a piece of string out of my pocket and undid my trousers, pushing them down to the knees, then strapped the magazine tightly to my thigh. That way I was able to saunter to the green-house without anyone suspecting a thing, unless they thought it was odd that someone so jittery with a stiff leg should be trying to saunter. I had it all planned.

The green cigarette pack was opened to reveal ten potential sins snug inside it. I drew them out a little like the pipes of an organ, like in the ads, and offered myself one. The match was struck and the end lit. I was careful not to breathe deeply, for I knew, from previous, less premeditated attempts on the dunes with the Mahers and the Maloneys, that I would only cough if I did. I turned the pages of the magazine. Not that I needed to, for I was already up and running in the trouser department. I got it out, what there was of it, and held it taut between thumb and forefinger, pulling the skin back so that it bobbed under the pressure, and set about admiring it.

There wasn't much to go on, compared to what had been sported by PJ, or by the unsmiling men in the magazine, but it was more or less what other boys my age had, and I knew that if I was bad enough it would grow. I took another sipping puff on the cigarette and turned another page of the magazine. Two ladies were nibbling on the same knobbly monstrosity, their bottoms facing the camera and their varnished fingers rearranging their surprisingly compli-cated fannies. Cunts, I supposed, was what I should be calling them now. I looked despairingly from these great receptacles to my own – what? You wouldn't say cock or knob or any of the words that implied a heavy-headed trun-cheon of flesh of the kind a lady might be tempted to shove inside her. Prick was the word that came to mind, and I didn't like it. And what if it never grew? And what if it did? How would I hide it? How did anyone? I resolved to start inspecting men's trousers to see how they managed. I resolved to do a lot of things. I was going to be as much like PJ as possible. Given our consanguinity that was not an unlikely ambition. I would find out what he had eaten when he was my age, and I'd get a pair of chest expanders like his. And I'd sleep with no pyjamas on and tell anyone who tried to wake me to fuck off for themselves.

While I was thinking all this I had lost concentration. The cigarette had burned to the stub and the thing in my hand had reverted to the prawn it normally was. Consistent badness wasn't going to be as easy as it looked, but still, a good start had been made. I stowed everything in a box of rusty trowels, nodded to David Bowie and went in for the dinner.

Even though it was the school holidays I didn't get another chance to go out to the greenhouse until after Christmas itself, which was a day up to the usual standards. There was Sara to be picked up and jiggled when no one else was interested, and Ash to be visited, somehow, once a day, and all the help that Bridey needed in the kitchen, and the bar, which was busier than usual, to be minded.

It was getting to the stage where I would look forward to Mass of all things, as a time when I could switch my mind off and do nothing, which, as a would-be delinquent, got me top marks for ignoring God in his own house. I'd see the stations of the Cross and remember how, not too long before, I used to prostrate myself in front of them if I was alone in the church, and was scalded to think how God must have despised me for it. And only the night before, at midnight Mass, with the full church and the smell of drink and the hymns sung more as if they were songs, I had decided that if God really wanted me, he'd have to come after me himself. He'd have to admit that he needed me as much as I needed him. I felt like I'd looked God in the eye for a second and survived to think the tale.

There were two days in the year when the bar was supposed to be shut, by law. Good Friday was one and Christmas the other, and we all looked forward to a day of rest, even if past experience showed that it was unlikely we would get it. Bridey put her foot down and said that the back door was being locked this year, and no customers were to be let in by it no matter how long or hard they banged. Willy dropped his head and promised her that it would be so.

The big news was that there was a fair-sized box under the tree, wrapped in three kinds of floral paper. *To Joseph from Aunty Netty and Aunty Sally* was written down one side in slopy handwriting, and the anticipation of it made up for the fairy lights not being in working order that year. I opened it to find a record-player. A small record-player, made of white plastic with white plastic speakers.

Kieran said it wasn't fair; that I was the pet. I ignored him. I had had a look in his room for my bag of chocolate and all I found was a few wrappers kicked under the bed. Kieran said that he never got anything nice, and the Bridey said that that was enough of that now on Our Lord's birthday: surely Sally and Netty must have meant for the record-player to be shared.

'He never shares anything. He stole the money they gave him for me.'

'Is that true, Joe?'

'No.'

'Well, you'll share this, won't you?'

'He'll break it.'

'You can't be selfish on Our Saviour's birthday.'

'He breaks everything.'

Kieran opened his own present from the same source. It was a book about football. He said he hated football and threw it across the room in disgust and went outside, where he sat on the wall of the tennis court in the drizzle without a coat on and smoked a cigarette, holding it down behind his back between puffs as if he couldn't make up his mind between defiance and dissimulation.

'Willy. Do something. He'll kill himself going on like that with the TB.'

'I'll redden his arse for him, that's what I'll do.'

'You're not going out there to make a show of yourself on the street.'

Brenda and PJ exchanged a look. Brenda groaned. 'The same as it ever was. Why is Christmas always like this? I'd forgotten what you two were like, otherwise I'd never have come back.'

'Nobody asked you to.'

'Leave her, Bridey. Things are bad enough.' Willy looked out at Kieran again and pity came unexpectedly across his features. 'You'd think Mairead would have sent him a card if nothing else.'

'Who's Mairead?'

'Never you mind, Big Ears. You caused enough trouble with that record-player.'

PJ was in the middle of winking at me in an I'll-tell-you-later kind of way when there was a great noise from the back of the house. He rose to his feet. 'What's that banging?'

Bridey looked as if she was going to cry. 'Jesus, they're started already. Could they not leave us in peace this one day of the year?'

Brenda couldn't stop herself remarking that Bridey had a funny idea of peace, but Willy cut across her, saying that he would go and deal with it.

'Don't let them in, Willy. Whatever you do, don't let them in this year.'

Them, you knew without going to look, would be Pakki Purcell and Eddy Darcy and Shipsy Maher. It was no good locking the yard gate against them. On Christmas Day they would climb the wall, broken glass tops and all, to get in for a drink. Good Friday wasn't as bad, being more of a holy day and less of a family occasion. If Christmas in our house was anything to go by, they could be forgiven for wanting to escape to the pub for a few hours.

Willy returned and Bridey was waiting. 'Well?'

'I said they could have just the one if they were quiet.'

'You promised.'

'It was the only way to get a bit of peace.'

'You promised me.'

'It's Christmas, Bridey. You can't afford to get the wrong side of your customers at Christmas if you want to keep them the rest of the year. I'll just go in and mind the bar for a bit.'

PJ snorted and put a hand over his face.

'And there'll be less of that from you.'

Willy went to the bar and Bridey to the kitchen. Kieran and his protest on the wall were forgotten. I gave Brenda and PJ their presents. PJ gave me mine. It was a record token.

'How did you know?'

He tapped the side of his nose, just as a scream from Bridey, which would have shattered the glass in the lighthouse, had us all running into the kitchen. She was standing in front of an open oven door and screaming for Willy. He seemed slow in coming, considering all the noise.

'Willy. Someone stole the turkey. I went to baste it and it's gone.'

'No one stole the turkey, Bridey.'

'Look for yourself.'

'I had to give it away.'

'Willy. Don't. Say you hid it for a joke.'

'I gave it to the Devlins.'

'The Devlins? The Devlins next door? What possessed you to give our turkey to a crowd of good-for-nothing knackers like the Devlins?'

'They had nothing, Bridey. I went round this morning to say happy Christmas and they had nothing. Not a crust in the house.'

'What were you saying happy Christmas to them for?'

'They're the neighbours. It's what you do on Christmas morning.'

'Not where I was reared it isn't.'

'They had nothing, Bridey. I had to do something about it.'

'Now *we* have nothing. What are you going to do about that?'

'We have the ham.'

'We haven't the ham. I couldn't afford a ham. Do you see a ham, Willy? I only had enough money for a turkey. You gave the Christmas dinner away when we're no better than beggars ourselves.'

Brenda seemed to think that was an appropriate moment to remind everyone that she was vegetarian, as if that solved everything. Bridey looked as if she was about to strike her, but PJ got there first. 'No you're not. You eat anything.'

'Only because I have to round here.'

PJ said it was only a turkey anyway and not the end of the world.

Willy jumped in, glad of the chance to get on to the offensive. 'You can keep your smart remarks to yourself, buster.'

Bridey threw the oven gloves at her husband. 'Leave him out of it. What has he ever done?'

'Exactly. My point exactly. What has he ever done? Calls himself a student. What did you ever see him studying? Has he ever had a job for himself? Has he ever put his hand in his pocket to put food on the table?'

'There was enough food on the table till you ran next door with it.'

'I've had enough.' PJ sounded calm, as someone in the eye of the storm might well be. 'I'm going.'

'Where are you going?' Bridey had to catch hold of the Aga rail to stop herself succumbing to gravity under the influence of this latest blow.

'Back to England.' He was already out of sight and his voice echoed from the hall like one long departed.

Bridey ran after him, calling out. 'You can't go back to England. Take no notice of your father. There's no ferries today anyway. Wait. PJ. Love.'

Eventually we sat down to a Christmas dinner of tinned salmon and all the trimmings. Between forays into the bar to see to the growing number of those who had escaped their own dinners, Willy made brittle attempts at starting up conversations, seeming less aware each time how hollow his voice sounded as it fell across the moroseness of the table.

'Won't it be great to have music in the house now and Joseph can be the DJ and isn't that a powerful machine altogether the very latest thing and did you manage to set it up yet so we can play a few records, Joseph?'

'I haven't any records yet.' Not to answer at all would have flipped Willy from strained bonhomie to red-faced anger, and to have answered cheerfully would have been to take his side and have the others lined up against me, so I had to mumble.

'That's no problem at all is it, Bridey? There's records somewhere in the house. You have records, haven't you, Bridey? Didn't I see them above in the press only the other day?'

Bridey answered with a look. It was not a kind look, but since it was the first look she had given him in several hours he took it as an improvement in their relations and sent me upstairs to ferret out Bridey's musical past.

There was plum pudding and sherry trifle, both sent down from New Ross and the works of Netty's hand, and received by Bridey with slighted pride. 'Does this woman think I can't cook anything at all?' When they had been reduced to crumbs in one case and what looked like a puddle of sick in the bottom of the bowl in the other; and when all three of the Glen Miller records that formed Bridey's collection had been played both sides; and the last of the drinkers had gone from the bar, leaving by the back door and crossing the yard with a weaving furtiveness and rum-and-black smiles imprinted on the corners of their mouths; and Kieran had gone off somewhere with Smut Maloney, after a row in which he was told that he couldn't go out at all because he'd been seen smoking and besides he was supposed to be sick and did he want to kill himself altogether? to which he responded that he'd rather be dead than living in a hole like this and since Bridey wasn't his mother he could do what he liked; and after PJ and Willy had collapsed snoring side by side on the same sofa, looking suddenly as alike as a father and son could, which was disturbing to me because while it was my ambition to be like PJ in every physical aspect, I had a hard enough time dealing with Willy with his clothes on and the idea that a body might lurk, its nakedness hidden beyond the greasy contours of his collar and cuffs, was enough to make me want to halt the growing process at the stage I was, baldy prawn and all; and after I had got enough wood and coal in to last the evening and Bridey and Brenda and I were sleepily passing a box of Quality Street from one to the other while I kept a hand on the handle of Sara's pram to maintain the gentle agitation she liked to sleep to, and the only thing keeping the rest of us awake was the plot of a film about a girl who had been born into high society and was now sewing shrouds in the attic to keep body and soul together while her beau from the old days hunted high and low for her to tell her he'd made his fortune in China and they could get married; that was when the subject of renovating the garden came up, in a roundabout way.

'I don't know why we're watching this rubbish.' Brenda waited for the ads to make her objection, and for a minute I thought it was the ad she meant, which was the one where black-faced minstrels danced about to demonstrate the delights of Lyons the Quality Tea.

'It isn't rubbish. It's a good film. They knew how to make a good film in them days. Not the smut you get now. I remember seeing this one when it first came out. You could go to the cinema then and watch anything that was on without being mortified.' Bridey dug her forefinger into the corners of the box in hopes of finding another coffee cream.

'I can't see the point of having a television when we have only one channel.'

'Well, Miss Hoity-toity, you should be grateful we have a television at all the way things are going.'

I volunteered that the Mahers had put a big aerial up and could get the BBC on it.

'The Mahers must have plenty of money. I never thought I'd see the day when we had to do without a Christmas dinner.' Bridey gave up her creamless quest in the sweet box, the corners of her mouth turned down. 'We're the nouveau poor.'

Brenda quibbled. 'Poverty is a state of mind. I don't see why everyone is so hung up on money all the time.'

'We've had enough trouble from the state of your mind, thank you. Now shush, the film is starting again. Look, the poor love hasn't a crust to eat. She's like ourselves.'

I had an idea. I would have kept it to myself, but four bowls of sherry trifle had had their effect, and recklessness had gained ground as nausea receded. 'We could grow our own food.'

'Don't be an eejit, Joseph. You can't grow food.' The townswoman in Bridey had never left her.

'Yes you can.'

'Don't contradict your elders.'

'I'm not contradicting you.'

'Be quiet, then, and don't be cheeky.'

'Sorry.'

'That's better.'

'But you can. Tell her, Brenda, how we used to grow our own food. There's loads of room down in the garden. If we grew our own food we'd never have to go to the shop.'

Bridey thought about that. She hated everything to do with the shop, even though she never deigned to cross the street to it herself. I'd be sent back with complaints more often than I was sent across for messages in the first place. Her thinking didn't last long. 'You can't grow bacon or sausages, or bread or baked beans or butter and eggs.' She reflected for a moment to think what she had left out of her kitchen repetoire. 'And how would you grow an Arctic Roll?'

'We could grow potatoes and cabbages and keep hens for eggs, and there's a pigsty in the yard.' I could hear my voice rising to a crescendo as I outlined the model farm that could be established behind the hotel. 'We could get a cow and make the butter.'

Willy shook himself awake and asked what the excitement was.

'He wants us to grow vegetables out the back.' There was a sneer in Brenda's voice, though I might have expected support from her.

'There's the man with the brains. He'll make Prime Minister yet.'

'Don't encourage him, Willy. He's big-headed enough.'

'I was talking to a man the other day had a Rotavator. He said you could do anything with it. Anything.' He paused to give us time to be as impressed as he was by the machine's omnipotence. 'From what he was telling me you could have the bit of garden out the back there up and running in half a day. Vegetables coming out of your ears.'

'Did he say you could grow Arctic Rolls with it?' As Brenda was sniping at both of her parents at once, neither of them took any notice.

'Young PJ here.' Willy slapped his hand hard on PJ's knee, giving it a monkey bite at the same time so that PJ woke screaming.

'Willy. You're hurting the child.'

'Young PJ here can do the rotavating. It might put a bit of muscle on him that you don't get lying above in the bed half the day with nothing between your right hand and the Devil.'

I might have gone red in the face at that, but nobody noticed in the general uproar following PJ's retort that he'd rather be a wanker than a pisspot.

On St Stephen's Day, or Boxing Day as PJ called it, as if there hadn't been enough fighting the day before, Bridey had ceased speaking to Willy on the grounds that he had shown too much eagerness in his offer to drive their son to the ferry at Rosslare. PJ was leaving us. I helped him get his stuff down from the room. I had thought that we were well on the way to being friends, though he never said a whole lot to me and I felt a gag close on my throat whenever I tried to say anything to him. I tried to think of some way I could stop him vanishing before I had discovered what would bind him to me. With no time left at all to find out more I realised how little I knew about him.

'Will you come back?'

'Of course.'

'When?'

'Or you could visit me for a holiday.'

'Where will you be?'

'I should get back to college before they pull the grant from under me. They like you to put in an appearance now and again. They know I'm ill. Not that that makes any difference. These people give you money and then they think they own you. More like a bloody stalag than a university. Maybe I should just jack it in. See how they like that. I'd like to see them running a campus with no students. See how far their value judgments would get them then.'

'Do you not want to go, then?'

'It's all right for you. You're an autodidact.'

'What's that?'

'Someone who doesn't need to be told what autodidact means.'

'Maybe you should stay. Willy'll be off again as soon as Christmas is out of the way.'

He laughed at me. I didn't know what to do. He was standing on the lino with his back to the window, one leg in his trousers, Y-fronts pale blue with navy piping, fag in the corner of his mouth, laughing out of the other side of it. Suddenly he looked like a Scully and I thought I mightn't miss him. But I didn't want to find out.

'Where's your college?'

'London. Don't they tell you anything?'

'Why does everyone always want to go to London?'

'Why not? It's got everything.'

'All those people?'

'That's the best thing about it. You can pick and choose who you want to talk to. You can be left alone if you want. It's not like living in a goldfish bowl like this place. Everyone you see is a stranger.'

'I don't like strangers. The people you know are bad enough.'

He looked at me, fag bobbing in the middle of his smile while he did the last few buttons up here and there on his going-away outfit, trouser ends bagged over his yet-to-be-elevated feet. 'The world better watch out when you're set loose on it.'

'Why?'

I was looking at the floor when I asked and when I looked up to see why he hadn't answered he was gone. As I came downstairs with his bag I heard him pacifying Bridey in the hall.

'I'd love to stay a bit longer, Mother. But I've got myself to think of.'

After he was gone I threw the runestones for him. I hadn't used them since they had made such a terrible prediction for Netty, but I thought if I concentrated harder this time I might get it right. They suggested that his immediate future was all love and roses. After that I didn't feel so bad that he had gone.

There wasn't a whole lot of time for feeling bad in any case. The day after was the day I brought Ash to Arthurstown to have his shoes put on. I rode him slowly on the verge all the way, but still the blacksmith tutted over the state of his feet. I said I was sorry and that I'd bring him sooner next time. Every six weeks, he said. I couldn't see how I could come up with the money again in only six weeks, but I said nothing and only nodded. It seemed that the saddle would never happen.

The day after that was the day that Willy came home with the Rotavator. He started it up in the afternoon and set to work churning the soil of the far garden. I tried to tell him to be careful where he ploughed but he was on a mission. Though at that time, in January, all the vegetation was a brown frosted mass, there were other months of the year when remnants of former cultivation would burst through the weeds. You couldn't tell that to Willy. He had made up his mind that we were to be self-sufficient and he drove the machine in straight lines, churning up sliced daffodil bulbs and smashed tulip bulbs and fractured paeony roots and pulverised lilies; ploughing into fragments the site of an asparagus bed and severing the roots of plum trees. He sweated and strained, stripped to the shirtsleeves in the chill wind, and I thought he was going to have a heart attack. By the time he had finished, the whole garden looked like the poached corner of a field where cattle mill to be fed in the winter.

'There you are now. The world ploughing champions below in Wellingtonbridge have nothing on it. That'd show that feckin' PJ what a man could get up to if he put his back into it. Professional student I ask you. Did you ever hear the like of it?'

We could hear the phone ringing in the distance and nobody answering it. Willy said that he had a bit of a thirst on him and retrieved his jacket and jumper from the fork of a tree. After he was gone I did what I could, but not with any great hope, pushing bits of bulb and root back under the soil, not sure whether I was saving weeds or treasures. As much to distract myself from that as anything else, I thought I might as well go into the greenhouse for a minute and have a quick look at the magazine.

I had a flick through and got stiff, but I hadn't the courage to light a cigarette or get my thing out for admiration because I couldn't be sure that Willy would stay inside, or even that he mightn't bring Bridey out to show her his great work.

Then I thought there was a terrible silence and I felt as if I were asleep and dreaming. I saw Netty fly over my head and I flew up to her and asked her where she was going, and all she would say was 'Lovely, lovely, lovely'. I couldn't get over the shame of having the magazine still in my hand, though she didn't seem to notice or mind.

When I was back to myself again I ran into the house where Willy and Bridey were staring at the kitchen floor.

'What's wrong?' As if I needed to ask.

'Be a good boy and go out to play.'

'You might as well tell him.'

'Your Aunty Netty is very sick. She had a heart attack this afternoon.'

'Thank God.' The words were carried on a gust of relief, 'I thought she was dead.'

They were looking at me as if I had sprouted horns and hooves. Before they could decide what to think the phone rang again.

'Don't answer it.' Bridey didn't take her eyes off me as she spoke.

'I have to. It might be news.' Willy went to the phone.

Bridey kept me fixed, as if I might make things worse if she blinked.

When Willy had finished mumbling in the hall he came back. 'She's dead, God rest her.'

Before he had finished speaking Bridey ran at me like you would run at a cat that's on the butter. I ducked and fled and didn't stop running until I was in Martin Foley's field and hit a black wall of tears.

Inch after inch I grew in the summer following my four-teenth birthday. Brenda would remark on it every time she came to see us from her castle in Taghmon.

She had started calling herself Isis and she wore acres of unwashed velvet that gathered the dust off the earth in her sweeping train, making her slight frame unsteady with the weight of so much nap and soil. There were crystals glinting in the gloom of her bosom and a crescent moon of mala-chite rested in the central parting of her straight black hair. Her eyes were carefully painted in a hieroglyphic style. Though she was not yet thirty, and the face beneath her disguise was still that of a child who has yet to acknowledge that life is a troublesome business, her costume rendered her ageless or, as she would have hoped, immortal.

The transformation had come about not long after the Christmas of Netty's death and PJ's departure, the Christmas I found out what happened if you defied God. One day she was eating salt-and-vinegar crisps in front of the Brady Bunch and complaining that she might as well be dead, and the next she had disappeared from our lives to become the High Priestess of the Cult of Ra, and the châte-laine of Osiris.

This Osiris was a German weirdo who used to come to the village once a week to visit Con Maloney, the father of

Christo and Smut and all the other Maloneys. Con himself was a tall, angular man in need of a haircut who seldom spoke or got spoken to, and of whom we were all slightly afraid. He had strange beliefs that put him beyond the compass of his neighbours. For his part he made no secret of his opinion that we were superstitious primitives and he was therefore impervious to the pity and amusement he excited. He and his wife Ita, a domesticated woman who was rumoured to have been a doctor once, and their anarchic brood lived at the top of the hill above the village, in conditions that could only be speculated on since nobody had ever been invited to cross their threshold. He was often away for long periods, lecturing, it was said, in America, where there were others who shared his unlikely convictions. He was a computer man, and it was said that he believed that one day these props of science fiction would become a part of everyday life.

As if that weren't bad enough he had Osiris dropping by every week or so in his star-spangled Jeep, the two of them closeted together for purposes that defeated the collective imagination of Duncannon. Osiris was, if anything, even less chatty than Con, but you got the feeling that his silence was more part of the act than in his nature. He had long white hair and a long white beard. He wore magician's robes on an everyday basis and a precious stone on every finger and every bare toe. His castle in Taghmon was a Norman keep with a cottage pushed into the side of it. The keep itself was ruined and open to the sky and had only been used as a cattle pen for as long as anyone could remember.

Somehow, probably while she was giving the sofa a rest and swinging her legs off one of the stools in the bar,

Brenda got to hear of Con Maloney's visitor, and somehow she contrived to meet him. I asked her, during the summer I grew, how she had managed it. Her eyes narrowed to slits of kohl.

'The Children will always find each other. We are so few now, we True Children, that the air is emptied of our messages, and when one calls to another across the ether it is like a clear bell in the silence. Osiris called me and I found him.'

For now that I was no longer a child Brenda would talk to me. She confided in me all that was being done at the castle. They were keeping a light burning for the return of Merlin; a beacon in the Dark Age, invisible to the world but perceptible to the Ancient Ones. 'We are the Chosen. By holding fast now to what is true we will earn our place among the elect in the New Age. When the weeds in the garden are withered, the Roses of Avalon will shed their thorns and bloom.'

These conversations always took place in the seclusion of the far garden, so she never had to look far for the metaphors. She sat on a rusty bar stool, her dresses draped to the ground below her feet so that she looked like a standing giantess. She would watch me as I worked and if I asked a question she would respond, though not necessarily with what you might call an answer.

'Who is my father?'

'Who indeed? I could give you the name of the man, but what good would that be? Was Leda ever called upon to name the swan?'

'Maybe she was.'

'I am telling you all I know, and all I know is that your

father was not the man I could name. He was an instrument merely; a tool; a phantom come out of the mists of Merlin's conjuring. It is best not to question such things. When the time is right for you to know it will be revealed to you.'

I dropped my hands back on to the ground and the weeds I was pulling from between the rows of lettuces. I was near the end of the row and then there were the strawberries to do. The soil in that garden was so fertile that weeds appeared as soon as you turned your back on them. Buttercups, in particular, were liable to spring, fully formed and from nowhere, in freshly cleared ground. There was never a day when you could look at it all and feel satisfied. You would always see something that needed to be done, and then notice fifty other things wanting while you were doing the one.

After Willy had laid waste with the Rotavator nothing more was done for a while. The machine sat rusting in the mud until it was hidden by a luxuriant new growth of nettles and bindweed, and the man who owned it phoned every week to ask when he could have it back, until he came to get it his exasperated self. In Willy's absence I was the one who showed him where it was. I stared at my feet in silence while he disentangled it and passed disgusted judgment on our family for being a crowd of shabby barbarian knackers. 'A place like this going to the dogs. You wouldn't credit it. There's tinkers would have more sense and be grateful for it.'

I wouldn't have thought I knew where to start, but here and there a peony, divided and scattered by Willy's cultivation, had braced itself among coarser competitors and opened out in bowls of cerise. I'd gently free it from the stranglers, and begin to pull up lines of nettles by the incestuous network of their yellowy roots. Then I'd start to remember the sound of Debora's voice telling me what to do and every smell and nettle sting would chase a memory out of a dark corner.

A man called Jimmy Byrne came to trap goldfinches among the pear trees and saw what I'd been up to. He told me that he'd bring strawberry plants with him when he returned, and he did, and he showed me how to cultivate them.

The following summer I grew tomatoes and sunflowers. Jimmy Byrne came back for more goldfinches and told me what had to be done about the fruit trees, and how to rescue the raspberry canes and the gooseberry bushes, and what tools from the shed could be used for what once the rust was scraped off them.

The more I did the more I remembered from the hOme, not just about growing things, but about everything. Entire conversations would come back and play in my head while it was bent over a scuffling trowel. What gaps there were in my garden knowledge were filled by Jimmy Byrne's disinterested monosyllabic promptings. Anything else could be learned from mistakes. I didn't like to ask Jimmy what he did with the goldfinches, but he said that they were the best singers on God's green earth so I assumed that it was nothing unpleasant, and there always seemed to be plenty more frittering around the garden after he had gone.

He never came the third summer, but by then I had nearly half the garden under some kind of control and potatoes were swelling under the ground and onions on top of it. That was about the time that Brenda began to come back from Taghmon for regular visits, blithe now to Bridey's remarks about her fancy dress and unmotherly instincts. She would look at Sara the way I remembered her looking at me when I was a child, the way a cat would look at a newly introduced pup, with rivalry and incomprehension and affronted dignity all crowded in her sluggish black eyes. Sara would look back at her with an impudence that brought them no closer. The child had no idea that the witchlike visitor she called Blender was her mother. Though, by and large, she was a stoic infant, when she did get upset and require comfort on a motherly scale it tended to be me that she turned to.

Long before the summer I grew I had passed through the humiliations of change, when a different voice came out of me every time I opened my mouth, as if I were possessed by demons, some squeaky and some gruff and some that could cross all the vocal ranges in the animal kingdom in a single red-faced word, and each sound I made more irritating to Bridey than the last one. There were worse humiliations still, like the day on the strand when all the Devlins and Maloneys were pointing at my togs and laughing. It was the first fine day of an April before I was thirteen. I was wearing the togs I had worn the year before, not realising that there had been a transformation in the meantime and what had always been neat and snug to my undercarriage was now swinging out of the leg of my togs. The jeers and hooting rang in my ears for weeks, and not only in my imagination: every time I crossed the street a witty voice would call out to know if I was on my way for a swim and had I got my rubber ducky. That was the hottest summer we had and I never went into the sea once, nor wore short trousers for fear of the fall-out. How the generality of men coped with it was a mystery to me. I thought maybe there was some kind of restraining garment I hadn't been told of, but there was no one to ask, and the most protracted of sly observations on the strand would bring you no nearer an answer.

The bigger that lot grew the more prone I seemed to be to spontaneous erections in unsuitable company. I'd be up in Ross and calling in at the shop to visit Sally, and listening to whatever she was saying about whoever was passing up or down the street, when the tightness would come over me like a cramp and I'd have to twist myself into a position in which neither Sally nor anyone looking through the window nor any customer who happened in could see the awful excrescence at the front of my trousers, at the same time trying to look normal and pretend to be paying attention to what was being said until the thing elected to deflate itself.

Knowing that it was all my own fault was no help. I had encouraged it by reading PJ's magazines, and had wished for it to be a decent size, a knob that would dwarf any painted fingernail that came into the frame. I hadn't predicted the consequences of the rest of me not growing in proportion. I still had the body of a child half my age as a background to this thing, the great dull head on it like the cap of a mushroom that seemed to be growing every time I got it out to look at it. In feet and inches I was still the smallest in the class, while in inches alone I was rapidly becoming a different kind of freak.

By the start of the summer of growing I was nearly reconciled to it, having evolved a variety of suitable postures and gaits for concealment, and having been several times to the swimming pool in New Ross where worse could be seen in the changing rooms, though none, admittedly, attached to a body as scrawny and undersized as mine. That was the first winter that I started going to the secondary school in Ross, taking the bus every weekday. The alternative had been to go to Ramsgrange, but I had had my fill of nuns with Sister Vesuvia and neither the long journey nor the fearsome reputation of the Christian Brothers could persuade me to continue with them. It was an early start and the bus didn't leave to bring us home until six, so there was always a couple of hours to kill after school, either going up to the pool for a swim, or hanging around in the shop in Mary Street talking to Sally.

She didn't get so many customers any more. Half the shelves were empty and some of the sweet jars had no more than a bit of sticky on the bottom. There were dead flies in the window and the ice-cream machine was long broken. The sparser her customers became the more abruptly she treated them, shouting to know what they wanted before they were in the door and grumbling to herself as she made a half-hearted attempt to find whatever it was on the shelves behind her. I asked her why she didn't retire for herself, and she said she wouldn't know what to do all day if she did, that she'd go mad if she had to spend all day above in the room with Granny Scully screeching downstairs every five minutes.

The time before the bus would fly past when I was standing in the shop with her and hearing the nicknames of everyone going past.

'There's Sueya Mooney.'

'Sueya?'

'He'd sue ya if ya looked at him crooked.'

'Did he ever sue you?'

'I never looked at him crooked. See that fella there, with the cap on that's too big for him? He'd be a cousin of yours. His grandfather was the Half-arse Scully.'

'The Half-arse Scully?'

'The Half-arse Scully that went off to London for himself in the days when they all wore tail-coats. He'd a been the brother of Joseph Scully's father. Anyway, he came back in a lounge suit thinking he was the height of fashion, only it was the first one that was seen in the town without the tails on the back and he was the Half-arse Scully till the day he died long after tails became the oddity. Did you ever hear the like of it?'

'No.'

She would beam at that, all the lines of her face uncrossing themselves for about half a second in which you would see that she might have once had charms.

'How come you were never married?'

'The cheek of you.'

'Sorry.'

'I never met a man was worth the bother of putting on a big frock and everyone lookin' at you. Could you imagine me walking down the aisle of the parish church and a big bunch of flowers? They'd all be laughing.'

'And why did Netty never get married?'

'Poor Netty. God love her. She had a fella was soft on her once and she asked him to tea and didn't Willy the scamp put Epsom salts in his tea and lock the lavatory door. He ran off and we never saw him again. Grand big farmer he was with horses and all. Did you ever hear the like?'

'No.'

Sometimes I'd nearly miss the bus by listening to her and

have to run down the Ryan's on the Quay and jump on it breathless. As often as not the bus itself was late and you stood waiting to see it cross the bridge, not resorting to the fug of the waiting room unless the weather was so bad you were washed inside it.

Christo Maloney used to sit beside me for the journey home. Having had similar feelings to mine about the nuns in Ramsgrange he had also opted for a town education, though he, reaping the benefit of his father's mechanistic views, was being sent to the Tech.

He asked me about England once and whether it was true that the people there had nothing but filth on their minds. We had passed Campile and the bus was fairly empty and I felt I could speak freely without being overheard.

'What makes you think I know?'

'Weren't you brought up over there?'

'Only when I was little.'

'Well, you must know something. Apparently they have cinemas over there showing nothing but films of people doing it and they have big camps where everyone walks round in their nip all day. And the schools have both boys and girls and rubber johnny machines in the hall and everyone does it in the toilets at breaktime.'

'You seem to know more about it than I do.'

'I'm only saying what I heard. Is it true?'

'I don't know about the schools and the cinemas, but the place where I was there were no holds barred.'

'Where was that?'

So I began to tell him stuff about the hOme. The bus was like a no-man's-land cutting through the dark countryside, and it didn't seem to matter what I said. I told him it was all a secret and that I had never told anyone before and he secured my faith in him by telling me his secret, which was that he wanted to be a zoologist, because he thought that animals were better than people and that the only way the world would be saved was if the people destroyed themselves before they destroyed all the animals. He had great hopes for a nuclear war and his plan was that when it happened he would be out on the Serengeti in his Jeep and after that it would be just him and the zebras.

'Not even your family?'

'I can't be sentimental with so much at stake. The people have to go. We are the lowest life form. If it wasn't for humanity everything would be fine. Did you see that programme about the hyenas?'

'I hate hyenas. They're disgusting.'

'They're beautiful. And who are you to talk about disgusting with all the things you got up to in England?'

'I didn't get up to anything. I was a child. I only saw it.'

'You could have ignored it.'

'How was I supposed to know?'

'Anyway, you can't say hyenas are disgusting with people carrying on like that in daylight.'

'That's the last time I tell you anything.'

'That's the last time I'll listen. Disgusting.'

By the start of the summer I had made a friend of my mother, or perhaps it was she who did the making, since I did nothing more than work in the garden as usual and she it was who came to watch me, moving the bar stool and arranging herself on it wherever I was, and I was able to ask her whether the hOme was really as bad as I remembered and whether we had been no better than animals.

'Have you been talking to Bridey?'

'Are you joking? She'd drown me before she'd let me talk about that.'

Her first appearance in the garden had been as the result of a row with Bridey, and she came through the small doorway in the high wall in a towering rage, striding along the path like a queen in Wonderland, leaving the ground dragged and leafless behind her. She stopped short on seeing me, and her muttering died away, as muttering will on the realisation that it is audible to another person. For several seconds she stood rigid, regarding me with the glassiness of one who is regrouping scattered dignity in the presence of a stranger.

'Hiya.'

'Coorg? It is you? I didn't know you. You're huge.'

I made a furtive glance down to make sure she wasn't referring to anything I wouldn't have wished her to notice, and then conceded the point by holding my arm out. The end of the sleeve was nearer my elbow than my wrist. I had just passed the five-foot mark by then so we were seeing each other eye to eye.

'Bridey says I'm growing too fast and I won't get another set of clothes until I stop.'

'That woman.' Rage that had been cauterised by aston-ishment began to flow again. 'She said she was going to have a Mass said for me. A Mass? For me? To save my soul. That woman wouldn't know what a soul was if it bit her on the arse.'

I laughed. I was less self-conscious about laughing now, because the sound that came out was nearer a baritone than a shriek.

She smiled. She looked about her. 'Someone's been busy.'

I felt taller still for the compliment. I had always been a bit secretive about the garden. Neither Bridey nor Willy had ever come into it. If I was wanted to mind the bar I would be shouted for from the back door, and I thought it was better to keep it that way. It was better to have nothing said at all than to have all your work diminished by one grudging or patronising remark.

'I just tidied it up a bit.'

The stool was near by and she moved to settle on it. She surveyed everything in comfort without questioning why a bar stool should have been placed there for her convenience. It was Sara who had brought it out to me the day before. She was always moving things from one place to another. She called it helping, and the greater and more cumbersome the object, and the farther she went, the more helpful she considered herself to be. The dragging of this stool from the bar to the far garden had been her greatest achievement yet, and I hadn't wanted to belittle her by replacing it straight away.

A shadow of puzzlement crossed Brenda. 'What do you do with all the food?'

'Nothing.' I shrugged. 'I tried to give some stuff to Bridey in the beginning, but she didn't want it. She said it was lumpy. It was tomatoes. She said if they weren't roundy they weren't fit to be eaten, so she threw them away. Only a pauper would be desperate enough to eat stuff out of a garden.'

There was a few minutes' silence to cover things that didn't need to be said about Bridey. Meanwhile I watched Brenda's features as she focused on one part of the garden after another with legible admiration.

'She's mad.'

'We all know that.'

It was the first time my mother and I had agreed on anything and it was a pleasant sensation.

'So why do you do it?'

'I like seeing things grow.' I returned to my task of tying wigwams of sticks together for beans to climb, the way I had seen it done in the library book. That was when I asked her about the people at the hOme being no better than animals.

'How much do you remember?'

'It depends who's asking. I can remember a lot of stuff when I'm doing the garden.'

'How old are you now?'

'Fourteen. Last week.' I meant no resentment and she took none.

'You're nearly the same age I was.' She left it at that. She might have meant the age she was when she fell pregnant with me or the age she was when she stumbled on the hOme, or something else I didn't know about. Whatever it was, she reflected on it for a moment. 'At least you didn't have to grow up in Luton.'

'What was that like?'

'Hell. Getting knocked up with you was the best thing that happened to me. It got me out of there.'

I couldn't say anything for a while after that. There was a knot I had tied the wrong way and it took a bit of time and a great deal of concentration to unpick the string.

The more I came to know Brenda the more I worried about her being in league with the Devil. She tried to explain that the Devil was a Christian invention cobbled together from Greek mythology and Babylonian numerology to discredit the both of them, but I could hear phrases that were not her own in the explanation and I knew that Osiris was the source. I asked her whether she was not afraid of going to hell, and she said that there was no such place. That might have been a tempting thought had I not been warned against temptation.

I had by this stage become almost reconciled to having some kind of role in saving the world, though it was not yet clear to me how it was to be done. That it could be done, that war and money and atheism and stupidity could be abolished, I had no doubt, but I kept changing my mind about where to begin. Should I start a new religion or stick with the old one and work my way up to the papacy? Would I have to become a politician? What I really wanted to be was a hermit living in the woods somewhere with a horse and a garden. I used to pray to God to find another Messiah and leave me alone, but I knew that was selfish, and with the world the way it was we didn't have much longer before something had to be done. Meanwhile, and keeping all these worries to myself, I had to go through the motions of youth.

The only good thing about secondary school was that

you got three months' summer holiday. That was three months of not having to feign attention while you were told things you either knew already or that were not worth knowing in the first place. You were told how ignorant you were if you didn't give the answer or called a know-all if you did. You had to be wary of using the right word for something because they'd ask you whether you had swallowed a dictionary for breakfast. So you said as little as possible while the bored and disillusioned man at the front tried to fill his forty-five-minute slot with as little effort as possible and one hand deep in his pocket under the cover of the desk while the slowest boy in the class read aloud, stumbling from word to half-word and making incomprehensible something you had read and understood the day the book came into your hands. If it was a man at the front, in jacket and trousers, heaving sighs of self-pity over being afflicted with boys either too stupid to be worth teaching or too clever for their own good, at least that was better, for all his lazy sarcasm, than any of the Brothers in their stale soutanes and extruded zeal. It was either the Brother whose only subject was how grateful we should be to the Brothers for giving us an education at all, or the Brother who patrolled the rows with his dead smell, pinching and tweaking all the more attractive boys while dealing out pain to the less attractive via the end of a leather, or the Brother who leaped about like a monkey, both physically and verbally, his one motif being the heartfelt assertion that Hitler was a great and much misunderstood man. The only sad thing about the last day before the holidays was the awkwardness of talking to Sally as if it didn't matter that you wouldn't be calling in for a while to kick your heels with her while you waited for the bus home.

'Do you ever play a game called White Horse these days?'

'No. What's that?'

'We were always playing it in the summer holidays when I was little. People complain about the children now, but we were terrible the things we used to get up to. I always had to be the White Horse. I don't know why but I suppose I was stupid that way and I did whatever I was told. Anyway, whoever had to be the White Horse would have a blindfold put on them and they'd be put with their back to some woman's door. And they'd always pick the door of some out-and-out bitch and then they'd all shout. White Horse, White Horse, kick down the door. And you'd have to kick the door and they'd all run away and leave you to face whatever woman'd come out hoppin' mad you'd kicked the paint off her front door and you trying to pull the blindfold off so you could run away and she screaming blue murder. Did you ever hear the like?'

'No. It doesn't sound like much of a game.'

'We were stupid in them days. We'd do anything. It's a wonder I'm still here.'

'There's no such thing as a white horse, you know.'

'Is that a fact? How did you make that out?'

'It's to do with the colour of the skin. Technically they're grey, or albino. Never white.'

'And I kicking down all them doors and getting screamed at for nothing. We were terrible ignorant in the old days.'

'Why did you always stay to be shouted at?'

She thought about it. 'I was too big. I wouldn't have got far anyway. Anyway, have you the holidays all planned?'

The only bad thing about the holidays was that

Duncannon was invaded by townies and, worse, Dubliners, although, having said that, it was the townies and Dubliners who generated the income I needed to buy seeds for the garden and horseshoes for Ash. On the hotter Saturdays and Sundays and bank-holidays, when it was likely that the strand would be crowded enough to make it worthwhile. I'd go up to Martin Foley's early in the morning and give Ash a good brushing and saddle him up. I had the saddle now, and it had been under my nose all the time, mouldering away in one of the outhouses at the back of the hotel. It was not a comfortable saddle to sit on, but it fitted Ash well enough with a folded blanket beneath it, and I getting to be a bit on the big side for riding him anyway. I'd lead him down to Ballystraw to save his back for the day ahead, but once we were on the sand I'd get up and ride him into the sea. He liked that and he'd paw at the waves and do a big shit that floated away in green dumplings across the surface of the water. It was like our message to the swimming townies to let them know what we thought of them before we headed for the shore to relieve them of their cash. It was five pence for a short ride and ten pence for a longer one, and I never let anyone get up on him that was bigger than myself, and I never let anyone go off on their own, no matter how great a jockey they claimed to be. Usually the reverse was the case, and the whimpering child was set on to the saddle by a white-gutted father who seemed to imagine that the sight of his blubbering offspring on the back of a pony was an ornament to his manhood. Meanwhile the mother would be pestering me with questions about how safe the pony was, which I would answer evasively for the pleasure of seeing her sunburnt cleavage wobble in terror.

The day after I asked Brenda about my father was a blazing Saturday, and Ash and I were on our usual patrol when we were hailed by a woman too English to stir herself from her rug, and with a voice that reminded me straight away of Fi and of cantering round in circles in a Devon woodland clearing.

I watched us approach by the reflection in her big sunglasses. We looked what we were, sloshing through the soft sand: undergroomed and reluctant; neither of us prepared to look anyone in the eye or do exactly what we were told. Ash had more cause for his sulky demeanour than I did since he had no choice in being there and would have been far happier to have been left above in Martin Foley's field, living it up with the heifers.

'Is that your pony?'

It was none of her business, but she had the sort of snotty voice that made everything her business. I looked around for children, but could see none that might be hers. Maybe they were in the sea, which meant that I would have to waste time waiting while they were being enticed out of it and dried.

'Yes?'

'Are you in the Pony Club?'

'No?'

'I thought not. That animal needs worming. And your tack is a disgrace. Where do you live?'

'Over there.' I jerked my head in the general direction of the village. It was becoming apparent that there were no children to be given rides and that she was merely passing the time of day with browbeating.

I turned Ash round the wrong way so that he kicked sand across her, and we started to walk off.

'You never turn a pony like that! Always turn him away from you!' She was standing up and brushing the sand off her. Another woman was running towards her, of the same hamper-and-headscarf type.

'I know.' I called it out without looking back, and I could hear the other woman fussing over her, and I could feel her finger pointing at me, and I heard what she said.

'That boy. That boy with the wormy pony. That boy with a touch of the tarbrush.'

I didn't have it in me to do any more business that day. I set off for the far end of the strand, shaking my head in response to any children who came running up with clammy coins in their hands and sand on their legs. I couldn't deny that the woman was right, it was only the way that she had said it, talking down through her nose to make me feel inferior and incompetent, and dirty too, assuming that was what a touch of the tarbrush meant. But what she had pointed out I had suspected for some time. The pony needed worming. He was skinnier than he should have been on the summer grass. I would have to find a way to do something about it, and that would involve money and a trip to Campile, and all without letting Bridey know what I was up to. For if Bridey knew she would tell Willy, and if Willy was reminded of the pony's existence he might sell him, the way he always sold every movable thing that might raise the price of a gargle.

When I got back to the hotel Bridey was pulling her hair straight with worry. 'Have you seen the child? Is Sara not with you? Jesus Mary and Holy Saint Joseph, if she's dead I'll kill myself. Sacred Heart of Jesus I placeall-mytrustinthee. Saint Anthony help me find her.'

'Did you go out to look for her?'

'How could I when I'm sick with worry?' Bridey hadn't set foot in the village in years. She would step outside the door and into Willy's car to go up to Mass or into Wexford for a bout of shopping, but she was no more likely to walk across the street than she was to swim to Ballyhack. 'I sent Kieran out to look for her two hours ago and God alone knows where he is.'

'God and Smut Maloney. I saw the two of them heading towards Fethard on Smut's motorbike.'

'Don't you be telling me that kind of thing when I've enough to worry about with one child dead in a ditch.'

'She isn't dead.'

'How would you know?'

I wasn't going to explain that to Bridey, but there was no way that Sara could be dead without me knowing about it. Since Netty, the dead had always passed me on their way to wherever they were going, even souls of people I had never known. I ignored the question and said that I would go and find Sara for her.

First I went and got the runestones. A quick throw told me to stay where I was. Given the state Bridey was in that would not have been diplomatic, so I went outside and had a look round for the sake of appearances.

I saw her blonde head first, beyond the wall of the tennis court, coming up the slip road from the strand. Then herself, carrying something bundled in the front of her dress, with her knickers showing to all the world. She was talking into the bundle, oblivious to everything about her, threading her way between cars and the bare legs of townies. I went to see what she had.

'You have to give me fifty pence.'

'What for?'

'For her.' She let me have a look at what she was carrying. It was a brown pup, of a non-breed that I recognised.

'Where did you get her?'

'Off Tommy Whelan. He said I could have her if I brought him fifty pee back. He's blind.'

'I know.' In all the times I had drooled over litters of pups in Tommy Whelan's house he had never offered me one on credit. 'Did you go there by yourself?'

She fended off my patronising with a sharp look. 'I have to bring the fifty pee back now. I promised. Don't tell Bridey anything.'

'We might have to tell her about the pup. She'll find out anyway. But we won't say anything about the money. I'll bring it down to him for you, if you like. What are you calling her?'

'Bell.'

Bridey, predictably, said that she had enough troubles in her life without having a dog in the house and that the pup had to go back where it came from. But because I was needed to mind the bar and there was no one else to take her back to Ballystraw, Bell stayed the night. By the morning Bridey was feeding titbits to her and talking to her as if the fat brown creature in her lap might become a receptacle for the love that all others had failed to comprehend or reciprocate.

It was never apparent that Brenda had a motive for coming to see us so often, and it certainly never occurred to me that I was the object of her visits, though if I had thought about it the short and brittle exchanges she had with Bridey were hardly worth repeating on a weekly basis, and Sara's existence was not a fact that troubled her unduly.

Maybe I assumed that she came out of habit, and because coming was no effort to her, accompanying Osiris as he drove to Duncannon for his regular meetings with Con Maloney. I might have thought that she took some kind of pleasure in the two of them flaunting through the village in their costumes and the blue Jeep painted with constellations, and her stepping out of it at the door of the hotel and dragging her yards of velvet over the step while Osiris carried on up the hill. It was certainly Bridey's view that she came for no other reason than to shame us.

That Osiris had never shown any interest in coming inside to meet Bridey might have been a crumb of comfort, were it not for the fact that no snub cuts deeper than that which comes from one who is denying you the opportunity to snub them first. 'And who does he think he is anyway? A dirty war-mongering Protestant German? Wasn't Martin Luther a German that caused all the trouble when he married the nun? Ita Maloney might have him in her house, but I wouldn't have him in mine.'

By degrees, and while emphasising the secrecy of it, Brenda began to tell me what was going on in Con Maloney's study. At first she told me that they were devising a way to make astrological projections on the computer. Con himself was astrologically sceptical, as he was sceptical about all pseudo-sciences, including, it was said, Catholicism, but he was keen to show that computers could do anything and everything, and horoscopes were as valid an end as any when the means were the object of the exercise.

That established, she began to hint that this scheme was merely a cover for a greater and more secret project, tied in to what she termed the Work being undertaken in Taghmon. Once, when I was close by her, she bent low from the waist and whispered to me that they were looking for the Holy Grail. Then she glanced nervously at the wall that separated the far garden from the road to the harbour, and we heard the footfalls and laughter of passers-by filtering through the carnose leaves of the fig tree. The far garden may have been a private world but it was not an impregnable one. She raised her voice to change the subject.

'You should come and see our garden soon. You'd like it.'

'Why? What's it like?'

'Not like this. It's very different. I think you'd really love it in Taghmon. It's a bit like the hOme was, without all that communal bullshit. Or the vegetarian crap. And we don't make up stupid rules all the time.'

'Doesn't sound much like the hOme.'

'Well.' She smiled. 'I've told Osiris a lot about you. He's very interested in you.'

'What did you tell him?'

'Stuff. You know, about your destiny and that kind of thing. About your powers. He thinks you should be called Horus.'

I said that I had enough names to be going on with.

The Sunday after that Willy detained me in his car for one of his little talks. We had been up to Mass and back again. There was a long sermon about how sinful it was to think. Thinking had caused the fall from Eden and thinking had been at the root of the Reformation. It was all the thinking clever clogs who were going round saying that God was dead. Thinking was the work of the Devil and God had given us our brains not to use them but as a test to tempt us. We could prove ourselves worthy of God's love by abstaining from unnecessary thought in the same way that we proved it by abstaining from unnecessary action in a certain physical department. The brain was an organ of pleasure and should be mistrusted as one.

The part of this sermon that had troubled me was when he, an aged priest of red jowls and nasal hair, had quoted from scripture. 'The Bible clearly tells us, in black and white, the Word of Our Lord Himself, no less: "To think is to be damned for ever for the mind is the source of all evil."'

Now there was a Bible in the hotel, left behind by the previous owners, who, having been Protestant, were encouraged to possess and study such a thing. I had read it, from cover to cover and in secrecy, for want of anything else to read in that house, and I had no memory of such an injunction, not even in the letters of St Paul, who was not averse to prescriptions against human nature. It was hardly credible that the priest could have invented the quotation, but it set me in a daze of thinking for the rest of the Mass and the short journey home and, though I was anxious to get inside and get hold of the Bible and put my mind at rest, the next thing I knew was that Willy and I were alone in the car, which was pulled up facing the ball alley opposite the hotel, and he was saying something about Martin Foley.

These little talks had happened once or twice before, always trapped in the car and always with the two of us staring straight ahead at that concrete wall. The previous time he had tried to draw me out on the subject of self-abuse, saying that he had done it himself at my age and he knew the temptation all too well and wanted to set my mind at rest about it in case I thought I was a freak and not just a sinner. I had no idea what he was talking about. It crossed my mind that it might have been masturbation but the possibility was instantly dismissed. I decided that he either meant I was abusing my back by digging in the garden or abusing my eyes by reading too much, so I nodded and promised not to overdo it, and he clapped his hand on my knee and said he was glad we were able to have everything out in the open and so long as I didn't do it more than I could help myself. It was only later that night, after a particularly elaborate bout of knob-wrestling, that all his words slotted into place and I nearly swallowed the pillow in delayed embarrassment.

I had vowed never to be caught alone in the car with him again, but now here we were, and all on account of my becoming distracted by thinking too deeply.

'Martin Foley says you have a pony above on his land.'

'Was he talking to you?'

'Where did you get a pony, in God's name?'

'You gave him to me.'

'I did not.'

'Asfaloth. You got him off a fella in Clonroche.'

'That pony? I forgot black about it. That was a fair while ago.'

'What did Martin Foley say?'

'He was after me for money. For the grazing.'

'He never said anything to me about money.'

'Of course he didn't. Where would you get money?'

'I dunno.'

'Is that where you go off to all the time?'

'Where did you think I was going?'

'I thought you were going somewhere. Anyway, he's after me for money and I haven't got it. But I know a fella might buy a pony.'

'I'll get the money.'

'We'll say no more about it.'

Maybe I should have been grateful that Martin Foley had waited four years before asking what was due to him, but I had been slipping him the odd large bottle without charging and thought that was all the rent he wanted. I wasn't stealing, because I kept count of the drink so I could pay Willy and Bridey back when I was older and rich. Four hundred and eighty-seven large Guinnesses, priced at 19p in the beginning and rising to 26p for the last one.

I said a fair few prayers that night. The praying had been dropping off recently as I began to think about some of the words in them and wondering whether it was really the sort of thing that God would want to hear, night after night telling him how great he was, as if he were a shy little thing and needed a boost to his ego. Then there was the difficulty of knowing whether to say them before or after the other. If you prayed first you went to sleep in a state of sin, besides being distracted by a horn calling attention to itself below the sheets when your mind was supposed to be on higher things. If you pulled the plank first you were inclined to fall asleep in the middle of the prayers, besides there being no guarantee, given the wandering a mind can get up to while attempting communication with an elusive God, that you wouldn't be ripe for another pull by the time you hit the final Amen. I should have been able to resist temptation altogether and keep my hands above the sheets, but there was no way of getting to sleep at all with a thing like that sticking out of the middle of you and a parade of hoors dancing across the ceiling. The solution I eventually hit on was prayers first, then a thorough deboning, followed by a brisk act of contrition and sleep. That Sunday night, however, the sky was falling in on me and there was neither horn nor doubt nor sleep to stem the litany.

It was Bridey who had to tell me that Willy wanted me to have the pony in the yard for Tuesday afternoon. By then I had talked myself into thinking that it might be all for the best. Ash was too small for me and I wasn't able to look after him properly; to worm him or to shoe him as often as he needed it. There might be a child somewhere in Pullein-Thompson land who could give him a better life, and maybe he'd even have other horses to live with and not have his tail chewed by heifers. I decided to write a letter to this unknown child, explaining Ash's likes and dislikes, greeds and phobias. When the men came to put him into their trailer I handed the letter to one of them and explained who it was for. They were hard men, cigarette-in-the-corner-of-the-mouth men, and their trailer wasn't a proper horsebox but more of a sheep trailer, and you could see the whites of Ash's eyes as he stood in it. Willy was not on hand to witness it.

I handed the letter to the man and he looked at it as if he had never seen a letter before, and he listened to what I was saying as if I were speaking a foreign language, and he said nothing himself. He went over to the other man and mumbled a couple of words and the two of them stood and laughed at me, cigarettes flapping in the corners of their mouths.

Still the obvious didn't occur to me until after the trailer had pulled out of the yard and I turned and saw Kieran standing in the back door in his stocking feet. His eyes were puffy and his teeth were stained with nicotine, but his voice was the same as it had always been. 'Poor nigger. His little pony's gone to the knackers for dog meat. Ha ha.'

I didn't know where I was going. I went down to the far garden and came back again. All I had seen there was a memory of the frightened pony under the fig tree with his quarters drawn up, and him trotting away under the apple trees until he turned and stood his ground and took his chances by letting himself be caught by me. I turned left out of the gate and went down to the harbour, but that was full of people, of townies gaping at the boats and pointing at nothing over the rotten smell of the sea.

Smut Maloney ran into the back of my leg with the wheel of his motorbike, laughing and revving while I flailed my arms to stop myself falling into the low-tide mud.

'Are you up for a spin, young Scully?'

'Where are you off to?'

'Wexford, but I'll drop you down the road anywhere you like.'

'Could you drop me in Taghmon?'

'That hole?'

I shrugged.

'Are you off to see the wizard?'

'Will you?'

'Hop on so.'

Once in the lee of Smut's back there was no time for repentance. Every partial second was taken up with the challenge of adherence and the light-headed immediacy of death. To begin with I was unsure how to arrange myself, but the combination of necessity and his repeated exhortations to hang on and the ergonomics of the bike soon put me in my place. Fists locked into his waist and thighs rammed to the undersides of his and arse stuck out like a bimbo to avoid any more intimacy than was absolutely vital. I had the horn and the last thing I wanted was for the backscape of black leather in front of me to become aware of it.

Of all the people who took notions, Smut was among the more volatile, and he liked to have witnesses to his feats of brinkmanship. I assumed that some other passenger had let him down at the last minute and that was why he had asked me along. Why I had taken him up on it was another matter. Sometimes, when my knee was tantalising the surface of the road on a bend, or when we spliced the gap between an oncoming lorry and the one we were overtaking, a voice in my head might question why I had asked to be taken somewhere I had no conscious intention of going, but there was never time to give it consideration before the next brush with dustdom. I was biting the dust already with all the grit lodged in teeth peeled bare by velocity.

Taghmon, as Smut had indicated, was a hole. The dog who scratched himself in the street and was the only visible moving thing looked as though he might have had ambitions to be somewhere else once upon a time, before Taghmon had bludgeoned him with hopelessness. There was no sign of the paradise that Brenda had described.

'Well. There you are.'

I had got off the bike, but still had one hand on the pillion to try to appear steady on my feet. 'Thanks for the ride.'

'I wouldn't mention it. That's how rumours get started.'

He winked. I wondered for a moment of fluster if he had felt the horn, but I couldn't imagine that he'd be this good humoured about it if he had. My attempt at a knowing laugh was eclipsed by his flashing teeth and pockmarks.

'Thanks anyway. I'll see ya, then.'

'Do you know where you're going?'

'I'll find it.'

'Ask in there.' He nodded at the house across the road which showed inconclusive signs of containing a post office.

The spectral child in sole occupation of the business said that I would have to ask his mammy, and came with me to the door to point out which pub his mammy might be found in. Smut was still across the road astride his machine and grinning. I gave the kind of wave that was supposed to show that he could leave me to my own devices. He responded by taking out his tobacco tin and papers.

The pub turned out to be the manyplies of the village, where all the life missing from the street was being fermented into a state of contented excretability. By the time I had located the mammy I was looking for I had ten other mammies to help me with my enquiries.

'Isisanosiris?'

'They live in a castle.'

'There's no one lives in a castle in Taghmon, boy.'

'Maybe near Taghmon?'

'Is it a Mr Isisanosiris or a Mrs Isisanosiris?'

'Both.'

'What do they look like?'

'Well. Not normal.'

'Do you think he means the quare lot?'

'That isn't a castle. That place? That's no more a castle than I am.'

'Would they be lunatics, this lot you're looking for?'

'Well.'

'That's them so. The German in the frock and his English doxy.'

'What do you want to see them for?'

'I have a message for them.'

'What is it?'

'I don't know. A message.'

'Well, pardon me for asking.'

'Sorry. Do you know where they live?'

'It's out the road there. You can't miss it.'

We missed it a few times, scrambling up and down lanes and tracks, some so deep that the mud of winter still festered in their bottoms, where dead trees arched overhead and dust flew out of ivy at the noise of the engine. There was a hooded crow, shameless, on every gate, or on every obstructed gateway where a gate should have been, and all the fields were flat and reedy. The wheels slipped from under us and the engine stopped and I said that maybe we should give up, but Smut laughed and said that this was great altogether. The two of us were shrouded in mud, an inch thick on our feet and legs and thinning upwards to tiger stripes across our faces.

'I wouldn't mind seeing what the set-up is there anyway.' He winked again. 'For all the times he comes into the house he never says a word to any of us, only shuts himself up in the office with the oul fella.'

I couldn't think of anything to say, because the last thing I wanted was to have Smut with me when I turned up.

He went on. 'Christo told me you were telling him it was one long orgy the place you were staying over in England.' He was grinning at me expectantly, his tongue clamped between his teeth. I wanted to run off across the rushy field.

There was a cough somewhere the other side of the ditch and we looked up and saw a man's head looking back at us.

The tractor had no wheels. Stumps of axles rested on big stones, and the man sitting in the driving seat was similarly denuded, both his ears being chewed off by frostbite. Smut called out to him to ask where the wizard's castle was and he rose in his stirrups and pointed over the hedges, and suddenly it was there, a square stone tower not three fields away. There was no guarantee that it was the castle Brenda lived in, but I was prepared to take my chances rather than get back on Smut's bike and have him talk about things he shouldn't have known.

'I'll be seein' ya so.'

He took it in good humour, winked, and went off in a muddy wheelie.

'Grand evening for it now.'

I jumped, startled that the man on the tractor should have the power of human speech, and quickly replied that it was indeed, noticing that my voice had a squeak at the edge of it, and set off towards the castle, it being one of those situations where the unknown has its attractions.

It was not three fields and not six either, and there wasn't a straight line you could take across two of them, and no plant in any of the hedges that wasn't more thorn than stick, and no hedge that didn't have a ditch either side of it that could swallow a hurley team. The castle seemed farther away the nearer you got to it. I didn't cry or anything, but I got into the state where that would have been an option when I was a couple of years younger. The one comfort I had was that when my body was found and brought back to Duncannon, Willy would see the error of selling horses to the knackers.

It was the smell which hit me before anything else. Like flowers but spicier and capricious on the wind, engulfing for one pace and eluding for the next. After that half a dozen grey geese with orange beaks spotted me the same instant I saw them. They set up a clamour, loud enough to clear the bar at closing time. I thought I saw a unicorn, but it was only a white horse standing under a tree with a branch sticking out at the right angle to make the illusion. I reminded myself that there was no such thing as a white horse.

I realised this field was no field but a garden, and the first scent I had detected was supplemented by others, some heady and some sweet and some you couldn't describe which were somewhere between pleasure and poison. Everywhere, across the ground, were little mounds of earth at random, some fresh and some overgrown and all about the size of an infant's grave.

I looked up and the tower was above me, as sudden as when I had first seen it, but full scale now, rising sixty feet above my head. I looked down again and there was my mother, smiling at me as if I was expected.

Tired as I was I couldn't sleep on the narrow settle they gave me for a bed. The cottage that was dependent on the tower was not much more than one room, the walls of which were as thick with whitewash inside as they were out. Not that you could see much of the wall for all the furniture, of black oak, twisted and carved and wedged in place. There was a table in the middle of the room with great machines on it that sprouted hanks of wiring. A small screen, like a little telly, showed a constantly fluctuating and pulsating line, the green light of which flickered over the grotesqueries of candlesticks the size of coatstands and thrones that clawed the ceiling. When I had asked what the telly thing was for, Brenda told me it was *The Dark Side of the Moon*. It must have been obvious that I didn't understand what she was on about, so she held up the Pink Floyd album cover. 'It's a computer-generated graphic representation. We believe in the power of incantation but Osiris doesn't like the noise. This is kind of like the modern version of a Tibetan prayer wheel.'

They were sleeping in the other room, if a space that small could be called a room. There was a little bathroom as well. You could sit on the lavatory and have a shower at the same time. The settle I lay on was shorter than I was and only just wide enough so I didn't fall off it if I balanced on my side and kept still. There was a sliver of velvet cushion between my bones and the wooden seat. I thought about sleeping on the floor, but there wasn't enough space on the floor to stretch out.

When you can't sleep you think, whether you want to or not, and when you don't want to think is when the worst things come into your head. I thought a lot of things about Christo Maloney and none of them good. I thought about my own stupidity in imagining that I could trust anyone. It was obvious that I could never go back to Duncannon now. I'd die before I'd walk down that street with all of them knowing what they did about me.

So, that bridge burnt, I thought about the place I had come to, and it seemed that getting there had been no accident. I thought about Brenda and how, for all her strangeness, she had become the nearest thing to a friend, if only because it didn't matter what I said to her since she knew it all already. Then, for some reason, the Devil popped into my head, and I began to wonder whether he was present in that place. Bridey was always saying that Brenda was engaged in the Devil's work and here I had walked into the centre of operations of my own free will. I prayed a bit and double-crossed myself and kept my wrists crossed tight over my heart for protection.

I thought back to what had led me there, and it all seemed to stem from my doubting the word of the priest on Sunday. That had resulted in Ash being sent to the knackers, which had led to me being tempted on to Smut's bike, and Smut had a skull and crossbones dangling from his left ear, which could easily have meant that he was an agent of the Devil, and he had given me the horn, as if to lure me into the unthinkable. I nearly thought the unthinkable, Smut unpacking the bulge in his jeans, but there was a black fear that stopped me before the point of no return.

I may have slept a little. I may have dreamed I was in Mervyn's lap and nothing there to tremble me. One minute it was pitch dark at the window and endless Pink Floyd flicking green across the room, and the next everything was stricken with a light as grey as rain-clouds. There was the noise of a latch lifting. Brenda and Osiris were getting up and the night was over.

'Are you awake?' Brenda's whisper sounded as though she was still asleep herself.

'Yes.' I began to unlock my limbs from cramped shirring.

Two figures threaded their way among the furniture. They were white in the sullen dawn and it was a white too glimmering to be fabric. Before I had time to focus on them properly I snapped my eyes shut again.

'What's wrong?'

'Nothing.'

'Why are your eyes closed like that?'

'You've got nothing on.'

'So? Coorg, I'm your mother.'

'I know.'

'Stop being ridiculous. Coorg, open your eyes. The body is nothing to be ashamed of. Didn't you learn anything at the hOme?'

'I don't know.' I did know, but I hadn't known then what I knew now. You can't go back to pretending that something isn't a sin after you've been told that it is.

'My poor baby. They really got to you, didn't they? All that Catholic propaganda.'

'I suppose so.'

'It's okay. If I got over it you can get over it. What you're forgetting is that Bridey fucked my brain up when I was your age too. Free your mind. You don't have to believe what they told you.'

'Thanks.'

'Now. Come on. That's enough of this. We're going into the tower to greet the dawn. The Sun God is rising from the dead. Just slip your things off and come with us.'

'I'm grand here, thanks. You go ahead.'

I heard a 'ho ho ho' sound like someone being Santy Claus. It took a few seconds to work out that it was Osiris laughing at me. There was a hairy moment when the two of them squeezed past the settle where I had drawn myself up into a ball with my face crushed to my knees and coloured spots dancing on my eyelids. Something touched me and I didn't want to think what it was.

When I heard a lot of muffled chanting and I was sure that they were safely in the tower I put my runners on and bolted for the garden to avoid their return passage.

People are always saying that the early morning is the best time of day. I suppose if you like your world to be cold and damp and monochromatic and populated by nauseatingly cheerful early risers, it might be. A saner person could wait until the day had got itself started before quitting the certain comfort of the bed. But this was one of the mornings that must have started the rumour.

The sky was pink and blue. A flat layer of mist hovered over the level fields. Trees, floating on the mist, glistened in dew. A perfume, sharper and sweeter than the scents of the night before, drifted on the stillness. By the time Brenda came to the door to ask whether I was ready for breakfast my runners were soaked from the grass and I was shivering. Fortunately she was decent by then, redraped in velvet and her face freshly plastered and painted.

Papers had been shoved aside at one end of the table and there was a plate of salami and foreign cheese and odd-shaped bread, and two glasses of what looked like cider. The door from the bathroom was open and Osiris came through and stretched his arms over his head so that his robes spread out like a peacock's tail. It was the first time I had ever heard him speak, and his voice was as deep as a yawn.

'That was one good shit I did. You should have seen it. Real nice.'

Though, out of hunger, I had just got my head round the idea of eating cheese for breakfast, that took some of the edge off my appetite. He and Brenda raised their glasses to each other and dealt with the contents in one swallow. Brenda had a funny kind of smile on her face. There was an ammoniac smell. My stomach was on edge already, as if I were nervous or something, and that smell was all it took to induce a flush of nausea. I went to the bathroom in case I was going to be sick. The heavy smell Osiris had left lingering in there ensured that I was.

The day was hot before my head was clear. I had found a hammock screened by bushes and I was just dozing off when Brenda appeared with a plate of sandwiches.

'You used to love hammocks when you were little.'

'Did I?'

'How did you sleep last night?'

'Grand. It was a bit tight.'

'We could sling a hammock for you to sleep in.'

'Did you make the sandwiches?'

'Why?'

'I just wondered.' I'd never known her take the trouble to feed anyone but herself, but I couldn't say that.

'Osiris made them for you. He thought you might be hungry since you missed breakfast. He likes cooking.'

'He doesn't say much.'

'He doesn't need to.'

'It doesn't cost anything to say hello occasionally.'

'When your words have power you can't afford to waste them.'

'Like telling everyone what a big poo you did?'

'He's very keen on you. He likes you a lot.'

I looked away. It was disturbing to think that someone should like me. I didn't want Brenda to see that she had hit a weak spot. 'What are all the little graves for?'

'Little graves? Them? They're part of the Work.'

'Of course they are.'

'There's no need to sound like Bridey.'

'Sorry. Anyway, what are you burying?'

'Not burying. The opposite.' She looked around, as if there might be someone listening in the bushes. 'I can tell you about it here. We're protected.'

'By what?'

'Do you believe in fairies?'

'No. I mean, not now. I used to think they might be spacemen that got stranded or something. You know, the things you think when you're younger.'

'You could be right. Nobody knows where they came from. Fairies is just one name for them. We used to call them spirits at the hOme. Some people call them angels.'

'And you think they protect you?'

'We're doing their Work. They protect the Work.'

'Which is?'

'What I'm going to tell you now is more than a secret. If you tell anyone else you could lose your life. You could put us all in danger. Do you know what the Holy Grail is?'

'I suppose.'

'What do you know about it?'

'It's lost.'

'Exactly. We are going to find it. It's here. Somewhere. Osiris has spent his whole life tracking it down, all over the world. And he knows for a fact that it is buried here.'

'Get out of it. What would the Holy Grail be doing in Taghmon?'

'Waiting for the right person to find it. Like the sword in the stone. All those little graves are places we've dug already.'

'Why don't you get a JCB in?'

She gave me a look.

'All right. Why don't you get the archaeologists in?'

'It's a secret. It has to be. Even Con Maloney doesn't realise what his computers are really being used for. If archaeologists found it they'd put it in a museum and no one could use it. Besides, they couldn't. I told you, it's like the sword in the stone. Only the right person can find it. Osiris has realised that it won't be him. He's been living on top of it for years. It would have been found by now if it was meant to be him. Only Merlin can use it.'

'What for?'

'To save the world.'

I hadn't realised there were so many hairs on my body. They were standing out like the bristles on a nailbrush. The blood was thickening in my veins and my heart was having a hard time pushing it round. 'Come on. How's an old cup going to save the world?'

'It is a vessel. It's what it contains that's important.'

'And that is?'

'The only part of Christ that was left on earth when he was taken into heaven.'

'I thought you didn't believe in Christ.'

'We don't. Well, not in the usual way. We believe he was a being who was sent to save the world and he had extra-ordinary powers. But the time was wrong.'

'You'd think if he was so great he'd have known that.' I could have bitten my tongue for the blaspheny that came off it. Maybe the Devil was controlling me already. 'So, anyway, is the time right now?'

'We think so. But there are vested interests who want the world to stay the way it is. They wouldn't survive in the New Age. That's why it has to be a secret.'

'You're stretching it now.'

'Am I? Have you forgotten already what happened last time?'

'Last time what?'

'You don't remember being taken to see Marc Bolan?'

'No.'

'The wizard? You don't remember that?'

'Was he Marc Bolan? Get It On Marc Bolan? The Twentieth-century Boy? He wasn't, was he?'

'He could have done it. He had the power to pull it off.

All the children had their heads in the right places. He could have been the second coming.'

'So what happened?'

'He got nobbled, that's what happened. He got bought off by the establishment. They tumbled to him and they turned him into a shitty little pop star.'

'Was he going to find the Holy Grail?'

'Who knows?'

'Did he ever come to Taghmon?'

'I'm not telling you any more if you won't take it seriously.'

'Sorry. So which bit of Christ got left behind?'

'You can work that out. He was Jewish.'

'And?'

'And if he was Jewish he was circumcised.'

'So?'

'You do know what a circumcision is?'

'Yes. Oh my God, you're not serious. Jesus, that's disgusting.'

'No it's not. It's perfectly natural.'

'Since when is chopping the end of your thing off natural?'

That made her think for a minute. 'What I mean is that the foreskin is a natural thing. It's not disgusting.'

Discussing foreskins with my mother was making me shrivel so I said nothing.

'It's all there. In the Bible. Joseph of Arimathea was present at the circumcision and he was given the foreskin which he brought to Camelot. After the Knights of the Round Table were defeated the Grail was brought to Ireland for safe-keeping. That was when Ireland became the land of saints and scholars, because the Grail was being kept here.'

I didn't know what bible she'd been reading, but it was more up to date than mine. 'Why Taghmon?'

She looked irritated. 'It was the ley lines or something. Wolfy knows.'

'Wolfy?'

'I mean Osiris.'

'I thought the Round Table lot were the ones who didn't know where the Grail was?'

'Look. You can quibble about anything you want. You just have to believe. Do you want to save the world or not?'

I was looking up at the green of the leaves; birch leaves. The principal sensation was vertigo. I was not in a hammock at all but standing on the point of a needle thousands of feet up in the sky, like Jesus being shown the cities of the world. I couldn't answer either way.

You could hear her exasperation. 'What do you think all of this has been about? I told Osiris about you and he said that you were the Merlin. Like they said you were at the hOme. He said I had to get you to come here to find the Grail. What the hell do you think I was doing facing Bridey every Wednesday to go and talk to you in that garden for?'

'I thought you wanted to be my friend.'

'Don't be so childish. You don't need friends. It's the Work that matters. Well.' An audible breath. 'You're here now and that's what matters.'

'Maybe I can't stay.'

'What are you going to do? Go back to Bridey? You can't deny your destiny. You're sulking now.'

'Maybe I'll go back to the hOme. I'll find Debora.'

'That bitch. What do you want her for?'

'She was nicer to me than you were. She didn't pretend.'

'Didn't she? She handed you over to Bridey.'

'It wasn't like that.'

'How would you know what it was like? She was always jealous because I had a child and she didn't. She tried to steal you from me and when that didn't work she helped Bridey steal you. You're my son. You should stay with me. Osiris wants you here.'

'I don't care what Osiris wants.'

'You should. There's stuff to do and not much time. We have to find the Grail soon. And we have to make a new grail, for insurance, in case they get to you. We have to bury your foreskin somewhere safe for the people of the future.'

I walked off. Round the other side of the house Osiris was getting onto his starry Jeep. Brenda was following me, still talking about this and that. I asked where Osiris was going.

'Duncannon. I'm staying behind with you today.'

'I'm going with him.'

'What's in Duncannon for you?'

'I'm worried about Sara.'

'Sara?'

'Your daughter.'

'I know who Sara is. Sara's fine. Children have a way of looking after themselves.'

I didn't say anything else then. I opened the door of the Jeep and got in. I told Osiris that I was coming with him and he shrugged and pulled the corners of his mouth down the way foreign people do when they think you're wrong but can't be arsed to argue.

All the lampposts and all the telegraph poles all the way home were plastered with posters left over from the elections in June, and I wondered that I hadn't noticed them on the way down the day before.

Bridey asked me where I'd been. I said I'd been out. She said I must have been up early because she hadn't seen me leave. She didn't look at you when she spoke any more because her eyes were always on the pup in her lap.

Sara was fine. She had been looking after herself.

'Who went off to see the mad mammy, then?'

Kieran had turned sixteen the previous March. He had been avoiding school one way or another for nearly four years now, and spent the time defying his lungs, one way or another. When he wasn't out fishing on the trawlers he could be found, if anyone could be bothered to look for him, in one of the sheds, with a packet of Woodbines and a third-hand copy of *Health and Efficiency*. The result was not an improvement in his social skills.

Not that I was acquiring many social skills by going to school either, unless it was the skill of attracting as little attention as possible, of avoiding being sat on and thumped by characters who might have been Kieran's soulmates, had he known them.

For reasons best known to themselves, there were girls in the village who lusted after Kieran. They would sit on the wall across the road and ask me to take messages to him, and play self-consciously with the ends of their hair when they saw him cross the street to the shop, working up the courage to call out to him when he crossed back again. If he chose to acknowledge them they would fall backwards off the wall in tittering paroxysms. I used to look at him and wonder what it was about his sly and puffy face that made him so attractive, but wondering was as far as I ever got, and it was neither safe nor pleasurable to look at him for long.

To give him his due he was the first person in Duncannon to call himself a punk rocker. He cut up his old Bay city Rollers scarf to make a tartan tail for his denim jacket, threaded a bit of chain through a self-inflicted hole in his earlobe and somehow acquired a pair of Doc Martens that laced nearly up to the knee, which lent weight to the enquiry that was his response to anyone naïve enough to attempt a dialogue with him. 'You lookin' for a fuckin' kick in the head?'

I was hoping that no one would hear about the trip I made to Taghmon. I was trying not to think too much about it myself. What is there to think when your own mother has those kinds of designs on you? The Devil came to the end of my bed now when I didn't know whether I was asleep or awake, and stood there looking at me. I had drawn myself to his attention and he knew where to find me. I thought sometimes about becoming a priest to get protection from him. Celibacy was easier now that I was less inclined to draw my foreskin back.

You can hope what you like, but Smut must have told Kieran about our adventure in the back of beyond, and now Kieran was letting me know that he knew. I ignored him and went on polishing glasses. It was not yet opening time and the bar was shuttered and quiet. There was a strong smell of unopened pub hanging in the air; of ash and slops and aerosol furniture polish. Kieran hung on the door latch while he was thinking of the next jibe.

'Did they put a spell on her little hoochy-coochy can't talk now?'

I told him to fuck off and picked up a basket of empties to take them through to the yard for sorting. He followed, and watched while I dropped bottles into crates. I hated doing the bottles, with the sticky necks and the putrid waspy smell.

'Didja see any ridin' while you were out there? Betcha ould Fritzy the wizard have his work cut out keepin' on top of that wan.'

I straightened and looked at him. It was meant to be a warning. By then Sally had told me enough about his family history for a cutting remark or two to be forming in my own mind.

He went on, in a falsetto Englishy voice that was supposed to be an imitation of Brenda. 'Ooooh, Fritzy, Fritzy, what a big pole.'

'His name is Osiris, and he's German, not Polish.'

I was pleased to have held back from saying what I could have said, but Kieran hadn't got it. For one moment of incomprehension his face opened and his expression was left vulnerable, and I saw a chance that I couldn't resist to shut him up completely.

'At least I've got a mother who's sober enough to talk to. Have you heard anything from Mairead lately?'

That done, I turned to finish sorting the bottles. Maybe the clink of glass covered his footfalls or maybe he just launched himself off the doorstep like a rocket, but the first I knew of his reaction was when he landed on my back and I fell head first into the basket. In all the glassy noise I'm not sure I heard the bottle being broken across my skull, but I felt it. In the fractured second of consciousness left to me I also felt a kind of satisfaction.

The dull headache lingered, on and off, for several days, but I was peculiarly happy and didn't mind anything, not even Bridey losing her rag at me for forgetting things. All the troublesome parts of my brain had been shut down and it was like a holiday from thinking and remembering. So when Mrs Devlin came into the house, screaming like a parrot and saying that she would have us all arrested for kidnapping, I smiled at her and asked, like a genial host, whether she would like a word with Bridey.

There was stiff competition in the hall that day, between Nuala Devlin and Bridey Scully, each asserting their own respectability at the top of their registers and venturing into tones unknown to humanity to express long-held doubts about the respectability of the other. From what I could gather, among the piquant reminiscences of vanishing Christmas turkeys from one and the florid allusions to a house full of pagan satanists from the other, the nub of it was that Kieran and Patsy, the elder Devlin daughter, had privately contrived between the families an alliance of a biological nature, and had removed themselves to a place unknown in anticipation of their discovery. Or, as Nuala Devlin described it, that gurrier put Patsy up the pole and fecked off with her. Both women expressed concern that, should the facts become public knowledge, they might not be capable of living with the shame, apparently unaware that the volume of their discussion could be the reason why an unusually large number of people were sitting on the wall across the road to warm their backs in the sun.

Bridey, Sara and I took the afternoon bus to New Ross, with Bridey making regular interruptions in her rosary to remind me that this was no laughing matter. She had locked the pub and left a note for Willy to feed the pup, if he ever came home. In Ross we went to Mary Street to leave Sara at the shop.

Sally asked me what was wrong with me.

'Nothing.'

'There's something wrong with you. You're not your-self.'

'Never mind him. He's always odd. It's Bell I'm worried about. I should have brought her along with me.'

'He's not himself. Look at him. You'd think he was hit over the head with a frying pan. I don't think you should be taking him to Dublin on a hot bus.'

'He's grand. I couldn't go on me own. On a bus. Sacred Heart of Jesus, what did I ever do to deserve this? I suppose poverty and riches can never be hid.' She thumbed her engagement ring, as she always did when she trotted that one out. 'And the state of me. I didn't even have a new pair of tights to put on.'

Sally gave her a tight-lipped once-over. 'The more rakish the more takish, they say.' Then she put her big hand on my forehead to feel it. 'Could you not wait for Willy to come home and drive you up?'

Bridey drew her head back and looked her sister-in-law in the eye. 'It's not the christening we have to be in time for.'

We walked from where the bus set us down to North Great George's Street. Bridey plucked at me with a distracted kind of violence all the way, saying that I should watch where I was going and not be bumping into the people and she should never have brought me in the first place but what could she do? It was the first time I had been in a city of any size and I was struck dumb with the horror of it. I never imagined the air would smell so bad or that there could be so much compression from legions of strangers. As the crowds thinned at the top of O'Connell Street, her pace began to show reluctance. On the corner of North Great George's Street she told me to wait for her there, then changed her mind and told me to come with her. At the half-rotted door with twelve doorbells she did the same again.

The staircase trembled under our feet and the litter on it grew deeper the higher we climbed, and then the woman who opened the door at the top of it was called Mairead and I realised that I was facing Kieran's mother. She looked like an older, thinner version of Bridey, and seemed so thrilled to see us that you were inclined to overlook the stains on her jumper and the half of her teeth that were missing. She stood to one side to invite us in and said that we must be desperate for a cup of tea.

I already knew the word stench, and I had thought that I knew what it meant, but it wasn't until we went into that flat that I had any concrete idea what it described. Slurring like Martin Foley at the end of a night, Mairead put the kettle on. She waved a hand at the cockroaches and filth and said she was sorry for the mess but she hadn't had a minute to tidy up that day, she was so busy with one thing and another, and if only she'd had warning we were coming.

Bridey cut across her. 'Mairead, this is Joseph.'

Mairead held out the tips of her fingers to me and nearly curtseyed. I took the scarred, filthy hand and shook it gently.

'Joseph, I've heard so much about you. I'm your granny's sister. Her baby sister, isn't that right, Bridey?' And suddenly she looked like a baby, with her watery, toothless eagerness to please. 'Your granny's a saint, aren't you, Bridey? God love us, where would we all be without her? Are you up for the shopping, is it?'

'No. We are not. Has Kieran been here yet?'

'Kieran? No.'

'He will be.'

Since we had entered the flat, Bridey's face muscles had flexed no more than was necessary for the formation of words, while her sister's had been stretched to breaking point in cheery appeasement. Now Mairead's face was altered, inverted instantly to the miserable opposite.

'What have you done to him now?'

'I've been a mother to him, which is more than can be said for some. I didn't send him down the country for a little holiday and then not enquire after him in five years.'

The appeasement returned. 'Bridey. Bridey, love. You know I have problems. Don't I do everything I can? As God is my witness.'

'He's got himself in trouble.'

'What trouble?'

'Little pictures have big ears.' Bridey indicated me. Perhaps she forgot that I had been present that morning when the situation was discussed in gynaecological detail at a volume that moved off the decibel scale and on to the Richter.

'Is the law after him? Is he on the run? God help him, I wouldn't wish jail on anyone. It's worse than being dead.'

Bridey moved towards her sister and whispered.

Unpinned by relief, Mairead's eyebrows shot towards her hairline. 'Jesus, is that all? I thought you said it was him that was in trouble.'

'It's bad enough. The two of them ran off.'

'What made you think they'd come here?'

'He has a photograph of you in the drawer above in his room and he left it behind. If he was going anywhere else he'd have took it with him.'

'God, Bridey, you should have been a detective. What age is she?'

'Sixteen. The same as him.'

'He's never sixteen already? God, Bridey, don't children make you feel old? I'd say you're wrong all the same. I'd say they're gone over to England to sort themselves out. They'll be back in a few days and no one the wiser.'

'That's murder.'

'That's easy for you to say.'

'Jesus give me strength. Whatever they did, they hadn't the money for England.'

'We'll have a cup of tea anyway; as you're here we might as well.'

I looked into my tea when she handed it to me, in an encrusted mug with spots of sour milk floating on top of it. I was wondering how offended Mairead might be if I didn't drink any of it, when there was a noise like a bee in a bottle.

'That's the doorbell.'

'It must be them.'

'It may not be.'

'Look out the window, Joseph, and see who it is.'

Glad to be able to get my head outside the flat and breathe some comparatively pure smog, I wrenched the sash up. A sprinkle of paint flakes fluttered over the street and down the sheer brickwork towards the top of Willy's cap, recognisable at any distance or angle.

When he came in he wasn't given the chance to say hello.

'Did you feed the pup?'

'What pup?'

'Did you not read the note I left?'

'Of course I fed the pup. What do you take me for?'

'What did you feed her?'

'I didn't feed the pup, Bridey. I wasn't home yet. I called in to Mother's and it was Sally told me where you were. I came straight up.'

'She'll be starving with the hunger. You can go home now and feed her and you can take Joseph with you.'

'Now I'm here I may as well stay, until Romeo and Juliet put in an appearance in any case. How will you get home otherwise?'

Mairead interposed. 'Will you take a drop, Willy? I know you like a drop. I haven't a drop in the house, but we can send Joseph down to the pub at the end of the street. He won't be a minute.'

Willy looked as though he might accept the hospitality, but Bridey interrupted the jingling of change in his pocket. 'The sooner you're gone the sooner the pup gets fed.'

'I can't leave you here on your own.'

'This is my family, Willy. I'm the one that has to deal with it.'

You might have described the way he looked at her as something like admiration.

'A saint. The woman's a saint.' Willy repeated this conviction to me at every set of traffic lights until we had cleared the suburbs of Dublin. 'Did you know your grand-mother's a saint, Joseph?'

'What did Mairead go to jail for?'

'Who told you that?'

'She did.'

'Don't be listening to her, and I wouldn't be telling anyone else you heard it. Brilliant woman, Mairead. A scholar. If she hadn't gone to the university she could have married any man she wanted. Now you see where commu-nism will get you.'

'Is she a communist?'

'The fecker she married was, or something like it.'

Anything more that Willy had to reveal about Kieran's origins was lost on me. I slept, heavy-headed, all the way home. Once or twice I woke to find myself alone in the car, parked outside some pub or other on the side of the road. I don't think he ever stopped for more than one, and we made good time, considering.

I fed the pup, and then for some reason I had trouble finding my bedroom. All the doors in the house seemed to be in the wrong place. When I woke next day it was after-noon and strange. The pub was still shut and Willy had gone away again. I had the whole place to myself; all the rooms and landings. I got some croquettes and an Arctic Roll from the freezer. The Aga was out. I watched telly for a little bit and then switched it off. It was better having no human voices around the place at all.

I never heard all of what happened in Dublin. Bridey and Willy came home late at night and Kieran was with them. Patsy too, apparently, though she was sent straight round to her own house to face the music there. Kieran went up to bed without saying anything. He passed me on the stairs with no one looking and I made to duck the usual punch, but no punch came.

Bridey looked beaten and Willy looked old. He went to get himself a drink in the bar and she sat in the kitchen with her coat on and Bell on her lap. I offered to make her a cup of tea.

'Did you open the bar?'

'No.'

'Jesus.'

'I wasn't feeling well.'

'There's none of us feeling well.'

'Sorry.'

'The Aga's out I see.'

'It was out when I got up.'

'I suppose you weren't feeling well enough to light that either?'

'Sorry.'

'Go to bed. Get out of my sight.'

I went upstairs, but I wasn't sleepy. I got my record out,

the one I had bought with PJ's tokens. It was *The Best of Bowie*. I knew all the words of the songs by heart from reading the inner sleeve. The record itself was in mint condition. The day I brought it back from Waterford I had found the record-player with the arm torn off it. Kieran said he hadn't been anywhere near it, but he also said it was an accident. So I sang along with the sleeve, knowing some of the tunes from the radio. We could get music on the radio by then. The tunes I didn't know I had to make up for myself. I was sitting on the bed and singing one of these when I realised that I was behaving like a nutcase, and stopped. If I was a nutcase I didn't want anyone else to hear me and find out.

The banns were called for Kieran and Patsy, and he began to look very pleased with himself. He would snog her defiantly on the street corner and try to talk to Willy as if they were equals. I had fallen beneath his notice and I was grateful for it.

The Saturday before the wedding Willy took Kieran and me into Wexford to get new clothes for us. Bridey said there was no point in getting me an outfit until the last minute because of the rate at which I was growing. It was not entirely a successful expedition. By the time we had found something that Kieran was prepared to wear and Willy was prepared to pay for the shops were closing. We drove back along the New Line in squally weather, with me in the back trying to think of a way to explain my empty-handedness to Bridey. There was a long silence, which Willy broke in his usual way by sermonising about money.

'They have a nerve the prices they were asking. It's not like the clothes are built to last like they used to be. It's all about money. That's all there is to it. If you could get money out of the people that owe it. The money I'm owed would shock you. Please God there's a fella in Gusserane due to make a big payment and this time next week we'll be staring solvency in the face.'

There was a hiatus while Kieran and I concentrated hard on nothing out of the window, before Willy cranked himself up again.

'All about money. Well, you'll be a married man in a few days' time and then you'll know all about it. Are you looking forward to it?'

I saw a smirk on the corner of Kieran's mouth. 'I'm looking forward to getting a ride whenever I want it.'

It was a good thing the road was straight and there was nothing coming in the opposite direction. Willy tried to sound patient by way of contrast to his driving. 'And you don't think there might be more to a marriage than that?'

'What else would there be? Isn't that the reason you married Bridey if you were honest?'

'God help us.' Willy glanced in the rear-view mirror at me and had nothing more to say. The day of the wedding he was late coming into the church.

The first three days back at school were given over to a retreat. A squad of priests descended on us. Instead of lessons we had prayers and talks and solemnness. The man who took over our year was young, with charismatic teeth and hair. He had the unnerving habit of looking you straight in the eye when he spoke to you. On the first day he talked a lot about Christ's mission on earth. On the second he told us about a priest's work and said that, although it was the duty of everyone to strive to be

Christlike, it was the privilege of a priest to emulate Christ as much as was humanly possible. The third morning he mentioned the second coming and I found myself paying a bit more attention. It was written, he said, that Christ would come again. Nobody knew where in the world he would be born or to whom or when it would happen. For all we knew, he said, the New Christ might be sitting in this very classroom at this very moment. He might have meant it as a joke because when nearly everyone laughed he laughed along with them.

In the afternoon we had to go and see him one by one in the science room. The blinds were down to make it dark like a quarter-acre of confessional, and the Bunsen burners and taps were gleaming like religious artifacts on row after row of altars. Over the smell of chemicals and floor polish you could smell the soap that he used, and it was like a woman's soap.

He said that he had been taking special notice of me in the last few days and he could see that I had a very special relationship with God. I thought that was perceptive of him since I hadn't put my hand up to answer a single question he asked. Which, he said, was why he was glad to have this chance to have a private talk with me. He asked me if I prayed.

I had stopped being nervous. I said that I did, but not as much as I used to.

He said that we all had our time in the wilderness. Even the saints were sinners first. Our Lord had taken the trouble to show us that God had a human side. So long as I was trying my hardest then God's plan would be revealed to me.

It was all the way you would imagine it, with stillness in

the room and dust in a sunbeam. He put his hand to the side of my face and asked me to pray with him. I had not been touched like that for a long time and it made me feel faint. I don't remember what prayer we said.

Back in the classroom, at the end of the retreat, we all had to say what we wanted to be when we grew up. There were some who said they didn't know but most said they wanted a job in the bank. There were five of us who said we wanted to be priests and were rewarded with the smile you get when you give the right answer.

There was a great sense of relief as soon as I said it. For some time I had wondered whether that was what was to become of me; to be a man in black with pallid hands. I heard the words come out of my own mouth and I knew that it wasn't true. I could no more be a priest than I could live in Taghmon and walk around wearing a bedspread. Sometimes it is only when you say the lie out loud that you recognise it for what it is.

Over the next couple of weeks I began to notice that there was something strange going on at the hotel. Furniture would disappear. I'd get home from school and go to do my homework on one of the tables in the big dining room, where guests used to eat when there were guests, and there'd be no table, or tables. Just congregations of chairs around table-shaped spaces. We ran out of large Macardles in the bar and no new stock came to replace it. Then the draught Guinness ran out and the Carroll's cigarettes. I asked Bridey and she told me not to be plaguing her with questions. I said that the customers were wondering and she told me to tell the customers to feck off for themselves, she was scalded with customers. Then there was a Thursday I came home and the bed was gone from my room. Bridey said there were plenty more beds in the house, what was wrong with me? I moved my stuff up to PJ's old room at the top of the house and came down again to mind the bar.

There was a townie customer who asked for ice. I stalled him as long as possible because there were strong words filtering through from the kitchen. Willy and Bridey were having a discussion and I didn't want to interrupt. At the first sign that things had gone quiet, and after the fourth sarcastic remark from the customer, I picked up the ice bucket and took a deep breath.

Things had only gone quiet because they were having a staring match. I stood in the doorway and waited for them to see me. Bridey said that she didn't want the whole festering village to know her business.

Willy was using his patient voice. 'We have to tell them some time, Bridey, come on now, surely you can see what it's like for them not three weeks married and the state she's in and before they know it there won't be a roof over their heads.'

'And if we do tell them she'll be straight round to her mother and you might as well paint it in big red letters down the middle of the street outside. No. They'll find out soon enough.' Then Bridey saw me. 'And here's Big Ears as usual. What are you doing standing there?'

'I have to get ice.'

'Ice. Jesus spare me. Ice.'

I went through to the fridge. The ice trays were metal and your fingers stuck to them.

'Joseph?' Willy had his arms folded and he was staring at the floor.

'What?'

'You'd be better staying home from school tomorrow.'

'Why?'

'The hotel is sold. We might need a hand moving a few things.'

'Jesus, Willy.' Bridey turned away and went off before I could be sure whether she was crying.

'All right so.' My fingers were stuck fast and burning.

'Good lad.'

I ended the day lying naked on PJ's bed and the horn came swiftly. I held it and looked at it and wondered whether it would ever be any use to me. There was a crucifix on the opposite wall that Bridey had put up to keep watch over her son. I wondered what the half-starved, beat-up Jesus had under his loincloth. Then I remembered about the Grail and decided to put the light out.

I was woken by a death in the early hours. That was not unusual, but this death was stronger than any previous one. At first I couldn't work out who it was had died. Usually, if I didn't recognise them they would tell me what their name had been; whisper it in my ear when I flew up to intercept their flight path. This person was formless. He embraced me before flying on. The dead had never embraced me before. I thought, as he disappeared, that he looked like me. A stray notion came into my head, as I descended, that I was the one who had died.

That was the last time a death ever woke me. It was also the night I stopped growing. The height I was then is the height I remained. The forecasts of gigantitude were wrong. It takes more than one summer of growing to be huge.

The next day Brenda came and found herself unwelcome.

We were all either putting things in boxes or moving boxes or stacking boxes. Even Kieran and Patsy were lending a hand. They were taking their imminent homelessness calmly. Patsy said it would make it easier for them to get a council house of their own.

Brenda came swooping in with a gait that had to have been rehearsed. I had avoided her since the time I went to Taghmon, slipping out of the back of the house as she came in the front, to go somewhere I could be throwing stones at the sea until long after she was gone. This time I couldn't get away. She made straight for me and put a hand on my shoulder, while looking about her at the boxes and rolled carpets.

'Change. Change. All change.'

Bridey said we were busy and asked her what she wanted.

'I wanted to see my son.'

'There he is. Have a good look. We're still busy.'

'So I see.'

'The hotel is sold. The bank have all the money. We're paupers now and anyone that wants can see it. Poverty and riches can never be hid.'

'All change.'

'If you can't help, try not to be a hindrance.'

'Does nobody listen to the news around here?'

'I'll news you in a minute.'

'He's dead.'

'Good.' Bridey turned her back on us and started to climb the stairs, doing it slowly enough to show us that she was not a well woman and all this work was beyond her.

I waited until she was out of sight before I said anything. 'We're going to live in Ross.'

'Are you?'

'Apparently. I'm not dead keen on the town.'

'You can come and live in Taghmon.'

'No thanks.'

'You don't understand. Everything's changed. He's dead.'

'Who? Old Wolfy?'

'No. This is important. Come with me.' She pulled me towards the back door.

'Where?'

'Into the garden. I need to talk to you.'

'I'm busy. If I skive off I'll be kilt.'

I went with her. We walked to the far garden and it began to rain. She looked around her. 'This is all a bit –'

'I know.'

'Weedy.'

'I haven't been out here for a while.'

'Anyway.' She turned and looked at me in a way I didn't like. 'Marc Bolan is dead. He died last night in a car crash.'

'So?' I tried to sound as if it didn't have anything to do with me, but I was thinking, so that's who died in the night.

'Don't you see? Don't you remember everything that was prophesied?'

'No.'

'You're being obstreperous.'

'I think you mean obstinate.'

'You know what I mean. Why are you being like this? This is your big chance.'

'To do what, exactly?'

'Everything. You can do everything. You can find the Grail. Osiris is sure of it. Make the world a better place.

Now that Bolan is out of the way you can step into his shoes and become the new Merlin.'

'What if I have other plans for myself?'

'You can't escape your fate. It will follow you.'

I had an awful feeling, but I managed to keep it to myself. 'You know what, Brenda?'

'What?'

'You want to grow up and cop on to yourself.'

I could hear Bridey screeching for me. I said I had to go. I recognised the awful feeling. It was vertigo, but not the dizzy kind of vertigo you get in your head, more the kind of physical vertigo you have when you're dreaming, that numbness that spreads out from your chest until your whole body feels both heavy and weightless. It felt as if something or someone was taking over and filling out my flesh. I turned to get away from her and, as I did, I had a falling sensation. I could see my legs moving in the normal way, but all I could feel was falling. It was all I could do not to hold out my arms to stop myself.

My mother followed me down the yard, her skirts dragging in wet anthracite dust. 'I'm applying for custody. We've looked into the law. You're still a minor and I'm still your mother. I want you to come and live with us and you don't have any say in it.'

I turned. 'Brenda.'

'Yes?'

I thought of a lot of things to say to her. I don't know why I said what I did. 'Your goddessy make-up is dribbling down your face. You look stupid.'

I needed to get back inside the hotel. If anyone could stop this happening it was Bridey. She'd send Brenda packing for herself. The feeling was as strong as the one I had had when I turned my back on God and his black uniform. Only now, what was left? With God and the Devil out the window, only Bridey remained. Bad as she was, Bridey was constant. She'd never asked for my immortal soul or threatened to cast me out if she couldn't have it. I wanted to get back inside the hotel and be told what to do to make myself useful.

Bridey stood rampant in front of the Aga, thrusting a magazine in front of her with a trembling fist. 'What is this?'

'I don't know. What is it?'

'It was under your mattress.'

I looked. Painted nails and hairy bollocks. 'It's not mine. Not my mattress.'

'That was your clothes in the room. That was your pyjamas on the bed. So whose mattress is it supposed to be?'

'I only moved in there last night. Remember?'

I didn't have to say anything else. You could tell from the expression on her face that she was working out who had occupied the room before me. I was surprised that Kieran hadn't scoured the bed springs in PJ's wake and found it, but there it was, all the busty ladies and horny men crushed in Bridey's fist.

She took the poker in her other hand and I thought she was going to hit me, but she used it to raise the cover of the hot ring on the Aga. The hole glowed a pale red. Living mice would be dropped into that hole from their traps when they were caught, cast into hell for the germs they carried. She threw the magazine into it and poked the writing bodies down with the poker. There was an eruption of flame.

'Mam?'

'What?'

'I want him to come and live with me. In Taghmon.'

I thought there was still a chance for me. I thought Bridey would never let Brenda have me back.

'You can do what you like. I'm sick of the lot of you.'

Bridey, somehow, had hit upon a spell to change the world. Not the whole world maybe, but the whole of the world that I knew. She had removed the last plank of certainty from under my feet, and while I was still falling through the collapsing structures of my mind I still had time to observe how she had done it. It was not so much the words themselves as the force behind them, like she had tapped through the crust of the earth beneath her, so the words were propelled as deadly as lava with all the might of hell pushing from behind. Languorously destructive words that bore down slowly, spitting hot rocks at the periphery. Those words could never be taken back; they would petrify and remain.

I thought I was still standing there, but when I stopped thinking that I found I was walking on a road. It was the road to Ross, though at first I didn't recognise it, and of course what I felt was terror, as you would if one minute you were watching your grandmother transform herself into Beelzebub and she cast you out and the next minute you were alone on an empty road sure of nothing except that the devil had greater power than he had ever let on, and the ditches either side were full of nothing but briars and brambles arching over to tempt you to run under three times, to say the word and join the winning side as any sensible person would. I only kept walking because I was afraid that if I stopped I would die in the devil's country. Though I was wishing for sanctuary I had no great hope of it.

There were no cars. There was no wind or rain or sun. Nothing but grey and silence and the fall of my own two feet and the twitching of spiders on dewy webs strung from one thorn to the next.

The road twisted as it slipped past me and there was a shift in the landscape and the abbey was suddenly below me, floating in river mist and lit warm by a pillar of candescent sunlight, though the source of light might well have been the abbey itself piercing the cloud above, and a greenfinch broke the silence with that one note of anguish and complacency. Of course I thought that the abbey must have been where I was going all along.

The sign said to get the key from the cottage and I don't remember whether it was a man or a woman who gave it to me. The abbey grew in size as I crossed the field towards it and as it got bigger it appeared more ruinous. In the distance it had been a delicate tracery of stone, but as I came nearer and the stones grew larger I began to wonder what was holding them one on top of the other in broken and unbroken arches for the hundreds of years since the place had been abandoned, and I realised that there must be more than mortar to it. And once I was inside I felt safe as I hadn't done since before Bridey and Willy had brought me along on this visit, which had stretched now to a decade.

I walked over every inch of Dunbrody and ran a hand over every stone I could reach and found stairwells in walls and stood in great empty windows high above the ground.

There was a place where you could suppose the altar had been but that was dank; and the place I felt holiest was a cloister or the remains of a cloister where even on a day as grey as that I could feel the memory of sunshine and shadow. I began to think how I could stay for a while.

I took the key back without locking the gate and I don't remember whether it was a young person or an old person who I gave it to, and then I walked up the road a bit and doubled back by the edge of the river, the stench of the mud flats serving as a reminder of the evil in the world outside the abbey and the goodness within.

Once I was inside again the thinking came fast. From those high windows I could look out squarely on the whole accretion of monsters that had been chasing me harder and faster with every month of my life. I remembered everything and found a place for it in the pattern. There had been no accidents or coincidences. I had been born for a purpose and everything that had happened so far had been to keep me safe until I was ready to fulfil the purpose. At the hOme they had talked about overthrowing the establishment and here they talked about defeating the devil. It was the same thing, but here they couldn't see that the establishment was the devil; that the rich were rich because they had sold their souls; that the church was a skin of lies over a body of tradition; that the world was nearly at the point of being beyond redemption.

The more I thought, the stronger I felt. I became nearly certain of everything and certain of nearly everything. The monsters camped around the abbey had faces now and I knew my enemies. The only thing I didn't know was whether I had a friend. I thought of my mother and all I thought was how stupid she was, digging holes in Taghmon when all the time the Grail was here in Dunbrody buried under the cloister garth. I didn't know that until I thought it and once I had thought it it was obvious. Having found the Grail the last thing I would have wanted to do was dig it up so it could be gawped at and fought over. Better to leave it under the ground so I would always know where to come and find sanctuary.

Debora kept coming into my mind: her face before me and her voice beside me and the song about her never far away, her sunken face still like a galleon. If I had an ally it was going to be Debora and if I was ever going to discover whether I was alone or not I would have to see her first. I was sure if I went to Devon I would find the place where the hOme was. Maybe she would still be there. Nothing, I reminded myself, happened for nothing. It would not be hard to track down someone I was meant to, especially if the future of the world was at stake.

It was dusk, cold and damp by the time I had decided that I could hitch-hike across on the ferry somehow; probably convince a lorry driver to take me. I didn't look old enough but I could make up for that by talking old. I began to shift myself from the corner of the great arched window I had been sitting in when a movement in the field that was not a cow or a horse caught my eye, a dark shape moving along the track from the road.

I don't know what paralysed me. It can't have been fear when I had just found my place of safety. I thought maybe that I was spellbound. Whatever it was I stopped breathing as soon as I heard the gate rattle under a testing hand and the oath of exasperation. There was a cursory shout to enquire if there was anybody still in there and the clank of iron as the gate was locked properly. By the time I was breathing normally the figure was half way back across the field.

Perhaps I had no fear of being locked in. Perhaps I thought I could still leave if I chose, drop from a window to the soft grass and roll. And to begin with it was exciting to be in there in the pitch blackness, feeling my way around the stones and feeling the presence of all the dead monks in the holy ground. I sat on the mound in the middle of the garth and felt the power of the Grail beneath me and with a seeming suddenness the cold of the night. I had no coat on me.

A drop is a long way down when you can't see the bottom, and I hesitated, trying to remember from daylight what distance away the ground was, and then convinced myself it was as near as made no difference and let go my hold on the stone and tried to spend the time of falling rolling myself into a ball, without any real success. I fell on my side. My shoulder hit one stone and my leg another. The shoulder hurt more than the leg at the time but it subsequently turned out that they were equally broken.

The odd car passed on the road so I knew by the head-lights where it was and I knew that even by inches I could reach it eventually, and I somehow thought I was still heading for Rosslare and Devon, that there would be a motorist who would pick me up and take me to England because that was where I was meant to be and if there was anything seriously wrong with me the only person who was fit to deal with it was Debora.

I might have passed out more often from the pain if I

hadn't been so benumbed with the cold, and sometimes I would drag myself over a cow pat and feel the heat of it for a precious minute, and sometimes I would stop for a cry, knowing that I was doomed. I was up against forces that had defeated better men than me for centuries, millenia, and I wasn't even a man yet by most standards. I cried with hopelessness when I realised that inching myself across that field was only the latest in a long line of punishments and that I would never reach the road, being condemned to drag myself in agony and darkness through all eternity. You can find the Grail if you like, so long as you understand that this is not so much the risk you take as maybe the inevitable consequence.

I didn't know the rules of the place I was in, or whether it was still within my power to capitulate. If I called the devil and apologised, would he mend my shoulder and my leg and make the sun shine in the middle of the night? I knew I should never have left the abbey. To be locked in had been a test, and I should have stayed where I was, on vigil, all night, by the Grail. I realised that heaven was punishing me as much as hell was.

I think that was the last thing I thought. What followed was not in the control of my reasoning. Looking back the way I had inched, there was a glimmer of white horse; a light that seemed sometimes perfectly like a white horse and sometimes no more than a glimmer. And then the dead in legions came out of the sky to accuse me of having failed them, and to escape the blackness of their scorn my soul left me and flew up about the universe, and when it came back to me they were gone, they and their basilisk eyes, and so was I.

I was found, blue, in the morning. The man who came across me called the police to say there was a dead boy dumped in the field beyond the abbey. He declined to identify himself, a precaution which may have had something to do with the circumstance of my being found with my flies open. He had taken his commission for finding me by way of a fumble, which could only make you wonder what kind of isolation a man would have to endure all his life to be tempted by the cold unvaunted penis of a dead boy in a field. The kind of life maybe in which a boy's first sexual contact with another person might be one in which he plays the role of a corpse.

To die of broken bones and hypothermia, you'd have to leave it a few hours longer than I did before your body is happened upon by a sex pervert with a conscience. The first person I saw after I came to was a nurse. The fact that I was conscious after a week of hovering between this world and the next seemed not to strike her as hard as the emptiness of the bowl on the bedside locker.

'What happened them grapes?'

'I was starving. I ate them.'

I had woken with a feeling in my stomach as if I hadn't eaten for a week, for the obvious reason that I hadn't, and there was a bowl of grapes in reach of my good arm, white grapes, yellowy green, lustrous and blooming, and what else should I have done with them?

'If you vomit them up you can clean it up yourself.'

'Okay.'

'I suppose the doctor will be wanting to see you now you're awake. You were trouble enough while you were under.'

'Sorry.'

'Sorry didn't wipe your arse.'

The nurse went. I watched the articulation of her disproportionate haunches under white nylon as she worked her way steadily and resentfully among the beds, hanging charts at the feet of them with the slow carelessness of a glacier depositing moraine, and I thought that if I had an arse like that to wipe every morning I might find myself a job that didn't involve the arses of others.

She left the curtains open behind her and now I could see all the old men responsible for the hawking and farting and groaning and wheezing that had welcomed me back to the land of the living. And the bright spark in the bed opposite who seemed to be waiting for my eyes to rest on him so he could make a friend of me. I fell asleep.

The doctor asked me questions, but none of them memorable. He stuck his finger up my arse for no apparent reason and whispered a lot with the nurse – another nurse, a boss nurse in navy with a lemon-sucking expression and bones that were not content to lie quietly under her shrivelling skin. The doctor was young and clammy and halitosic. He smiled at me a lot, but not convincingly.

Then a gard came, in a uniform, to ask questions. He mostly wanted to know whether I had been alone; whether I had seen anyone else at the abbey at all. He was more interested in that than in what had happened, so it was easy to seem like a stupid boy who had run away from home and panicked at being shut into the abbey. I kept staring at this gard who was younger even than the doctor, but handsome. You never saw a handsome gard with no belly or jowl or watery eyes or sarcasm and I wondered if he was an imposter. For some reason he was trying to get me to trust him, and for the same reason, without knowing what it was, I knew that trusting him would be a big mistake. I fell asleep while he was still asking preposterously gentle questions.

Then I opened my eyes on Sally, and closed them again.

So far, everything had been new. Unpleasant maybe, but at least dissociated from my past life. I had been able to pretend that I had been born into a new world and that as soon as I could walk I'd be able to disappear and never be heard of again. Not as Joe Scully anyway.

I had nothing against Sally. But if she knew where I was then so did Bridey and Brenda and I might as well have sent a postcard to hell itself telling them where to come and get me.

It was rude not to open my eyes, and you can only be rude for so long.

'The craythur.'

'Hiya.'

'You must have been desperate altogether.'

She made me cry saying that, but she waited until I was finished before she said anything else, the whole great crumple of her sitting by my bed. She looked sad, but she wasn't trying to muscle in on my sadness with tears of her own as another person might.

'Sorry.'

'You've nothing to be sorry for. It's the rest of us should be sorry. I want to make you an offer I should have made years ago. Netty was always saying we should, but the two of us were afraid of Bridey if you want to know the truth. Anyway, not to be tiring you out with the details and the state you're in, and you don't have to give me an answer now, you'll be here a few days yet, would you like to come and live with me in Mary Street when they let you out?'

'I wanted to go to Devon. I wanted to find the hOme.'

'All right so. I'll cut you a deal. You stay with me for a while and have a bit of normality the same as any child in the town can have and you can go above to the discos in the Five Counties or whatever it is you want to get up to, and the two of us will make a trip to, where is it, Devon in the school holidays and I won't make you do anything you don't want to except maybe have a good wash for yourself now and again.'

'What about Sara?'

'She won't be far away. Willy and Bridey are after landing themselves one of them shocking new council houses above in Nunnery Lane and she spends half her time below with me in the shop as it is. So your best chance of keeping an eye on her will be to hang your hat on my hallstand.'

'Well.'

'That's enough talk for now. You don't have to give me an answer. I brought you a few more grapes to be getting on with. There's nothing like white grapes for healing the sick. And a few old chocolate bars to hide in your little cupboard there. Lick your arse and all.'

After she was gone I was still awake and the bright spark in the bed opposite had his chance to make my acquaintance. He looked like an assistant in a draper's shop, which was exactly what he turned out to be.

'How are ya cuttin there?'

'Hiya.'

'I'm Mike. What's yours?'

'Coorg.'

'That's a queer name. Is it short for something?'

'No. It's just queer. I used to have a queer life.'

'Would you listen to your man. Anyone would think he was a hundred.'

I closed my eyes. That was enough for now.

FRANK RONAN

Dixie Chicken

After Rory Dixon's car sails over a cliff into the Irish Sea, his widow cries murder. The police, though, insist it was an accident and his friends concur: who could possibly have wanted to kill someone so widely adored? Even God considered him special. Yet as the tale unfolds of Rory's charmed life, he emerges as an unexpectedly complex figure, a man with many facets – and secrets.

'From the first startling death with the blasting stereo and the damaged brakes one is led compulsively, and often hilariously, through a landscape that includes incest, adolescent despair, drug abuse, suicide fixation, sex killers, corrupt politicians, repulsive old lechers, necrophiliacs [and] unfrocked priests.' *Independent*

'An enthralling mystery as well as an effective satire. Its blasphemy makes *The Satanic Verses* look like, well, chicken-feed; but it is also thought-provoking and hugely entertaining' *Daily Telegraph*

'A deeply funny tale of sex, death, corruption and infidelity . . . Ronan is a very gifted storyteller: the narration from Him upstairs is a perfect tool for the plot . . . As more of [Rory's] complicated life is revealed, the humour becomes ever blacker and ever funnier. A wonderful book, highly recommended' *Time Out*

'One of those novels that stand rereading periodically because it is so full of clever ideas, and funny, too . . . Most intriguing and philosophical of all, is Ronan's idea that poor old God, much to his chagrin and embarrassment, never actually knows where suicides go when they die. You could almost weep for him.' *The Times*

'A compelling mystery story which is also a wicked satire . . . a seriously funny book' *Belfast Telegraph*

SCEPTRE